"Hate me if you will, Leah," Nicholas grounded out, his own voice hoarse and edged with fury she did not understand. "Yes, give me your hatred. Yet I will have something else as well. By Zeus or Hades, I will have it."

Her hands came up to push against him, but it was useless. Nicholas's other arm now encircled her with its hard, sinewy strength, and Leah could do nothing more than utter a strangled protest before their lips captured parted softness.

Passion flared between them as though renewed with the vengeance of Ares. Trembling, and struggling for breath, she once again sought to push him away, only to moan when he gathered her closer....

THE FATES

THE FATES

A Novel

Tino Georgiou

iUniverse, Inc.

New York Lincoln Shanghai

The Fates

iUniverse books may be ordered through booksellers or by contacting:

iUniverse
2021 Pine Lake Road, Suite 100
Lincoln, NE 68512
www.iuniverse.com
1-800-Authors (1-800-288-4677)

Because of the dynamic nature of the Internet, any Web addresses
or links contained in this book may have changed
since publication and may no longer be valid.

This is a work of fiction. All of the characters, names, incidents, places,
organizations, and dialogue in this novel are either the products of the
author's imagination or are used fictitiously.

ISBN: 978-0-595-46433-3 (pbk)
ISBN: 978-0-595-90726-7 (ebk)

Printed in the United States of America

To my mother, my father, and my sister, a caring and loving family—a family with honor. Also, a special dedication to Jena, Mike, and Keith.

CHAPTER 1

▼

Asia Minor.... 14th century

The wind was the worst so far. Fierce, relentless, chilling everyone to the bone in spite of the protective layers of wool and linen.

"How is it the accursed place could look so fertile when winter is upon us?"

"A trick of Lord Hades, no doubt, meant to lull us into a false sense of well-being."

Hearing the exchange behind him, Nicholas Constinos allowed a faint smile of irony to touch his lips. He frowned in the next instant and shifted in his saddle. His eyes, so dark a brown as to appear fathomless narrowed imperceptibly while they traveled across the surrounding countryside. It was a wild, untamed beauty of undeveloped land spread before him. Gentle hills were mantled in thick, wild grass, dark and dense woods still offered a canopy of leaves in spite of the lateness of the season, and a multitude of sparkling streams and rivers wound their way through the perennial, legendary green. The air was heavy, charged with the unmistakable scent of rain.

There would be a storm before nightfall.

"It is said these woods were inhabited by ghosts." Riding at his old friend's side, much the same as he had done for the many years past, Josh Leonidas directed a curt nod toward the near by woods. "A paradise for spirits, both good and evil."

"A living underworld, more like," muttered Nicholas.

"Pray that Lord Ares never hears of your ingratitude, my old friend," sarcastically said Josh.

"Ah, but I am grateful." Once again, the merest flicker of amusement, however mocking, set aglow within the piercing, gold-flecked intensity of his gaze. "Grateful enough to risk death upon these haunted woods."

"With that would he given you reward close to home." Josh grumbled traitorously, he said to Nicholas.

"Where would the challenge lie in that?"

"Faith, man. Are you not yet weary of these challenges?"

"Yeah," conceded Nicholas, his deep-timbered voice lowering as well. "It was for no other reason I agreed to this madness."

He tightened his grip on the reins and cast a quick look over his shoulder. Nearly forty soldiers, squires, and men-at-arms had made the choice to come with him.

Now walking in a double column along a narrow, mud-choked path, they were fully prepared to follow wherever he led. To the depths of Hades and back, if need be.

The thought made his ego swell with pride—and filled him with a sense of responsibility even greater than what he felt when he was in the midst of battle. These were his men, by Zeus. He held their fate in his hands.

For a fleeting moment, the late afternoon sun broke through the clouds, lighting fire in the short, rich brown thickness of his hair.

He was not handsome in the underweight model way so fashionable among the men and women on television today. Tall, powerfully built, his features tanned and chiseled and his manner one of supreme confidence, Nicholas looked every inch the magnificent specimen that he was.

"Unless my eyes deceive me, Nicholas, we are fast upon our final destination," Josh noted, with a wry smile of his own.

He, too, earlier had instinctively lifted his head to the brief, benevolent warmth of the sun's rays. Neither as tall nor as commanding as the man beside him, he was nonetheless a force in his own right. Indeed, he was a lady's man and he made the maidens pulse quicken at naught but a glance, wide-set hazel eyes, and short blonde locks. And with his fair share of women, his heart, as yet has remained unscathed. In that respect if no other, Josh and Nicholas had much in common. "Karabey," he murmured, toying with the reins gripped in one gauntlet-clad hand. "A curious name." He sighed and shook his head before remarking prophetically, "yet no more curious, I'll wager, than either the keep or village it graces."

That said, he watched as Nicholas's gaze followed in the direction ahead of him. The sun had disappeared once more, returning the chill to the November afternoon and the gray, unwelcome pallor to the sky above. In the distance just ahead, the location they were heading rose like a great marble beacon. With four corner towers standing tall and forbidding beneath the boiling heavens, a five-storied keep bearing the tell-tale marks of past wars, and a massive, jagged wall providing a barrier to any who would demand entrance to the courtyard within, the parameters seemed impregnable.

Impregnable and cold and strangely out of place on the sloping lush landscape.

"An unearthly place if ever there was one," was Josh's first assessment.

"Nonetheless," said Nicholas, "it's mine." With his face set in a mask of grim determination, he glanced to his men and led the way onward.

The gate had been opened, surrounded by the dark waters of a moat, apparently in full anticipation of the new lord's arrival, yet no one ventured forth to bid him welcome when he approached the main gate. A banner should have been flying from the ramparts.

There was none.

His gaze flickered eastward. The main village itself could be glimpsed a short distance away, nestled in a valley across the river.

A tidy little collection of thatched-roof cottages, marble buildings, and narrowed cobbled streets, it seemed the very picture of rural quaintness. Oddly enough, however, there was no sign of activity during what should have been the busiest part of the day.

There were no men crossing to-and-from the shops, no women fetching groceries or children playing, not even dogs scampering about. If not for the columns of smoke being whipped aloft from several of the chimneys, and the distinct, resounding chime of the marbled-temple bell carried across to him on the wind, Nicholas might well have thought himself surveying a ghost town.

He tensed. A sudden, sharp uneasiness crept over him, but he urged his well-trained mount purposefully across the river and through the gate. Without hesitance, the other men followed. Their horses' hooves thundered upon the cobbled streets to announce their progress into the center courtyard.

They were met by an unexpected, almost eerie silence.

The courtyard was deserted. Worse than that, its spacious, muddy grounds were littered with a sickening array of debris. Bits and pieces of broken furniture, fetid straw, horse dung, rotting food, and stagnant water—all combined to produce a ferocious stench that made even the most hardened of men catch his breath.

Nicholas drew the sleek black animal beneath him to a halt and swung down from the saddle.

His eyes glittered harshly. A single muscle twitched in the clean-shaven ruggedness of his cheek as he battled the surge of white-hot anger rising deep within him.

Disrepair and neglect were painfully obvious at every turn.

The thatched roofs of the stables, dog kennels, and servants' huts sported gaping holes. The wooden kitchen looked dangerously ramshackled; a fire had reduced both the bakehouse and laundry to a pile of blackened rubble The vegetable garden, as well as nearly all the fruit trees, had been stripped-down. If evidence pointing to the fact that some of the damage had occurred only recently, it would have been easy to believe the palace had been abandoned years earlier.

"It appears the constable has been somewhat remiss in his duties," Josh observed cryptically. He dismounted and signaled for the others to do the same. The jingle of spurs and the creak of a wooden footpath filled the cold air, made even heavier by a disappointment none would voice.

"By the gods—" Nicholas grounded out. He sliced a narrow, furious glare at the keep, then turned and strode abruptly toward the outer stairway.

His leather sandals connected almost soundlessly with the weathered steps as he climbed to the second floor. He flung opened the unlocked, iron-clad wooden door and strode inside the darkness of the main hall.

Damp and musty-smelling, and every bit as filthy and cluttered as had been foretold, it offered none of the comforts, the cold, hungry travelers would have desired. There was no fire blazing in the crumbling stone fireplace, no tapestries or rushes to chase away the prevailing chill, no wine or food to warm the empty bellies of the men who waited outside.

Nicholas listened to the wind howling mournfully through the cracks in the thick marble walls. His expression now stoic, he slowly drew off his leather gloves and dropped them to the surface of the only table still standing—albeit precariously—in the room. He looked up toward the high, oak-beam ceiling. There was little doubt in his mind that the rest of Karabey Palace would yield more of the same dilapidation. "Karabey," he murmured, then allowed his mouth to curve into a brief, humorless smile. His reward.

"Constable!" Josh bellowed as he suddenly materialized in the doorway. "Show yourself at once!" There was, of course, no immediate answer to his angry summons, and still none after several long seconds had passed. Visibly perplexed, he looked to Nicholas.

Their gazes met in the pale gray light. "Where in Hades is the lazy jackal?"

"Gone. If ever he existed."

"Gone? But were you not told—?"

"What I was told doesn't matter." Nicholas's tone was quiet, edged with more than a touch of bitterness.

"It's a mistake, surely!" Josh hastened to reassure him.

"Yes. My own." Removing his fur-lined mantle, he tossed it impatiently aside. He lifted his arms and folded them across the bold, hard-muscled expanse of his chest. Glancing down, he caught sight of the coat of arms displayed on the front of his banded crimson tunic—a golden raptor, with a dagger-tipped wreath of laurel above.

His eyes darkened with memories he tried, and failed, to obliterate.

"More fool I for ever thinking my fortunes changed," he said, half to himself.

"You must appeal to Lord Ares at once!" protested Josh, swiftly closing the distance between them. He reached to grasp Nicholas's arm. His own eyes were full with faint hope. "I cannot believe he would have our blood freeze in such a place!"

"He would have us do his bidding," Nicholas asserted evenly. "You forget, Josh—we are here not for our own pleasure, but for his. I was charged with holding Karabey. And that is exactly what I plan to do."

"We could leave at first light. Yes, and hasten back to Greece before the court has taken off!"

"We will not return to Greece." With an air of weary resignation, he picked up his gloves and gripped them tight in one hand. His gaze made another quick, encompassing sweep of the hall.

"For better or worse," he decreed somberly, "we are here to stay." Tempted to provide further argument, yet knowing full well that it would avail nothing at present, Josh reluctantly acknowledged defeat.

He dropped his arm back to his side and schooled his features to impassivity. "What would you have us do?" he asked.

"Make ready for the coming night. Break out the last of the provisions, and gather whatever wood can be found. The men must at least have a hot meal. Zeus knows, they'll find little enough warmth inside these walls." He wandered across to the fireplace, bracing a hand absently upon the smoke-blackened stones. "Tomorrow, we'll begin repairs."

"Tomorrow," Josh echoed. Giving a curt nod, he pivoted about and moved back to the doorway. He had yet to step outside before Nicholas's voice halted him.

"Josh?"

"Yes, my lord?" The look that passed between them was one of silent understanding.

"Make it known I will freely release any man who wishes to leave."

The words were spoken in a voice that was very low and level; the effort with which they were uttered was not lost on Josh.

"None will accept the offer," he said. Suddenly his mouth curved into an impulsive, boyish grin. "Like it or not, Nicholas, you will have sufficient company in your misery." With that, he was gone.

Nicholas stared after him for a long time. Then, cursing himself for a fool, he brought the leather gloves slapping against his leg and headed off in his friend's wake.

All was quiet.

The storm, mercifully brief, had left a multitude of shallow puddles glistening beneath the stars. Though it had only a short time earlier lashed at the earth with a single-minded vengeance, the wind was now little more than a faint, whispery breeze that caressed the hills and stirred the rain-washed leaves of the trees.

Standing alone in the fire-lit darkness of the master bedchamber near the very top of the keep, Nicholas directed a pensive glance downward. The squires and men-at-arms were temporarily quartered in the great hall below. They slept upon the cold marbled-floor, their blankets spread as close to the heat of the fire as safety would allow. Josh and the five other elite, who would normally have sought the comfort of private rooms above (as befitting their more exalted station,) had chosen to remain in the hall as well. It was by far the warmest and driest room at the palace. Outside on the battlements, four men had been posted to stand guard at each corner of the towers.

The new lord of Karabey lifted a hand to the thick, rough-hewn mantelpiece above the fireplace. For him, the hours had crawled by with agonizing unhaste. His eyes moved back to the flames dancing on the other side of the hearth. The firelight played softly across his face and cast long shadows upon the wall. Behind him, a huge four-poster bed, carved from solid oak, offered but a damp and lumpy respite from the day's worries. The rain had snaked in through the broken tiles of the roof, wetting both the mattress and the faded, heavy brocade curtains left undisturbed by the palace's plunderers The only furniture in the room consisted of a small table beside the bed, a massive yet empty wooden trunk, and an ancient-looking chair that had already proven itself capable of bearing the weight—though only briefly—of Nicholas's tall, muscular frame.

He was too restless to sit.

Still deep in thought, he turned and wandered to the arched window, noting idly that two of the nine lead panes of glass were missing. The night air wafting into the bedchamber was cold, and scented with a potent combination of wood smoke, wildflowers, and the rubbish in the courtyard below Inhaling deeply nonetheless, he gripped the edge of the stone sill. His eyes clouded with sudden pain, a pain dulled by time but never quite forgotten, while his mind drifted with a will of its own back across the past. What a fool he had been all those years ago. What a young, romantic dreamer.

My heart will always be yours, dearest Nicholas. Lauren's betrayal still haunted him, still served to make his blood run hot.

Damn the woman! Would he never be truly free of her?

He muttered another curse underneath his breath and flung a glowering look up at the fading brilliance of the moon. The first muted, tentative colors of the new day had already begun to light the sky. He turned from the window and moved back to resume his troubled stance in front of the fire. He was tired. Dear Zeus, he was tired. And he was in Anatolia. He released a long, uneven sigh and closed his eyes for a moment.

It was then, in the rare and peculiar stillness just before the dawn, that he could have sworn he heard the soft, lilting strains of a woman's voice …

CHAPTER 2

▼

Her eyes, full of uncertainty and nearly as blue as the blanketing sky, strayed to Karabey once more. Towering ominously above the village, out-lined against the endless blue of the sky, it served as a hated, inescapable reminder of an earlier takeover. Of other strong and battle-hardened men from across the Aegean sea who had tried, yet failed, to break the spirit of the Turkish people.

"The morn has long since fled, Leah Baal, and yet you tarry still."

Leah started guiltily. Dull, tell-tale color stained her cheeks as she turned back to face the old woman who stood regarding her from the house's narrow doorway.

"I-I have much to do, it's true," she stammered. She forced a smile to her lips and nodded politely at the tiny stoop-backed seamstress dressed in black. "Langdon will be wanting his new coat. Good day to you Margaret Hellyer, and my gratitude once more for finishing the job so quickly." She balanced the large wickerwork hand basket on her left hip and prepared to set off down one of the town's cobbled paths. Margaret, however, unexpectedly chose to ignore the farewell.

"They'll find no welcome here," the old woman pronounced.

Her ancient features creased into a sudden, deep frown while her gaze sought the five-story palace across the Banaz river. She drew her faded shawl more closely about her and shook her silver, wimpled head for emphasis. "None at all."

"Who?" asked Leah, feigning ignorance.

"Sent by Hades they be." She touched her hand to her forehead, then spat on the ground in a clear expression of disgust.

"Have you seen them?"

"No. But others have. Yes, and found themselves the worse for it."

She shook her head again while muttering, "Black-hearted rogues, they are Spawns of Lord Hades himself, come to steal what will never be theirs."

"Was it fear of their thievery, then," asked Leah, "that prompted all doors to be shut against them yesterday?" A faint, quizzical smile tugged briefly at her lips.

"Sneer if you must, child. But none in this town would pay *him* respect. He and the others are to be shunned, now and forevermore. Even the oracles have declared it so."

"So that is why the temple bell was rung." Strangely enough, the sound of it, reaching across the landscape to where she'd been seated alone in the gardens at Ponceel House, had chilled her to the very bone.

"And you'll be hearing it again, for there are many more prayers to be said." Margaret advised. She then leaned closer to reveal conspiratorially, "The new lord sent three of his elite to the marketplace not long after the sun broke this morn. After food, they were, and women to do the cooking and cleaning."

"And what came of it?"

"They walked away with naught!" Her pale gray eyes shone with triumph, and she cackled gleefully. Leah found herself unable to share in the laughter.

"He has the right to use force, if need be," she warned. "Surely defiance will only bring trouble."

"Trouble? What would you, a mere maid, know of trouble?" the widow scoffed.

"Enough to realize that Lord Ares' men will not be driven away so easily," Leah replied, her voice underscored by more than a touch of defensiveness. "I've been in southern Anatolia these three years past, remember? I have heard—"

"It matters not what you've heard." Margaret cut her off. "We'll not do their bidding. No, nor part with any of our victuals to warm their bellies. Come time for the feast of Artemis, they'll be away. Back to Greece." She uttered the prophecy with a conviction both thorough and steadfast, then fell easily into the old language with, "Από το Θεό, τους θα πάνε!"

"Mayhap they believe themselves in Hades already," Leah parried quietly. She glanced at Karabey again while Margaret, impatient now, disappeared inside the house and closed the door.

The sun blazed directly overhead, spreading warmth across the timbered, windswept slopes and setting Leah's hair aglow.

She had secured the thick, honey-colored tresses in a single long plait down her back—and had rebelliously disdained the use of a veil or a wimple. Her clothing had also been chosen out of a characteristic preference for comfort and simplicity rather than an eye toward social dictates. Of plain, deep blue wool, with long fitted sleeves and a rounded neckline, her gown was laced close to her body down the front. And while modest by most any standard, its clinging fabric served to accentuate the slender, well-rounded comeliness of her figure.

If not for the hooded mantle fastened about her shoulders, she might well have drawn even more attention while on her rounds through Karabey. But she gave little thought to her appearance as she heaved an audible sigh and idly maneuvered the basket—laden also with two books borrowed from one of the local oracles and new writing materials to join the cloak as a gift for Langdon Fogus—

onto the curve of her other hip. Curiosity rose within her, curiosity to see for herself what manner of men had come to enforce the latest infuriating and arbitrary restrictions against her people.

Black-hearted rogues, Margaret had called them. Perhaps they were that, mused Leah. Perhaps worse. Yet truly, all that mattered was their purpose in coming. For that reason alone, the invaders were to be despised.

Her eyes blazed with vengeful anger before she forced herself to look away from Karabey. Setting her leather ankle-high sandals along the cobblestones with practiced ease, she headed toward the makeshift tables set up in the midst of the central marketplace. The village was bustling with its usual midday activity. Karabey, although small, was fairly prosperous, claiming as it did the advantage of lying only forty miles downriver from the important city of Troy. Still, it was much like a small kingdom unto itself—*with a king whose subjects would gladly revolt.*

There was much to be done, especially after the hours sacrificed to the symbolic abeyance of the previous afternoon. Leah's crystal gaze swept the proceedings with found indulgence. A rickety, lop-sided cart loaded with fresh vegetables rolled over the arched stone path on its way in from the many outlying farms.

The clatter of people walking echoed throughout the streets, along with the sounds of laughter and music and the merchants' singsong hawking of their wares. Women were caught up in the endless, age-old cycle of cooking, scrubbing, sewing, and tending to their young. Men toiled in the nearby fields, set their hands to the cleaner yet no less worthwhile pursuit of shop keeping, or merely sat and passed the time with a mug of ambrosia and a circle of like-minded cronies. Chimneys jutting out of thatched roofs offered up the thick, ever-present curling of smoke; the smell united, hopelessly, with the even more pungent aromas of animals and food and human waste.

Leah emerged into the crowded square and repositioned the basket again before sailing forward. Her eyes sparkled at the tempting array of foodstuffs for sale—fresh strawberries and olives, pears and apples, figs and walnuts, milk and butter and cheese, puddings and sausages, wild game, meat pies and vegetables, and everywhere, loaves of freshly baked, whole-meal bread. The scent of spiced punch wafted from a huge black pot simmering over an open fire. Margaret Hellrey's widowed daughter stood behind a table displaying some of her mother's handiwork.

And one enterprising young man (little more than a boy, really) had taken it upon himself to gather a profusion of wildflowers and now offered small bunches at the princely sum of a half dra' each.

Watching the children who scampered to-and-fro in the sunshine, Leah smiled to herself, then quickly sobered when she recalled that there was still no proper school in the village. The oracles did what they could, of course, but it was little enough.

Very few families could afford to send their children to private schools in Thrace the way her foster parents had done. And Troy, while a good deal closer, was nonetheless too far distant for a daily trip.

Her spirits lightened once more when she caught sight of a group of young women gathered on the outer fringes of the open-air market. She hastened toward them. Having ventured into town all too seldom following her return from southern Tarsus at summer's end, she was eager to hear the latest gossip before making any decisions. The three years she had been away seemed like an eternity. But she was home now. Home in Karabey.

In spite of her superior education and families one-time wealth, the villagers accepted her as one of their own. They cared nothing of her privileged upbringing, but they were duly impressed by her heritage.

The Baal's, after all, had been powerful chiefs in the southern part of Anatolia—before they had lost both their land and their status to taxes. Drifting northwards, they had gained a certain notoriety as outlaws. Leah's father, had inherited the streak of 'mischief.'

Rascal he might have been, and a bit of a wastrel as well, yet he had clung fiercely to his Turkish roots and had been much loved by his neighbors When the great war against the Bulgarians had carried him off, along with his beautiful and devoted wife, the people of Karabey had honored his memory by erecting a small marble monument bearing his name in the town square.

Leah glanced down at the memorial on her way across the square.

The sight of it never failed to stir her heart.

"Good day to you, my love."

She drew up short, her eyes flying wide before lifting to meet those of the smiling, raven-haired young man who had suddenly moved to block her path.

Her temper at the sound of the endearment on his lips—innocent enough, perhaps, to be called 'my love' by such an old friend—and she resisted the impulse to scold him for it.

"I am surprised to see you here, Peatro Conrad," she told him.

Her color deepened as she observed the way his gaze traveled over her with an unnerving familiarity.

"Surprised you should be, Leah Baal." With an expression of mock severity, he said accusingly, "Have you forgotten the promise you gave me?"

"Promise?" Her bewilderment was both obvious and genuine.

"To ride with me this morn."

"Oh, I-I am sorry, Peatro." Full of contrition, she directed a significant glance down at the basket balanced on her hip.

"Langdon—"

"—gave me leave to search for you," he finished for her.

His gray-brown eyes twinkled, his angular and lightly freckled countenance shadowed by the wide, turned-up brim of his battered felt hat. He was dressed, as was his usual custom, in a simple cote-hardie of rough woolen fabric. His sandals were worn and caked with muck, giving evidence of the fact that he had spent the better part of the morning in the stables. "No matter," he insisted, "I will see you home."

"But I've not yet finished my errands."

"Then you shall have my help." He took her arm and began leading her back toward the food tables. There would be no gossip this day.

She did her best to conceal her disappointment.

"Are you not away to Troy tomorrow?" she inquired casually.

"I am."

"Will your mother be going as well then?"

"No." His fingers tightened possessively about her arm; he cast her a look of such tenderness and affection that her throat constricted in sudden alarm. "She would think it kind of you to pay her a visit in my absence. To discuss the wedding."

"Oh, Peatro." She sighed, halting and pulling her arm, gently yet firmly, free of his grasp. Her eyes were full of silent entreaty when they lifted to his face again.

"Have I not told you—?"

"Often enough." The smile that touched his lips this time was one of wounded irony.

"I have been away these three years past," she reminded him, quick to lower her voice as she glanced nervously about. She would not have the whole of Karabey know the intimate details of their courtship. Especially since it was a courtship in which she was a highly reluctant participant. "You must grant me more time."

"More time? We have known each other since childhood." He curled a hand about her arm once more and drew her over to the relative privacy of an alcove bordering the marketplace. "Was it not your own father's wish, Leah Baal, that we should be husband and wife?"

"It was indeed," she was forced to admit. She flushed guiltily.

"Yes, and my father's as well. It was agreed between them when you and I were but babes." Fighting the urge to pull her close, he assumed a more businesslike air and confided, "I have spoken to Langdon. He would see us wed before the year's end."

"What?" She gasped, her eyes growing round as saucers before she shook her head in a vehement denial. "It's too soon, Peatro!"

"Is the thought of marriage to me so distasteful then?" he demanded sharply, almost angrily.

"No. No, but ..." Her voice trailed away, and she searched for the kindest words with which to put him off. Sweet Hera, how could she ever hope to make him understand?

Mercifully, the fates intervened.

Before she could speak again, a commotion broke out in the village square The sudden thundering of horses' hooves shattered the here-to-fore peaceful camaraderie of the marketplace. A woman's terrified scream pierced the air, followed closely by another and yet another.

Leah gazed in horror at the seven horsemen who rode through the crowd with no apparent thought to the townfolks safety. Mothers frantically snatched up their children, merchants scurried to insure their tables were not upended, while the rest of the assembly looked on in shocked and silent disbelief.

The plates of mail worn by the invaders glinted harsh and cold in the sunlight, the banner carried by the lead man identifying them as the new lord's men. A path cleared for them. They drew their mounts to an abrupt halt.

Josh Leonidas swung down from the saddle. He wasted no time in striding purposefully to the stone, slate-roofed well in the center of the square. Withdrawing a parchment from his tunic, he swiftly unrolled it and held it aloft for all to see.

"By order of Sir Nicholas Constinos, Lord of Karabey," he proclaimed in formal, ringing tones, "I am posting this document in which are set forth the statutes of Troy. Surely, there are some among you who can read. The words are clearly written." He turned and secured the parchment to one of the well's supports with a sharpened peg. Behind him, a belated murmur began to rise from the crowd.

"What be these statutes?" a bearded, barrel-chested man demanded, stepping forward to confront Josh.

The man had heard of the new laws, of course. They all had.

Yes, and sworn revenge against those who had created them.

"Rules by which we must all live," Josh answered, his mouth curving wryly upward for a moment. "Be fore-warned—they shall be strictly enforced." He directed a curt, wordless nod at the six men-at-arms under his command. They dismounted as well now intent upon following orders—previously issued—to gather food. By force, if need be.

"To Hades with your rules!" someone called out.

"Yes, and may it please your Lord of Karabey to know we will soon be putting fire to his rules!"

Shouts and curses, given voice in both Greek and Kurdish, sounded from all quarters as the seeds of unrest took root.

The men-at-arms found themselves struggling in the midst of an increasingly angry and defiant crowd.

Josh scowled darkly and lifted a hand for silence once more.

"Sir Nicholas is a patient man, but his patience will soon wear thin!" he cautioned. "He owns Karabey and all that is within it. You will honor and obey him, else—"

"Από το Θεό, τους θα πάνε!" a woman's shrill voice intoned.

Clearly the desire for a poisonous pain to afflict the enemy was shared by others.

"And may Hades roast the heart of Lord Nicholas Constinos!" another woman added, her outburst rewarded by a roar of agreement.

Josh opened his mouth to speak again, but never got the chance. With no prior warning, a rock came hurtling toward him. It struck him full force upon the cheek. A small stream of blood trickled down his face.

Raucous, approving laughter erupted in the crowd. The men-at-arms hastily shoved their way back to Josh's side, their hands moving to the hilts of their swords in preparation for a battle they would fight gladly.

"Hold fast!" Josh bit out. His eyes gleamed hotly, yet he managed somehow to keep his temper in check. *Reason instead of might,* Nicholas had advised. By all the gods on high, what reasoning could there be with these savages? he asked himself. "Take care," he warned the townsfolk, raising his voice to be heard while his narrow, furious gaze swept the crowd "Set a course of rebellion, and you leave us little choice but to cut through it!"

To emphasize his point, he suddenly drew the sword from its scabbard at his side. The other men did the same. With a loud, collective gasp of furious startlement, the crowd instinctively quieted and fell back.

Watching from the alcove, Leah's eyes filled with horror. She took an instinctive step forward, but Peatro's hand caught her about the wrist.

"Stay!" he whispered.

"Are we not to do anything then?" she shot back, her sense of justice outraged by the menacing sight before her.

"Not yet." He shook his head and repeated, "Not yet, Leah."

"Henceforth," Josh instructed gravely, "there will be no resistance.

We will take what food we need this day. At first light tomorrow, you will send a wagonload of fresh provisions. *And* people to work at the palace—cooks, servants, carpenters, laundresses, and a blacksmith.

There are many repairs to be made. At week's end, Lord Nicholas will begin an inspection of his holdings."

This time, there were no jeers or insults offered in response— merely dagger-laden glares that spoke volumes.

While Josh and three of his men stood guard, the other three hastened to fill sacks with meat, bread, and vegetables. Once they had secured the bulging cloth sacks to their steeds, all seven sheathed their swords. Josh paused briefly then, a faint humorless smile playing about his lips while he settled himself more comfortably in his saddle.

"A final warning." The gleam in his eyes hardened. "My liege would deal fairly with you, for he is, in truth, a fair-minded man. Yet for good reason have his enemies called him 'The Raptor.' Defy him, and his retribution will be both swift and deadly."

He reined his horse about and rode away. The men-at-arms followed close behind.

Everyone began talking all at once in their wake. The marketplace sprang chaotically to life once more, its rebirth with a great mélange of complaints and curses of prophecies of doom.

Leah dropped her basket and pulled away from Peatro.

Making her way through the tumult, she hurried to the center of the square to read what was written on the parchment. The wording was stiff and formal, yet it was still possible for most who listened to glean their significance.

"'Regarding the loyal subjects of His Majesty, King Franklin Sie-maszko,'" she read aloud, translating for many townsfolk who could not decipher what was written.

"'These statutes were duly passed by a special Parliament con-vened in the city of Troy, in the year of the gods, thirteen hundred and ninety-nine.'" She took a deep, steadying breath and continued.

"'There shall be no intimate relationship between the Greek and the Turkish in either marriage or concubinage. There shall be no trade with the Turkish. There shall be exclusive use of the Greek language, even by the native Byzantine, and only Greek names shall be used for children. Any ancient Byzantine laws are hereby prohib-ited, with common law prevailing in all matters. There shall be no contact made with Turkish musicians, poets, and singers in view of the danger of espionage. The Greek shall have the right to lay claim to the choicest farmlands …'"

There were other statutes, less significant yet equally offensive, but she could not go on. Although her tone had remained admira-bly even throughout, she was seething with outrage. The men and women crowding close about her stared at one another when her voice trailed off; a mixture of shock and furious bewilderment was clearly written on their faces.

"What does it mean?" asked a young woman cradling a tiny, heavily swaddled baby in her arms. Her question was directed at no one in particular, and she did not wait for an answer before wander-ing away to find her other children.

"Why?" Someone else posed the inevitable. "In the name of Zeus, why have they done this?"

Leah knew why. Hadn't she heard rumblings of the impending travesty while at her aunt's house? She hadn't wanted to believe that the Greek leaders, for all their anger and prejudice toward her peo-ple, could be so foolish as to drive an even greater wedge between the two lands. The Ottoman controlled Anatolia. But they had never been able to truly conquer the proud Greek race across the land.

"The Greek fear that those who came before have grown more Turkish than the Turks themselves," she said, repeating what was common enough knowledge among the Turks.

"They have reason enough to fear," claimed Peatro, suddenly materializing at her side now. He turned and addressed his remarks to the others. "Two hundred years ago, the Greeks invaded our land. They sought to break our spirit—but found their own bending instead. Having failed then, they are set to try once more!" His countenance was flushed with an anger every bit as righteous as Leah's, and he scowled vengefully while slicing a hot glare toward Karabey. "Are we to be forever treated with contempt in all the lands?"

"Surely we can still dare to hope for a peaceful coexistence," the newest of the town oracles put forth. Looking very young and slight in her long robe of sheer white wool, she stepped forward and lifted her hands in an earnest appeal for reason. "I know Oracle Victoria herself has recommended separation and defiance at all costs. But no good will come of that. How can it? No, I say we've little enough choice but to submit. Do we not know what sort of violence these men are capable of? Perhaps, after all, Lord Nicholas may be persuaded—"

"This is his land, Oracle Lydia," Peatro snapped in a burst of impatience. "He'll not be persuaded to anything!"

"The oracle is in the right of it." Ronald Cayden, a blonde-headed giant of a man who had inherited the job of blacksmith from his father, towered above the crowd as he came forward. Folding his massive arms across his leather-aproned barrel of a chest, he took it upon himself to point out, "Were we to prove stubborn, Lord Nicholas and his men could easily cut us to shreds. They have the right."

"The right, you say?" a buxom woman in a bright red shawl gasped indignantly. "May Hades have mercy on your soul, Ronald Cayden! Are you of a mind to let him treat us however he pleases?"

"For all our talk, we will do as we are bid," Ronald said in his deep and gravelly voice. "Or see Karabey doomed."

A sudden, involuntary shiver ran the length of Leah's spine.

She listened to the townsfolk's responses to the blacksmith's words, listened to their heated arguments and foolhardy plans of rebellion, and felt her heart grow heavier. Shaken by what she had seen and heard, she fled back across the square to retrieve her basket.

Peatro gave chase.

"Come, Leah," he said, reaching the basket before her. He lifted it and clasped her arm as he had done earlier. "I will see you home now."

"No." She reached out and took the basket from him. "Truly, Peatro. My head is pounding and I would prefer to walk alone."

"You should not trouble yourself over what has happened." There was more than a trace of condescension in his tone, and even his eyes seemed to hold a special patience reserved for children and imbeciles.

"Should I not?" She rounded on him with startling vehemence, her own eyes ablaze. "This is my home as well, Peatro! I would not see Karabey, nor its people, come to any harm!"

"Let us fight the Greeks, Leah. Not one another," he exhorted soberly. When she pulled away, he was unwise enough to reiterate, "I have Langdon's permission to ride back to Ponceel house with you."

"Yes, but you have not mine!" Her angry steps led her away from him now.

"I will not allow you to go without my protection now that those Greek jackals have come!" He was in hot pursuit once more, but she quickly outpaced him. "Think, Leah, what could happen—"

"There are other dangers to be avoided!" She flung the retort back over her shoulder, then finally disappeared from view around a corner.

Her thoughts and emotions were in a chaotic whirl now as she walked homeward. The problem of dealing with her would-be betrothed paled in comparison with her worries over what would follow the disturbing incident with the Greek in the town square.

Already volatile, the situation with the new lord would be made a far sight worse by the preposterous 'laws' his armed men had posted. By the blood of the gods, she thought with an inward shudder, where would it all end?

She felt her spirits lift somewhat when she caught sight of her home in the distance. Nestled within a pastoral, tree-dotted valley less than two miles distant from Karabey, the estate had once been among the finest in all the land. And would be again, she vowed, if they dared to hope for any true justice in the world. The four-storied, gray stone manor house, covered by a thick tangled of ivy and in sore need of repair, lay at the end of a long narrow path. The outbuildings were, for the most part, crumbling and empty. Only the gardens were not greatly altered from the days Ponceel house, filled with the sounds of music and laughter, and with the brilliance of a thousand candles, had welcomed guests from as far away as Rome. Those times had long since fled, but the memory of them still burned brightly. And other memories as well, thought Leah, a sudden shadow crossing her face.

She had been scarcely ten years of age when she came to live with Langdon and his wife, Louise. The arrangement had been only natural, given the fact that Langdon and Leah's father, though not of the same blood, had regarded each other as brothers. The childless couple had welcomed her with open arms, had loved her as their own. She had been happy at Ponceel house these many years past.

And she would now do anything within her power to repay her foster parents for their care and kindness—except marry Peatro.

She frowned, whispering a quick prayer for guidance when she saw that Langdon stood waiting for her on the front steps of the house. Stopping only a few feet from the house, she hastily smoothed down the folds of her gown.

One look at her foster father's stern countenance was enough to warn her of his displeasure.

"Did Peatro not find you then?" he demanded tersely. His brown eyes, full of reproach yet not unkind, narrowed across at her. With his swarthy complexion and gray-streaked, black-as-midnight hair, he looked like Lord Hades himself, ready to pounce should he be crossed. But Leah knew differently. She knew that beneath his rough and burly exterior beat a heart that held neither evil nor malice. And it was to his softer instincts that she still hoped to appeal.

"He did." Turning calmly about, she lifted her hands to retrieve the basket she had napped on her back. "We chanced upon each other at the marketplace."

"And did he not tell you I gave him leave to bring you home again?"

"Yes, but I-I felt the need to walk alone." Facing him once more, she determinedly steered the conversation elsewhere.

"There was trouble in the town, Langdon. The new lord sent men to warn us."

"To warn us? Of what?"

"Lord Nicholas would have us obey him. And the laws he is determined to enforce."

"Laws?" Puzzlement immediately gave way to remembrance. He nodded his head and said, "Ah, yes. The statutes of Troy."

"You have heard of them already?" Leah asked in surprise.

"I was in Troy a fortnight ago, remember? To petition the courts again for the return of your father's lands." His lips curled into a brief, bitter half smile.

"Much good it will do me now."

"It is much worse than any of us feared." Her arms tightened about the basket. "Our language and customs are to be forcibly suppressed. The Greek may not join with us in marriage—a blessing in disguise, if ever there was one—and they have been given the right to steal what little we have left!"

"You are to marry Peatro."

She blinked up at him in disbelief, her face paling. "How can you possibly speak of such things now?"

"There will be no better time for such things, Leah." He raised his hands to her shoulders. His solemn, paternal gaze locked with the sparkling blue defiance of hers. "Can you not see? We must remain strong within ourselves. So long as we keep to our own path, the Greek cannot hope to win. By wedding Peatro, you will gain much more than a husband. You will help to guard the future for us all."

"But," she protested, her throat constricting in alarm, "I do not love him!"

"You were promised to each other by your fathers. And you are long past marriageable age. Peatro has been patient enough."

"Perhaps he has," she conceded, "but—"

"I must go to Karabey now." His expression had grown distant, unapproachable. Releasing her, he moved to gather up the reins of his horse. "I would see for myself what manner of man has come to rule."

"Take care, Langdon." Her concern was for him now. All too vivid in her mind was the lingering image of the men, swords drawn, who had threatened the townsfolk only a short time ago. "He may well—"

"I have no fear of him, Leah. Lord Nicholas is but a man, flesh and blood, the same as me." He mounted up and paused to give her a faint yet reassuring smile. "Greek or not, he will one day answer to Lord Zeus for his actions."

Her head spinning, she nodded mutely and watched as he rode away. It wasn't until after he had gone that she remembered the gifts she had brought him.

A short time later, after she had told Louise of the day's troubling events, she was relieved to be able to escape into the gardens.

She liked nothing better than sitting among the fragrant, well-tended flowers and greenery behind the house. Many times, she had sought peace and solitude within its protective boundaries, either to read a book or compose a letter. Or to sing.

It's your mother's gift, Langdon was fond of remarking about her special talent. It was said that Leah's mother sang like a muse.

"A muse," Leah murmured to herself, then smiled ruefully.

There was nothing at all inspired about the wild, deep-seated yearnings stirring within her whenever she sung the ancient ballads passed down from generation to generation. For, almost without fail, the stories told of men who were strong yet gentle, men whose hot-blooded passions were well matched by the women who loved them. It was this particular, all too earthly legacy that returned again and again to haunt her dreams at night.

Perhaps Langdon was right, she mused, blushing guiltily at her own wicked thoughts. Perhaps it was time she married. Only, Hera help her, why did she have to become the wife of a man, however good, who had failed to ignite a fire in either her heart or her blood?

She heaved a long, rather disconsolate sigh and sank down upon a marble bench—the same bench to which she had wandered just before dawn that morning, when a sudden and unaccountable restlessness had driven from the warmth of her bed.

She could not have said why she had paused to catch up a small, elaborately carved marble figure on her way outside, nor why she had found herself singing such a melancholy tune as Apollo turned the sky into a magnificent blaze of color.

Most surprising of all, however, was the way the music had filled her with a longing more intense, more earth-shakingly powerful than ever before ... and left her with a strange sensation that someone else had shared the secret desires evoked by every rich and plaintive note.

CHAPTER 3

▼

"Make haste, Leah Baal, else you will be left behind!"

"Perhaps, Theresa, I should not come," murmured Leah, a sharp frown of indecision creasing her brow. Torn between an unshakable sense of misgiving and a curiosity made all the more acute from a long, restless night's worth of anticipation, she caught her lower lip between her teeth and raised her eyes to the palace just ahead. It towered more ominously than ever against the sky, looking for all the world like something out of a dream Yes, she mused silently, a dream filled with myth and mayhem … and a tall, broad-shouldered figure shrouded in darkness.

She swallowed hard. An involuntary shiver ran the length of her spine.

"We can tarry no longer!" Theresa whispered impatiently, then spun about and hurried off to join the others.

Leah bemoaned her own cowardice as she watched the four women approach the bridge. The plan was already set in motion; how could she be so fainthearted as to abandon it now? She glanced down at the coarse, gray woolen gown and tattered black shawl she was wearing.

Borrowed from Theresa, the clothing ensured that she looked much the same as the other local women who had been summoned to cook for the Greek.

The threats and warnings had taken seed among the Turks.

Rebelliousness had given way to a keen sense of self-preservation and a desire to discover for themselves what manner of men now held their destinies ransom.

Each day of the past week had seen increasing numbers of them venturing across the river to do the new lord's bidding. The sound of hammering and the stench of burning rubbish had become common enough throughout the daylight hours, as had the sight of wagons, laden with supplies, rolling across the narrow stone bridge. Many in the town, of course, had continued to preach defiance, and there was still a palpable air of uncertainty to be endured. But it was painfully obvious that Lord Nicholas Constinos had won the first round in yet another battle.

Leah heaved a sigh at the thought and frowned again. An image of Langdon's stern, disapproving features flashed into her mind. He had ordered her to stay away from the building.

Yesterday, however, when Theresa had told her of the latest summons, she had known she would find a way to go, even at the risk of angering her foster father. It had required a lie to escape from the house—an invitation to dine with Theresa and her family—and once that lie had been convincingly offered, she had ridden into town to the tiny house Theresa had shared with half a dozen younger brothers and sisters. She could only hope that the night's adventure proved to be worthwhile. And, Providence willing, that she would be safely home and in bed before Langdon suspected anything at all.

Her blue eyes lit with renewed determination. Resolutely squaring her shoulders, she cast a swift look skyward and followed in Theresa's wake.

Darkness had already begun to fall. The rising moon had become obscured by a drifting curtain of clouds, and the wind's mournful howling—"like a siren," some would have described it—gave no sign of relenting. The night promised to be cold and fierce, the sort that chased all living creatures into shelter and turned the air above Karabey thick with smoke.

Aware of the knot tightening in her stomach again, Leah pulled the borrowed shawl more closely about her in a futile attempt to keep warm. She walked arm-in-arm with Theresa across the bridge and through the gate, all the while plagued with a strange sense of foreboding. What possible misfortune could await her? Could it be that her instincts were warning her to take flight? No, she told herself bracingly, it was nothing more than a lingering guilt over the night's escapade that gave her pause. There could be no true danger in it.

Still … *was it not said that curiosity killed the cat?*

"Keep close once we are inside, Leah," cautioned the buxom, dark-haired Theresa, "and speak to none. Langdon would take a switch to both of us if he knew what we are about!"

"That he would," murmured Leah, with a faint, preoccupied smile.

"Yet, mayhap Louise would find it amusing I am to spend this fine Autumn eve amid the new soldier's pots and pans."

"And would Peatro find it so as well?" Theresa asked teasingly, only to be rewarded with an eloquent frown from Leah.

The group's progress was noted by the men-at-arms standing guard along the outer walls. The bailey, apparently deserted at first glance, was lit by candles that gasped and sputtered with each step. The mounds of rubbish were gone. The kennels had regained at least some of their former usefulness, and a new kitchen had erected atop the ashes of the old. There were still a good many repairs to be made—in truth, the repairs far outweighed the necessary funds—but work had ceased for the day. All was quiet.

Leah paused briefly and looked toward the keep. She had not been inside since she was a child. Her eyes widened, then filled with a disquietude of the memory of those long-ago explorations. Karabey had seemed a frightening place then, haunted by the spirits of those who had perished within its great walls. Even now, she could not ignore its effect upon her.

"In there." A man suddenly emerged from the shadows to direct.

Leah tensed, her gaze flashing with recognition. The fair-haired elite before her was the same man who had posted the statutes of Troy in the town square. She tugged the white linen wimple lower upon her head, watching from beneath her eyelashes while Josh extended an arm toward the nearby, marble-walled kitchen.

"Hasten yourselves, good women," he said. His mouth curved into a soft, mocking smile. "I fear we have long grown weary of our own cooking."

Leah's companions treated him to a collective frown of belligerence before sweeping haughtily past. Leah cast her own eyes downward as she followed the others into the small rectangular building.

It was warm inside, in spite of the many gaps between the stones. A fire burned along one wall, and in the center of the room sat a rough-hewn worktable that had obviously suffered from years of both neglect and abuse.

There were only a handful of battered cooking utensils and bowls in evidence. Chunks of freshly dressed venison rested in a huge, ancient bronze cauldron beside the fireplace. A basketful of raw vegetables lay waiting atop the only chair in the room, while cloth sacks full of flour, salt, and spices had been flung carelessly in one corner. No rushes or straw covered the dirt floor. The air was thick with smoke—and the pungent aroma wafting from the kennels across the courtyard.

"May the gods preserve us all, are we to work miracles this night?" grumbled Mabel. A sour, big-boned woman of forty, she had only come to keep an eye on the others.

"Hold your tongue," the silver-haired Mildred Haanz was quick to advise. She shot a meaningful look toward the doorway, though Josh had already disappeared.

"Would you have your family cast out, or worse yet?"

"Lord Nicholas would not dare to harm us," Angela Hadgie, a slender brunette whose voice lacked conviction. She had come at her husband's urging; he had coupled his words with a chastening smack to her rump when she had resisted. Sighing heavily, she moved to snatch up a large wooden spoon. "It will take half the night to make a meal fit enough to eat."

"It's not so bad," Leah asserted, with a brief smile. "We must only—"

"And what would you know about it, Leah Baal?"

Mabel snapped. She folded her arms across her ample breasts and eyed Leah reproachfully. "It's naught but an adventure to you! *You* stand in no fear of starving. No, nor seeing your daughter's maidenhead stolen by one of the men whose bellies we have come to fill!"

"Holy Hera above!" Angela took a deep breathe, her eyes growing round with horror at the thought.

"But is that not forbidden by the new laws?" Mildred pointed out.

"Would you trust the Greek to be ruled by laws, even those of their own making?" Mabel countered, with a sneer. "My own blessed mother, may Lord Hades rest her soul, was set upon by a Greek monster when I was but a baby. Yes, and forced to bear his bastard son!"

"Perhaps we should not speak of that," murmured Mildred, her gaze flickering uncomfortably to the doorway again.

"Perhaps we should not speak at all," Theresa put forth severely.

She picked up a wooden bowl and crossed to the sack of flower.

"Talk will not be putting food on the table."

None could argue with that. Mabel glared at Leah once more, then fell silent and plunged her hands into the cauldron to seize the venison. Mildred launched her own attack upon the vegetables, while Angela went to fetch fruit from the garden outside. Leah, woefully unfamiliar to the workings of a kitchen, hurried across to give Theresa a hand with the flour.

The night deepened. Inside the great hall of the keep, Nicholas stood silently before the blazing warmth of the fire.

He held a scarcely touched cup of ambrosia in one hand; his other hand was braced lightly on the mantelpiece above.

He stared into the flames, lost in thought, while behind him the five lesser elite who had swore him lifelong allegiance commiserated with one another over their shared misfortune of the past week.

"And would you truly have us believe, Patrick, that the fall you suffered yesterday was not of your own doing?" Josh challenged wryly, leaning back in the chair as he sat at the table with the others. He lifted his own cup to his lips and downed the last of the fiery liquid.

"Do not doubt it," the raven-haired Patrick warned, with a mock scowl of anger. Still young and impetuous, the last several days had seen him battling restlessness as well as the Turks who had come to Karabey to work. "I tell you, it was the half-witted little beggar from the town that caused me to be unseated. He may well have loosed the cinch deliberately."

"I am beginning to think there are no accidents in Anatolia," the graying elite seated opposite remarked in a think-tongued drawl.

Older, yet not considerably wiser, David Bandle was a brawny, good-natured man whose skills at combat had earned him the respect of his comrades. At the moment, however, it was apparent to his comrades that he was more than half drunk. "No accidents at all."

"No, nor women." This particular complaint, here-to-fore voiced, came from Brian Vamaskis. He was slender, sharp-featured man, six and twenty years of age, who had known Nicholas for quite a few years.

"At least," he clarified unhappily, "none we are allowed to honor."

"Honor?" echoed Patrick. His eyes gleamed with sudden and wicked amusement. "Is that what you are calling it now?"

"Mayhap the Turks have a far more 'lyrical' name for it," John Lanpolous interjected, his tone one of biting sarcasm. Like Patrick, he was inclined to miss the earthly pleasures of Greece.

"If so, we shall never know—" Patrick started to parry.

"*Enough.*"

Nicholas's low, deep-timbered voice resonated throughout the room. The five elite, lapsing obediently into silence, looked in unison to him as he turned to face them.

His expression was solemn, his eyes betraying none of the turmoil within him. "Would you make it more difficult than it is already?" he asked quietly.

"Are you never tormented by such thoughts, my lord?" Patrick demanded, with all the rashness of his youth. He was immediately subjected to a sharp glower of rebuke from both Josh and Brian.

"Yes," conceded Nicholas, his gaze darkening now. "But I am long accustomed to denying them."

"As am I," David muttered, half to himself.

"Once we have made the town more hospitable, perhaps we will receive visitors from Greece," Josh told them.

His eyes met Nicholas's, and his features tightened imperceptibly before he revealed, with a deliberate lightness of tone, "Indeed, I do believe Lady Thalia is to favor us with a visit soon."

"Lady Thalia?" Patrick visibly brightened at the name, but scowled in the next instant. "This horrid place could never be fit for that sweet lady"

"Ah, but her presence here would be a blessing, would it not?"

David pointed out in all earnest. The others at the table could not refrain from smiling, however briefly, at his words.

Nicholas's eyes warmed for a fleeting moment before he pivoted slowly back toward the fire. He felt himself accursed this night, felt a strong sense of dissatisfaction deep within him. He could not shake it; even the prospect of seeing his sister again gave him no respite.

With the firelight playing softly over the rugged planes of his face, he folded his arms across his chest and closed his eyes. All too soon, the time would come to seek his bed once more.

But he knew he would rest little. His sleep had been troubled since the first night he came to Karabey. And stranger still, his dreams were always beyond recall ...

In the kitchen, Leah hurried to set the dough beside the fire. Theresa was close on her heels with another apronful of vegetables to add to the cauldron suspended over the flames. A stew had been the unanimous choice of meal. It was far easier to prepare than separate courses, quicker as well, and would no doubt please the palates of the men who had been judged far less than deserving of any better.

Mabel had suggested, not altogether in jest, that a pinch of poisonous herbs should find its way into the pot. Her remark had been met with nervous laughter from everyone but Leah.

Down south, she had learned that words alone could bring disaster.

The older women were lost in conversation around the worktable now, giving her the opportunity for a private moment with

Theresa. She cast a surreptitious glance over her shoulder, then leaned closer to whisper, "I am away to the keep."

"Oh, Leah. What was I thinking to let you come?" lamented Theresa. She straightened from the cauldron, a frown of apprehension creasing her brow. "You cannot really mean to do it."

"Was this not the reason I came?"

"Yes, and you were ever one for misadventure."

"I shall return soon enough," she promised.

"What if you are caught?" asked Theresa. She shook her head.

"Take care, Leah. True and lasting sorrows could come at a moment's curiosity."

Leah recalled the similar course her own thoughts had followed earlier. Ignoring the sudden twist of alarm within her, she told herself that life passed too swiftly to be ruled by fear. Impulse was the privilege of youth, was it not? And her days of freedom would soon be gone—especially if Langdon and Peatro had their way.

"I am but anxious to look about," she murmured, which was true enough. A quick and harmless exploration of Karabey was all she sought. That, and perchance a glimpse of the man few had yet seen. She tugged the wimple from her head. The white linen would be spotted too easily in the darkness. "If I am caught, it will be simple enough to explain my presence here."

She turned and headed for the doorway. Hesitation gripped her once more, but she conquered it and stepped outside. Behind her, she could hear Mabel questioning her departure, and could also hear the loyal Theresa offering an excuse of light-headedness brought on by the fire's heat.

Her pulse raced as she stole, undetected, around the corner to the darkened back staircase of the keep.

The marble steps were narrow and precarious, cracked with age, but she gathered up her skirt and climbed to the top.

Mercifully the door she found there was unbolted. She opened it, slipped inside, and with every care closed the door behind her.

Her whole body tensed as she pressed back against the wall and waited to make sure she had not been heard.

Again, memories flooded her mind. She knew she was in one of the corridors leading to the great hall, knew as well that it was there Lord Nicholas and his elite were awaiting their supper. Indeed, she could hear the sound of their voices drifting across the cold marble floor. She glanced up toward the ceiling, her eyes widening at the sight of the ghostly shadows set to dancing with each soft hiss and crackle of the fire. The wind's mournful howling continued, whistling through the cracks in the outer walls and adding to the pervasive otherworldliness of the palace.

It was a night like many another … Why then should it feel so peculiar?

She shivered. Whether it was from the chill in the air or the fear of discovery, she could not be sure. She remained still and quiet, trying to make out what the Greek men were saying. Although every instinct told her to flee, she would not leave. Not yet. Not before she had satisfied at least some small measure of curiosity burning within her.

"I cannot lie," she heard one of the elite proclaim loudly. It was apparent that he was somewhat better for a drink. "Were I divine, I should still suffer—"

"Were you divine," another of them interrupted, "you would spend your days in far less noble pursuits than you do now."

"Noble, you say?" a third snorted disdainfully. "Do you call it noble, Josh, to spend each night fondling naught but a cup of ambrosia while thirsting for what is forbidden?" His remark elicited more than one ironic chuckle.

"So long as you remain true and loyal to our liege's cause, you may 'thirst' as much as you please." Leah recognized this voice; it belonged to the man who had directed her to the kitchen a short time ago. But, she wondered with growing impatience, which of the voices belonged to Lord Nicholas?

Her eyes strayed toward the winding stone staircase in the nearest corner. Seized with a sudden desire to explore a bit farther, she gathered up her skirt again and crept away through the shadows. Her footsteps were light and sure, and she was grateful for the masking drone of the elites' conversation as she crossed swiftly to the stairs.

A candle burned somewhere above, sending a soft, golden array of light spiraling downward. Leah climbed the first narrow and uneven step, then the second, praying that the elite would remain too preoccupied to look her way. She forced herself to proceed slowly, and felt certain triumph within her grasp when, safely hidden by the cold gray walls of the stairwell, she neared the top step.

Without warning, a hand closed like a band of iron about her arm.

A sharp gasp broke from her lips. Her eyes opened wide, her blood thundering in her ears as she whirled about. She found herself facing a man. *The most striking man she had ever seen.*

Though she was balanced on the step above him, he towered above her, making her feel small and vulnerable ... and more aware of her femininity than she would have believed possible. She could literally feel the heat emanating from his body.

He was trim yet muscular, undeniably masculine, his powerful shoulders and broad chest encased in a belted cote-hardie that was much the same color as the dark, sun-streaked richness of his hair. He was handsome, but in a more rugged manner than the other Greek men she had seen. His features were tanned and chiseled, and there was something about the way he held his head that bespoke a confidence few (in truth, if any) men of her acquaintance had ever possessed.

He looked for all the world like some legendary hero of old come to life ... like a flesh-and-blood apparition of one of the great warrior gods such as Hercules or Apollo or perhaps even mighty Zeus himself. But it was his eyes that commanded her full attention now. They were dark brown, steady and penetrating, flecked with gold. And they were burning down into hers with such smoldering intensity that she felt her very soul stripped bare.

A sudden, electrifying tremor shot through her. She was shocked to feel a wild leaping of her heart. Her breath caught in her throat. Her senses reeled. She lifted her free hand to brace herself against the wall for support, fearing her legs would give way beneath her.

The stranger's fingers scorched her arm, even through the protective fabric of her sleeve. He held her so tightly, so possessively, that she was certain her skin would bear the marks forever.

And still, she could not break the spell.

Nicholas said nothing. His gaze traveled over her with a bold and unhurried intimacy, drinking in the sight of her comeliness. She possessed the countenance of Athena—and the body of Aphrodite. Her thick, honey-colored tresses, set aglow by the candlelight, had been secured in a single long braid down her back, though several wayward tendrils curled beguilingly about her face.

The coarse woolen gown she wore could not hide the perfection of her graceful, womanly figure. Her breasts were full, her waist begged for the spanning caress of a man's hands, while her hips were at once slender and well-rounded.

She was beautiful, far more beautiful than most other women he had known, but it was more than that.

Much more.

Staring down into the wide, fiery blue depths of her eyes, he felt a strange and unfamiliar warmth course through him. She seemed like something out of a dream. It was as though she had materialized out of thin air, as though she was a siren called forth to tease and torment him on a night when he was plagued by a keen, unnamed discontent.

Yet she was definitely human. Her arm was soft and warm in his grasp. Her breasts rose and fell rapidly beneath the clinging fabric of her gown. He yearned to draw her close, to taste the sweetness of her parted lips and feel her soft, supple curves trembling against him. He longed to lose himself in her embrace ...

The temptation was almost too powerful to resist.

Almost. For, like her, he could not yet bring himself to shatter the bewitchment.

Time stood still as they stared at each other within the secluded, shadowy, confines of the stairwell. The elites' voices drifted up to them from the hall below, the wind moaned and lashed as violently as ever against the palace walls, but they were oblivious to all save each other.

And then, a sudden draft caused the candle above their heads to sputter. The flickering of the light sent them crashing back to reality at last.

Leah was the first to speak. Abruptly wrenching her arm free, she pulled herself another step higher and stood battling for composure while Nicholas's gaze remained locked with hers.

"Away with you, sir, or I will summon help!" It was not at all what she had wished to say, but the words had come of their own accord.

"Will you?"

She was stirred anew by the quiet and resonant deepness of his voice. And though he spoke soberly, she could have sworn a faint, mocking smile tugged at his lips.

"I-I must return to the kitchen," she stammered breathlessly. She attempted to move past him, but he blocked her path.

"You are from the village?" he demanded.

"I am." She tried, without success, to ignore the mingled excitement and apprehension his proximity caused. Hastily retreating once more, she moved to draw the shawl about her in a defensive gesture, then realized she had left it in the kitchen.

"So. You are one of the Turks." His tone, oddly enough, was one of weary resignation.

"Yes. And you are one of the Greek." Her own voice held a discernible edge, while her eyes flashed accusingly across into his.

Nicholas cursed the acute, inexplicable disappointment searing through him now. Of course she was Turkish, he told himself angrily. What else would she be? What else had he hoped for?

"I must go," Leah murmured, then added impulsively. "Lord Nicholas's patience is no doubt wearing thin. He will wish to dine before midnight."

"You have met Lord Nicholas?"

"There is no need." She feigned indifference, then could not resist adding, "if I *were* perchance to cross his path, I would advise him there will be no welcome for him in Karabey—neither this day, nor any other!"

"And would he take heed of your warning?" Nicholas queried, with a deceptive nonchalance of his own. The temptation she presented was as great as ever.

"Why should he not?" She swallowed hard, torn between the urge to flee and the considerably more foolish impulse to tarry in his company. "I speak the truth."

"Yet the truth you speak is disloyalty."

"I owe the man no loyalty!" she asserted, with a proud, defiant toss of her head. "He may own Karabey—he may well own everything that is within sight of the palace ramparts—but never shall he be able to claim the hearts and minds of the people!"

"Strong words from a kitchen wench, would you not agree?" he challenged softly. Intrigued by her spirit, and more drawn to her than he cared to admit, he continued to subject her to an unwavering scrutiny.

She felt branded by his gaze. "Indeed, sir," she murmured. "But even a kitchen wench holds freedom dear." Dismayed to feel dull color staining her cheeks, she hastily looked away. She folded her arms beneath her breasts and shivered. This time, there was little doubt that it was from something other than the cold.

Another silence rose between them, a silence filled with a tension so palpable, so compelling and mysterious, that they both knew the memory of it would not easily fade. A sudden impulse prompted Nicholas to raise a hand toward her, but he caught himself in time and settled his fingers instead upon the hilt of the silver-trimmed dagger tucked into the belt round his waist. He watched as the candlelight danced softly over the delicate, smooth-skinned loveliness of her face. She looked far more like a well-born lady than a simple farm girl. Her manner of speaking was certainly more refined than he would have expected. But, no matter what her station in life, *she was Turkish.*

"What is your name?" he now asked, his voice splendidly low and vibrant to Leah's ears.

"My name can be little interest to you. For I am only one of the villagers, am I not?" She raised her eyes to his once more. He was surprised to glimpse sadness as well as anger within them. "The new laws would have me naught but a slave. A slave in my own country." Why did she speak thus to him? He was an enemy. And dangerous in a way she would not acknowledge.

"You bear little resemblance to a slave."

She was certain she detected a note of amusement in his voice. Certain as well that he had held many a young women spellbound with those fathomless, dark brown eyes of his. She found herself wanting to touch him, to feel his hard warmth beneath her fingers and therein know that he was no less—*nor more*—than any other man.

"Perhaps," she suggested, with a remarkable evenness, "you make the mistake of judging me by Greek standards. We are different. More different, I dare say, than even Lord Nicholas would have it."

"Yes, it is so," he allowed gravely. "Still, no good may come of the difference," he pronounced in a voice that was little more than a whisper.

The words were directed at himself, not her. His gaze darkened, taking on the appearance of cold steel. His expression became grim and foreboding And when he moved toward her, Leah gasped and instinctively retreated another step. For a moment, she feared he would strike her.

"Away to the kitchen, then," he ordered curtly, his fingers clenching about the dagger's hilt. "And, in future, beware of straying."

She was startled by the change in him. A very real fear joined with the chaotic tumble of emotions within her, but she would not show it. Affecting an outward air of bravado, she gathered up her skirts and swept past him.

This time, he made no move to stop her. She could feel his eyes boring into her back while she descended the steps at a slow, measured pace. When she reached the great hall again, she raced across to the door, uncaring now if the group of elite should catch sight of her. She flung open the door and escaped outside. The cold darkness of the night welcomed her; she was glad of its chill.

Her whole body felt heated, and her legs were unsteady beneath her as she fled back toward the kitchen.

For several long moments after she had gone, Nicholas remained silent and pensive upon the stairs.

He cursed the way his heart leapt in her presence—and cursed as well the fever still raging in his blood.

For I am only one of the villagers, am I not? The memory of her sweet, lilting voice, of her beautiful face and damnably tempting curves, provoked yet another urge of desire within him. But the significance of her words could not be ignored.

She was Turkish. Yes, and therefore forbidden. His eyes gleamed hotly, furiously. With a muttered oath, he turned and descended the stairs at last.

CHAPTER 4

▼

"It is not safe to ride alone, my lord," Josh said, appealing to Nicholas once more, though he suspected his efforts were in vain.

"By the gods, allow an escort—"

"By Zeus and Hades, man," Nicholas grounded out in exasperation as he settled himself in the saddle, "would you have me appear the coward before my own men?"

"Your men love you too well to judge you. But I fear there are some among the Turks who would seize full advantage of your solitude."

"All the more reason to show courage."

He gathered up the reins and flung a swift glance toward the keep, satisfied to note the progress being made on the roof. Zeus willing, there would be no dampness within his bed this night.

His gaze lit with fleeting humor when it traveled back to his friend's upturned visage. "Take heart, Josh," he exhorted dryly. "Should I fail to return, know that Karabey will be yours."

"A great comfort indeed, sire," parried Josh, then cast a significant glance skyward of his own. "The skies threaten rain."

"When do they not?" With a faint smile of irony, and a look that warned against further argument, he touched his heels lightly to the horse's flanks.

Josh frowned after him, still greatly concerned at the prospect of the solitary ride. It was obvious to him that his liege had been troubled by something of late; he has been even more taciturn and withdrawn these past several days. Still, he had not ventured out alone since coming to Karabey. It was an act that could be viewed as both impulsive and perilous, not at all in keeping with Lord Nicholas Constinos's usual, battle-honed prudence.

I pray some good may come of it, Josh intoned to himself as he watched Nicholas approach the outer wall.

The portcullis had already been raised and the draw-bridge lowered. A steady stream of workmen had crossed into the bailey during the later hours of the morning. Steady perhaps, Nicholas reflected with an inward scowl of displeasure, but not yet plentiful enough. Unless there was a substantial increase in the number of Turks who showed themselves obedient to his commands, the repairs would take months, even years. And neither he nor his men could hope to find peace and prosperity for which they had so long yearned. But he was determined to put such thoughts behind him, at least for a while, as he rode away from the palace and into the welcomed freedom of the countryside. The scent of autumn wildflowers drifted on the wind, while the sun, its radiance more often than not obscured by the gathering clouds, hung low upon the horizon. The promise of rain, almost always too distant in Anatolia, filled the crisp November air.

Nicholas allowed the animal beneath him to set its own pace. His gaze searched idly for the farmers in their fields.

His fields, in truth, of course. He and Josh, along with several men-at-arms, had made a tour of the surrounding lands a few days earlier. They had also paid a brief visit to the village. And had been greeted with glares of pure malevolence for their troubles.

The thought of it prompted his eyes to glint dully. He had little doubt that, as Josh had observed, some of the people (the majority, perhaps) desired nothing more than his death. He was accustomed to finding himself the object of hatred—fully half his life had been spent in the presence of enemies—but he had never before attempted to force his will upon others on a daily basis. He had never before endeavored to make his home among those who would see him in Hades. The constant struggle weighed heavily upon him. And although he was loath to admit it, there were times when he longed to escape the responsibilities that had been thrust into his hands.

He sought escape from something else as well. Something far less explicable—yet all the more disquieting for its mystery.

My name can be of little interest to you. For the past three days and nights, he had been haunted by the memory of the beautiful, golden-haired Turkish woman who had faced him with such spirit upon the turret stairs. He had tried to forget her. He had tried to ignore the fire she had set to raging in his blood. But his efforts had proven entirely futile. Her face had risen in his mind with an alarming—inordinate—frequency. His dreams, vivid and memorable at last, had been of her.

His lips compressed into a tight, thin line, and he muttered an oath underneath his breath as his fingers clenched about the reins.

The restlessness deep within him had grown worse since the night *she* had come to the palace. His heart felt heavy, his soul weary and athirst. By the gods, why could he find no peace?

The glint in his eyes darkened. The ride no longer held any pleasure for him. He slowed his mount to a halt and prepared to rein about. Although the palace was not in sight, he knew he had not traveled far. He could see the smoke from the village in the distance. The surrounding landscape, an endless, an undulating panorama of gentle hills, gave up a silence that suddenly made him feel more alone than he had ever felt before. He shifted in the saddle and tensed as the cold wind swept across him.

And then his ears caught the sound of music.

He was certain it was a woman he heard. The lyrical, wondrously plaintive tune being sung with her voice drew his attention to the nearby woods. A peculiar and earthly setting for such a godly melody, he mused with a ghost of a smile. He quickly sobered, recalling how he had heard the same lilting strains on his first night in Karabey. The music had sounded strange and mystical then. It sounded even more so now.

Intrigued, he hesitated only briefly before dismounting. He led his horse along behind him into the thick shelter of trees. The music beckoned him onward. Its compelling harmony joined with an ever increasing curiosity to see who was singing with such sweet passion …

Leah sat on the grassy bank beside the stream, her long blonde tresses unbound and her woolen skirts sprawled about her as she sang. Her bare feet were tucked beneath her; in spite of the chill in the air, she had discarded her shoes and stockings in favor of a quick wade across the clear, tumbling waters of the brook.

It had helped little to clear her mind, though she had fervently hoped it might.

Ever since the night she had gone to the palace, her thoughts had been invaded by the tall, ruggedly handsome soldier. He was unlike any man she had yet known. He was Greek, of course, and had no doubt gained considerable honor and glory in the service of Lord Ares—indeed, it was not at all difficult to envision him in the midst of battle—but there was something about him that went far beyond his imposing physical appearance, far beyond the boundaries of either birth or loyalty.

The memory of his eyes, darker than the Turkish nights, had often sent a tremor through her these three days past. She could still recall, with disturbing clarity, the sheer power and masculinity he had exuded, and the commanding, deep-timbered resonance of his voice.

No good may come of the difference. His enigmatic words had echoed again and again within the secret realm of her dreams. Though her encounter with him had been brief, she had been profoundly affected by it. So much so that both Louise and Langdon had remarked upon her uncharacteristic distraction.

"It is not like you to be woolgathering so much," had been Langdon's comment only an hour ago. She had murmured a hasty, noncommittal response. It would be impossible to explain what had happened. Impossible as well to promise that she would think of the Greek man no more.

Theresa, of course, had not failed to notice her heightened color and lingering discomposure when she fled back to the kitchen on that fateful night. But she had revealed nothing of her meeting with the soldier.

She had remained in the kitchen while the others served. She had made certain to secure the borrowed shawl well about her head upon leaving the palace some two hours later. And when she had finally slipped into the sanctuary of her own room at Ponceel House shortly before midnight, she had collapsed upon the bed, breathless and trembling and in such a chaotic state of mind and emotion that she forgot to undress. Sleep had been a long time coming.

Heaving a long, eloquent sigh, she allowed her eyes to sweep closed. She cradled her pillow closer, she began singing a soft melody with a grace and expertise that had earned her the admiration of all who had witnessed her talent. Turkish tradition decreed that singers, both male and female, be accorded great respect, for there were few who could truly master the muse. But Leah cared little for that. She sung simply because her mother had bequeathed to her the love of harmony.

And because, whenever she sang, she could lose herself completely within the mesmerizing sweetness of the song.

The melody she sang now was another ancient one. It told of a beautiful yet naughty princess, of a king disguised as a peasant, and a humbling power of love.

Leah's mouth curved into a soft smile as she thought of the unabashedly romantic fairy tale. The wind rustled through the leaves on the trees and teased lightly at her hair, but she took no notice of it.

Oblivious to all else save the music, she might well have continued singing until darkness fell—if not for the sudden realization that she was being watched.

The sensation was acute, so much so that it penetrated the aura of peace and well-being with which the music had surrounded her. Her eyes opened wide. She raised her head and saw the man who had proven himself so difficult to forget ... the same man whose nearness had left her atremble with strange, highly unsettling emotions.

He stood quiet and motionless beneath the canopy of trees on the other side of the stream, only a short distance from where she sat.

The deep crimson of his tunic looked much the same as blood against the gently swaying foliage. His eyes, steady and glowing and even darker than she had remembered, seared across into the sparkling blue depths of hers.

Momentarily transfixed, she stared back at him in open-mouthed silence. But she glimpsed something within his gaze which caused a warning bell to sound in her brain. He was looking at her with a hungry, almost rapacious intensity, yet at the same time appeared to be struggling with himself. She would not venture a guess as to the outcome of the battle, but it was becoming clearer with each passing second that *she* was the cause of it.

A sudden shiver ran the length of her spine. Her cheeks burned hotly. Her throat constricted in very real alarm.

With a soft, unintelligible cry, she finally scrambled to her feet. Her thick blonde tresses tumbled riotously about her face and shoulders, her skirts swirling about her bare legs as she instinctively sought escape.

But it was already too late.

She had no time to flee, no time to do anything more than offer up a quick, frantic prayer for—*for what?*

Nicholas, crossing the stream in two long strides, was upon her in an instant. His hand shot out to close upon her arm. He pulled her none too gently about to face him.

For a moment, they gazed at each other, their eyes locked in silent combat. Nicholas felt his blood run hot with the fever she had put there. The sight of her enchanting dishabille, the memory of her face as she had sung, provided too great a temptation. He could not hope to explain it, even to himself. All that mattered was that she was before him again. He forgot that she was Turkish, that she was only a simple peasant girl, and that to touch her was forbidden. He forgot everything but the urge—nay, the *need*—to have her close.

Leah's heart pounded erratically within her chest.

She swallowed hard, fighting against the light-headedness she had felt in his presence before. She opened her mouth to speak, but no words would come. Once again filled with a potent combination of apprehension and excitement, she sought to pull away.

He would not yet allow her to go free. *He could not.*

He drew her closer. She whispered something unintelligible. His gaze flickered briefly, hotly—downward to where her breasts, swelling above the low rounded neckline of her bodice, rose and fell rapidly. And when his eyes returned to capture hers, she was almost certain she read an appeal for understanding within their smoldering dark depths.

Without warning, he threw all caution to the winds. He caught her up against him at last. She gasped to feel his powerful arms sliding about her. Her hands came up to push against the hard-muscled breadth of his chest, but he swept her close, so close that she could feel his heart beating against hers.

Urging her higher in his embrace, he bent his head. His lips, warm and strong and boldly possessive, came crashing down upon the parted softness of hers.

She moaned low in her throat and squirmed against him in a last desperate attempt to prevent the inevitable. It was no use, of course. His arms tightened about her with a fierceness that set her pulse to racing. She closed her eyes. An intoxicating warmth spread like wildfire through her body as she surrendered herself to the pleasure of his kiss.

His mouth ravished hers with a hunger that was both frightening and sensuously persuasive. His hand swept downward to the curve of her hips. She gasped when his fingers curled about her backside, but still she could not summon the strength to resist—not even when she felt the unmistakable evidence of his desire pressing against her. She gave another low moan, scarcely aware of the moment when her arms strayed upward with a will of their own to entwine themselves about his neck.

Her head spun dizzily as the kiss deepened. Never before had a man dared to touch her as he was doing. Never before had she felt these wild stirrings of passion deep within. What was happening to her? Surely it was wicked and forbidden and no doubt the work of Lord Hades himself ... but, oh, sweet Hera, *it was also Mount Olympus on earth.*

She was startled when his mouth suddenly abandoned its masterful conquest of hers and trailed a fiery path downward along the graceful column of her neck. Her eyelids fluttered open, and she knew a moment's uncertainty, only to suffer another sharp intake of breath when his lips settled upon the exposed, satiny curve of her bosom.

"Μην σταματήστε!" She gasped, scarcely aware that she was begging for mercy. Her eyes swept closed once more as her head fell back; her fingers crept farther upward to thread within the sun-kissed darkness of his hair. He brought his hand up to close, with a near painful urgency, upon one of her breasts. She caught her lower lip between her teeth and trembled at the shocking intimacy of his caress.

Swept up in the flash and fire of the moment, she felt as though she had become lost in one of her dreams. She could not think of where the delectable madness would lead, not with her senses reeling and every square inch of her body feeling gloriously, irresistibly alive ...

Nicholas gave a low groan and gathered her close once more, his mouth returning to capture hers. He knew his self-control was slipping away, just as he knew that he wanted her more than he had ever wanted any woman before.

Yet his desire, flaring hotter than he would of thought possible, was tempered with a strange tenderness, an urge to protect her ... *from himself?*

Reason hit him full force now. Dear Zeus, what had he become? Would he take her here on the ground? Would he steal her innocence and then leave her to pick up the pieces of a life dishonored?

No. He would not. By the blood of the gods, *he could not.*

With a silent, blistering curse, he forced himself to put a stop to the heart-stirring embrace. He tore his lips from hers and raised his head. His eyes, simmering like molten steel, raked over the flushed, upturned loveliness of her face.

Leah opened her eyes now as well and blinked up at him in stunned bewilderment. She caught her breath at the savage gleam contained within his gaze.

"Go," he grounded out. He released her as if the contact had suddenly burned him.

She staggered backward, her skirts tangling about her legs and her bare foot slipping into the stream before she regained her balance.

Fraught with surprise, confusion, and a feeling of disappointment so keen it had already become an ache, she struggled to find her voice.

"Wha-what?" she stammered out, hastily folding her arms across her breasts. Another shiver coursed the length of her spine. Gone was the man who had kissed her with such hot-blooded ardor. In his place was a dangerous, stony-face stranger who looked at her with an anger she could not comprehend.

"Go. Else you may well find yourself—" He broke off abruptly and turned away. His hand went to the hilt of his sword. It was an instinctive gesture, born of many years' practice. But the weapon would do him little good; the enemy he faced was his own deep-seated yearning.

Behind him, Leah's eyes sparked and blazed as all other emotions gave way, for the moment at least, to a furious, righteous indignation.

Uncrossing her arms, she balled her hands into fists and planted them firmly on her hips.

"Would you blame *me,* good sir, for your misdeed?" she demanded, with biting sarcasm. A sense of humiliation began to wash over her now, adding fuel to the fire.

"The blame ... is mine alone." He slowly pivoted to face her again.

His mouth curved into a brief, mocking half smile that made her legs weaken anew. "Though, if you were less comely, temptation would have long since fled." In actuality, of course, it was more than her beauty that had drawn him like a moth to light. *Like a moth to light,* his mind echoed. His visage grew taut with the effort it was costing him to keep his distance while his eyes traveled over her once more.

"So that is to be your excuse then?" Leah said accusingly, dismayed to feel herself blushing beneath his hot, branding gaze. She knew it was foolish to tarry any longer, foolish to risk a repetition of what had just happened, but she could not leave. Not yet. Not until she had reclaimed at least some small measure of her dignity.

"Because you think me pleasing to look upon, you believe you have the right to play conqueror?"

"You are indeed pleasing to look upon. And, in truth, the right is mine. But—"

"What do you mean?" His words struck another chord of fear in the pit of her stomach, yet she concealed her disquiet behind a show of fiery defiance. She stepped closer, tilting her head back to confront him squarely. It was difficult for her to ignore the way her heart quickened at his proximity, but she did her best. "You think because you are Greek that you may lay claim to everything in Karabey?" she challenged, her eyes narrowing up at him. "Well then, *my lord,* you have sorely underestimated us. Why, even if Sir Nicholas Constinos were to command me, I should not obey in this or any other matter!"

"Would you not?" Again the ghost of a smile touched his lips.

"No, and you may convey that message to your liege!"

"And who shall I say has sent the message?"

"Leah Baal. The daughter of Viggo Baal himself." She lifted her chin at the declaration, her proud demeanor a striking contrast to her becomingly tousled appearance.

"So, you are no kitchen wench after all," murmured Nicholas, frowning as he recalled the memorial he had seen in the village. The discovery she was of noble birth made little difference, save for the fact that it explained her educated speech and genteel ways. "Why did you allow me to think otherwise?"

"I was under no obligation to set your thoughts right," she replied, with more than a touch of defensiveness. "No, nor am I under any obligation *now* to allow myself to be-to be treated with such disrespect. I did not invite you to intrude upon my sanctuary." Her gaze fell. Quickly moving past him, she bent to wash her hands in the nearby stream, all the while trying in vain to forget how it had felt to be in his arms. Her lips still tingled from the sweetly savage assault of his. Her body was still plagued by a lingering—highly disturbing—warmth.

"I heard you sing. You sing well."

"I sing to please myself and no other!" she retorted, angrily whirling to face him again. "The new laws set forth by His Majesty, King Franklin Siemaszko, forbid you to listen to our music. And do they not also decree that you shall keep your distance?" She regretted the taunt in the next instant, for he suddenly advanced upon her. She backed away, her eyes growing very round, but he made no move to touch her again.

He stopped mere inches away from where she stood gazing up at him in breathless expectation. "Why are you here like this?" he demanded tersely. "Have you no husband or father to keep watch over you?" His gaze darkened at the possibility that she was wed.

"My foster father allows me the freedom to choose where I go."

"Do you not realize the danger of being alone in these woods?"

"I have never felt threatened before this day."

"Yes," he allowed in a low, strangely vibrant tone. "And so you should, Leah Baal." He did not elaborate, but the look in his eyes as he towered above her provoked yet another tremor. Again, she sought refuge in her anger.

"Lay hands upon me, Greek man, and I will see you hanged," she warned, though she knew she did not mean it. How could she hope to see him punished for what she had, in all honesty, encouraged?

Zeus help her, why had she behaved with such utter wantonness? She was lost to shame …

"Why did you come to the palace that night?" Nicholas asked quietly, interrupting her unhappy reverie. His question took her off-guard.

"It was idle curiosity, nothing more." She presented her back to him again and wandered across to the water's edge. Painfully aware that he was watching her every move, she sank to her in knees on the grass, and reached for her shoes and stockings.

"And was your curiosity satisfied?"

"Yes. So much so that I have given it no thought whatsoever since then."

"A falsehood indeed."

Startled, she inhaled upon a gasp and jerked her head up to meet his gaze. For a moment, she could have sworn he meant to close the gap between them once more. But he did not.

"We shall meet again," he promised solemnly.

A sudden rumble of thunder echoed across the hills.

Leah swallowed hard and cast a swift, worried glance up toward the sky. Her trepidation had nothing to do with the prospect of a rainstorm. No, it was the storm inside her that gave her pause, the storm that had been gathering since the night this man first crossed her path.

"Will you not give me your name?" she queried, with as much composure as she could muster under the circumstances. "I would know the name of the ill-mannered rogue who has dared to accost me!"

"My enemies, so I am told, call me 'The Raptor,'" he replied, with an undercurrent of irony. His eyes glowed as he watched her face pale.

"*Sir Nicholas Constinos?*" She breathed harshly in disbelief. "You-you are Sir Nicholas?"

"Yes."

She climbed slowly to her feet, her gaze filling with the awful realization at last. Her hand trembled as it lifted to her throat. "Why did you not tell me before now?"

"Would it have mattered?"

"No." She shook her head for emphasis. "But you enjoyed the deception, did you not? Yes, and sought to use it to your own advantage!"

The truth of his identity made his actions even more unnerving somehow. Perhaps because, as he himself had said, he had the right to demand her obedience.

As the master of Karabey, he was required to answer to no one, save Lord Ares. *He could do as he pleased.* The thought strengthened her outrage.

"Had I intended to take advantage," he pointed out gravely, "I would have done so. And left us both the wiser for it." His gaze flickered over her with a bold familiarity that made her face flame anew.

"You truly *are* a spawn of Hades!" she charged feelingly, unmindful of his exalted position. "The oracles were right to call you accursed."

"Think of me what you will," he replied, his own manner impassive. "It was never my intent to seek your good opinion. Yet, there is something between us. Something that cannot be ignored."

The hotly impetuous embrace had left him in as much of a quandary as she But there was no fear in him—only bemusement. And, strangely enough, a sense of well-being, the first he had known in a long, long time. The knowledge prompted him to look at her with no small amount of consideration, his gold-flecked gaze intensifying once more. If he were a superstitious man, he would have thought himself bewitched.

"May I well be damned for it, Leah Baal," he told her in a voice that was deceptively level, "I will not forget what has happened this day."

"It will never happen again," she vowed, adamantly scorning the truth of his words. "*To Hades with you,* Sir Nicholas Constinos!"

He said nothing more. His features inscrutable, he subjected her to a last thorough scrutiny. She closed her eyes against the fire in his.

And then he was gone.

Leah collapsed to her knees on the ground in his wake. Sudden tears gathered in her eyes as she wondered why her heart ached and fluttered so. No real harm had been done—had it? She had been kissed, *well and truly kissed,* yet nothing had been stolen save a measure of her pride and peace of mind. Why then did she feel as though she had lost a great deal more?

"Sir Nicholas Constinos," she whispered, still shaken by the discovery of his identity. It was worse than she had feared. Far worse. He was no mere vassal. No, by Zeus, he was the man set above all others ... the man she and everyone else in Karabey had sworn to hate.

We shall meet again. She caught her breath at the memory of his lips upon hers that filled her with a powerful mixture of delight and dismay. "Sweet Hera above, what am I to do?" she sent the urgent, heartfelt plea skyward, only to be answered with another deep rumbling of thunder that seemed to mock her confusion.

With her hands still shaking, she quickly donned her stockings and shoes, and raced back through the woods. The serenity of the afternoon had been shattered. And, to make matters worse, the drops of rain, cold and hard and stinging, began to pelt her before she could reach the safety of home.

Her clothing was very nearly soaked through by the time she slipped inside the house. She closed the heavy, iron-banded front door behind her, and leaned wearily against it.

She straightened and lifted a hand to rake the damp, windblown tresses from her face.

"Where have you been, Leah?" she suddenly heard a familiar voice demand. Her eyes, round with surprise, flew to where Peatro Conrad stood frowning at her from the doorway to the firelit library.

"You startled me, Peatro!" Guilty color flooded her face as she tensed and crossed her arms against her breasts. Her eyes sparkled with annoyance before she asked, "why are you here?"

"I am here to discuss the terms of our betrothal."

"Our betrothal?" She blinked hard and hugged herself tighter, trying not to shiver as the wind found its way into the once elegant house. Belatedly noticing that Peatro was clad in his finest cote-hardie, party-colored, and trimmed with fur, she found herself plagued by a sense of impending doom.

"It is time, girl," Langdon somberly decreed, materializing behind the younger man now. He lifted a companionable hand to Peatro's shoulder and gave Leah a look that caused her throat to constrict in alarm. "It's time."

"No!" she breathed unevenly in horrified disbelief, numbly shaking her head. "You cannot mean—?"

"We have settled the matter, Peatro and I," Langdon announced, again with a finality that gave her pause.

"You will be wed December Eve. The feast of *Artemis* will serve as your wedding celebration."

"There will be no wedding," insisted Leah. Her tone was edged with hurt and angry defiance. Her narrowed, flashing gaze shot back to Peatro. "You cannot force me to your will this way. You have no right—"

"You are Langdon's daughter by law if not by blood," he said, cutting her off. "And he has given us his blessing. He would see you happy."

"Happy?" she echoed. Striving to remain calm, she shook her head.

"There can be no happiness in a marriage forced upon me. I will not be your wife!"

"Leah, think before you speak." Langdon appealed to her now. His brown eyes held true affection, yet also growing annoyance. "You know it was your mother's wish for you to marry Peatro. You have chosen no other husband Indeed, your aunt's letters have told me how you refused every man down south who sought your hand." It was clear that his patience was ebbing when he demanded gruffly, "would you see yourself a spinster?"

"Better that than wed to a man who stirs neither my blood nor my heart!" she retorted, then suffered a sharp intake a breath as Sir Nicholas Constinos suddenly swam before her eyes.

"You are only a woman," Peatro pronounced unnecessarily. His own eyes lit with an ill-advised determination. "Mayhap it is time you were reminded of it. *And* saw the bargain sealed!"

Drawing away from Langdon—who refrained, wisely or not, from interference—he strode forward and caught Leah about the waist. She cried out and struggled against him, but he succeeded in pressing his mouth to hers.

It was the second time that day she had been kissed. Yet this embrace was nothing like the earlier one.

Nothing at all. Whereas Sir Nicholas Constinos's had set her afire, Peatro's provoked only furious indignation.

Lifting her hands to his arms, she pushed him away. Her eyes blazed wrathfully up at him; two bright spots of angry color rode high on the creamy smoothness of her cheeks. "I will not be treated so churlishly, Peatro Conrad! No, and I will not marry who I do not wish. By all the gods on high, I am a Baal! The blood of the Turkish chieftains run strong in my veins. No Baal has ever surrendered to the will of another without a fight. And no man shall lay hands upon me unless I choose to have it so." *No man?* A tiny voice inside her head challenged archly. Ignoring it, she looked to her foster father. "Will you not at least scold him for the dishonor he has shown me?"

Langdon would say nothing at the moment. In truth, he was stung by the reproach in her gaze.

"Very well." She refused to yield to tears or supplication. Her pride had suffered enough for one day. "Then say nothing." She pulled herself rigidly erect and declared, "know that I would please you in all ways, Langdon Fogus—save this one. You cannot ask this of me. No, nor command me to it, either." She looked to Peatro. "*There is no bargain.*" Her eyes, resembling twin pools of liquid blue fire, promised swift and well-considered retribution if he dared to press the matter further.

The two men watched as she swept across the dimly lit foyer and up the winding staircase. Once she was gone, Peatro turned to Langdon with a scowl of angry disgruntlement on his face.

"Hold fast to the promise that was given, Peatro," the older man advised grimly, then heaved a sigh while his gaze drifted upward.

"She will soon learn to accept it."

"She has already been granted twenty years in which to learn."

"'Ambrosia is sweet, but paying for it is bitter,'" Peatro replied, his mouth twisting into a humorless smile as he ran a hand through his thinning, overly groomed flaxen locks. "Bitter indeed." He, too, flung a glance toward the ceiling. "I could make an appeal to the new lord. He could command the marriage to take place. By law, we must seek his permission to wed."

"Greek law," grumbled Langdon, leaving little doubt as to his poor opinion of it.

"Sir Nicholas may take an interest," Peatro suggested as the thought took seed. He visibly warmed to the idea now, his gray-blue eyes filling with a renewed purpose. "A gesture of goodwill toward the people of Karabey, perhaps ... an example of his benevolence. Yes, he might welcome the chance to win favor with us."

"No." Langdon shook his head and argued, "we need none of *his* interference. It is best to settle this among ourselves."

"Have I not tried that already?"

"You cannot truly mean to enlist his aid. The man is our enemy."

"And will remain so. But an enemy can be of use, can he not?

I must follow my own path now, Langdon Fogus. And if the path should lead to the palace, then so be it."

"Do not play the fool, boy. You will but make matters worse," Langdon warned tautly, angered by the younger man's selfishness. "Think of—"

"Leah shall be mine," vowed Peatro. His pale, angular features became set in an expression of willful resolve, his tone defensive when he added, "Though I were forced to plead my case with Lord Hades himself, I would do so and be glad of the ally!" With that, he snatched his cloak from a peg beside the door and took his leave.

Blissfully unaware of his scheme, Leah stood at the window in her small, candlelit bedchamber and stared out across the rain-lashed countryside. She had stripped off her wet clothing and donned a fresh smock and kirtle; her hair was even more tousled as a result of the vigorous scrubbing she had given it with a length of thick toweling. Absently lifting a hand to the window's draperies, she allowed her fingers to tangle within the soft faded velvet. Her temper had not yet cooled from Peatro's insolence. The prospect of becoming his wife seemed even more distasteful than ever. But it was not the simple lack of affection—at least the sort required for marriage—that fueled her reluctance. It was also the memory of her brief yet passionate encounter with Sir Nicholas Constinos.

A comparison between his kiss and Peatro's had been inevitable. So, also, was a comparison now between the two men themselves.

One was young and untested, little more than a boy really, while the other, for all the impetuosity he had displayed this afternoon, was a man clearly hardened and honed by what life had offered him thus far. She could still remember the almost savage gleam in his eyes. Yet there had been tenderness there as well. And longing. A longing that seemed to speak to her very soul …

"You play the fool, Leah Baal!" she rebuked herself in a tremulous whisper, dismayed at the turn of her thoughts.

A short distance away, within the cold marble walls of the Karabey palace, another mind was similarly troubled.

Like Leah, Nicholas stood pensive and still, his gaze reflecting the battle that was raging within him. *She* is Turkish, the voice of reason proclaimed fiercely once more. The significance of that was greater than even she would realize. For he was a soldier of Sparta, sworn to honor and duty, charged with the defense of Greece's interests in Karabey. His own interests mattered little.

For the past ten years, they had mattered little. Could he now set them above the glory of Sparta?

Shaking his head, he resumed his seat at the table in the great hall. He was alone, and resolutely sought to return his attention to the ancient, tattered account book he had discovered in an old wooden chest, long ago plundered and neglected, that had been shoved into a corner of the room. What plagued him was temporary madness, nothing more. He would soon purge himself of the desire which had led him to Leah Baal. Never again would he tempt the fates.

Yet … his eyes glowed hotly of the memory of her body pressing against his, of her supple curves and sweet mouth. She had responded to him with a fire and passion that belied her innocence.

And afterwards, though her eyes had blazed with anger, he had sensed within her a yearning as startling and powerful as his own.

"Something that cannot be ignored," he murmured, repeating the truth.

The sound of approaching footsteps reached his ears. He frowned and pulled himself up from the chair again, his gaze growing hooded as he watched Josh saunter into the hall.

"I am sorry to disturb you," said Josh. His concern, and his curiosity, deepened when he caught sight of the forbidding expression on Nicholas's face. It was obvious that the solitary ride had failed to improve his liege's mood. "I have news to impart."

"Then do so."

"We have received word that Lady Thalia will arrive in two days' time."

"Two days?" echoed Nicholas, then swore silently. "She has hastened her journey."

"That she has," Josh concurred, a wry smile tugging at his lips. "She was ever headstrong."

"And shall have cause to regret it," Nicholas promised.

Fond as he was of his sister, he had neither the time nor the patience for her willfulness at present.

"Perhaps her presence here will help whatever troubles you," Josh ventured carefully. When there was no response he stepped closer, his eyes searching Nicholas's face while he prompted, "will you not tell me—?"

"No." His tone was quite low and distant. "This battle is best fought alone."

Josh started to press for more, but decided instead to change the subject. He smiled and folded his arms across his chest. "Do you recall, my lord, that we are to make further inspections of the farms tomorrow?"

"Yes."

"It has just this moment occurred to me that Lady Thalia's visit can be used to a particular advantage. I have little doubt that she brings a goodly number of servants with her. But, might she not enjoy the novelty of a Turkish woman as a lady's maid during her visit? It would, I think, represent a token of faith to the villagers, a small but significant show of trust. And if you are agreeable, I will set about finding a suitable—"

"That will not be necessary." Leah's face flashed across his mind as the idea took hold. Again, a sudden and irresistible impulse compelled him to declare, "I know of a woman."

His instincts warned against it, of course. He told himself the temptation would be too great, the danger too real. But he could not—*would not*—refuse the opportunity the fates had given him.

"She will serve as a companion rather than a servant," he decreed quietly.

"Surely it would be unwise to set her above one of Lady Thalia's own attendants," protested Josh, visibly taken back at the command.

"The woman of whom I speak is no servant." There was an edge of steel to his voice. Josh knew well enough to heed it.

"As you wish, my lord," he murmured.

When Josh took his leave, Nicholas moved across to the window and looked to the nearby woods. His eyes gleamed with both defiance and determination. "One way or the other, Leah Baal," he vowed, "we shall have an end to it."

CHAPTER 5

▼

The summons arrived two days later.

"Zeus help me, what am I to do?" murmured Leah, her face blanching anew at the prospect of what lay ahead. She sighed heavily and crossed back to where Theresa stood slicing carrots and cabbage to add to a thick mutton broth. "The message was delivered only an hour ago, by one of the young scribes from the palace." A shiver danced down her spine.

In her haste to seek Theresa's advice, she had forgotten to don a cloak; the delicate fabric of her vermilion brocade gown had done little to protect her from the morning's chill during her ride to the village. She instinctively drew closer to the fire now and swept a wayward lock of hair from her face while striving to calm herself.

"Does Langdon know of it then?" asked the buxom, dark-haired Theresa.

"No. At least the fates were merciful enough in that. He and Louise had ridden to Troy. They will not return for yet another day." Her fiery gaze dropped to the letter in her hand.

"Companion to Lady Thalia Constinos, sister of Sir Nicholas Constinos," she read again.

The arrangement was to be a temporary one, its duration no more than a few weeks' time, yet the thought of spending so much as a single day underneath the compelling, divinely handsome master of Karabey filled her with dread.

"I am no slave to be commanded at will!" she exclaimed, with indignation, then released another sigh and set to pacing restlessly about the small, cluttered interior of the cottage. Sunlight streamed in through the uncurtained window, adding to the warmth given off by the fire. The morning had dawned bright and clear, yet she was of no mind to give thanks for the rarity of a sun kissed November day.

"You must obey," Theresa told her, with surprising equanimity.

Leah stopped dead in her tracks and rounded on her friend in wide-eyed disbelief. "How can I possibly do so?"

"How can you not?" retorted Theresa. She set aside her preparations for the stew, knowing well that whatever she served her family for dinner would bring on a chorus of disapproval, and fixed Leah with a sage, cautionary look. "Think of what has come to pass of late. Sir Nicholas holds the law in his hands. He has the mighty Spartan army behind him. Your family—yes, and the whole village as well—could suffer if you were to refuse."

"The matter is between only myself and Sir Nicholas," Leah declared stiffly.

"Indeed. How so?"

"It is a personal ..." She started to explain, but left the sentence unfinished as her cheeks burned guiltily. With feigned composure, she presented her back to Theresa again and moved to the open doorway. She folded her arms beneath her breasts while pointing out, "Langdon will never give his consent."

"Then you must persuade him to it. Though, in truth, his consent is not needed."

"And what of Peatro?" Her mouth twisted into a bitter little smile as she distractedly lifted a hand to the door frame. The sun's strengthening rays caressed her face, while her gaze made a slow, halfhearted scrutiny of the narrow street running in front of the cottage. The familiar sounds and smells of the village were laid before her, the palace an inescapable sight looming above all else.

"Peatro would have it that we are betrothed. I can well imagine his anger when I tell him of the summons."

"He is a good man, though often enough a blind one," replied Theresa. A sudden shadow flitted across her pretty, apple-cheeked countenance, but she hastily concealed her distress. "If he values his life, he will not seek to interfere."

"His life?" Leah gasped. Dismayed, she whirled to meet Theresa's gaze again. "Do you truly believe Sir Nicholas would—?"

"He is Greek, is he not? What should he care if one of us met death?"

"I pray you are wrong. But still, I cannot go to the palace."

"Perhaps it will not be such an ordeal," Theresa offered unconvincingly.

"It may be far worse," murmured Leah. Then she declared, "It is time to draw courage and find out." Her eyes filling with determination, she squared her shoulders and announced, "I shall appeal to Sir Nicholas myself. I shall endeavor to make him understand."

Make him understand *what?* she then asked herself. That she was afraid of him? That she suspected the summons had little to do with his sister's need of a companion?

"I do not think him capable of a great deal of understanding," Theresa cautioned. She stilled the knife in her hand, a frown of genuine trepidation knitting her brow. "I have seen him, Leah. A tall and well-favored man, with eyes the darkest I had ever beheld. There is a hardness about him. One of the Greek men told Oracle Victoria that Sir Nicholas was as fierce and cold-blooded as the titans of old, and that the very sound of his name is enough to strike fear in the hearts of his enemies. The people here in Karabey fear him—and hate him as well they should—yet none of us know him.

Not truly. He has kept himself mostly at the palace thus far, but I do not doubt he means to bend us to his will."

"Nor do I," said Leah. Her pulse leapt wildly at the unbidden memory of his embrace, and she was aghast to realize just how often she had dreamed of his arms about her. Margaret Hellrey would in all likelihood pronounce her bewitched, and offer her a charm or even some foul-smelling potion in which to break the spell, but she knew that the passion he had awakened in her was neither other-worldly nor exaggerated by guilt. How could she face him again? *Why had he summoned her?*

"I will come with you," Theresa insisted. She began untying the strings of her homespun apron.

"No. I must go alone."

"But are you not wary of going among those monsters without—?"

"I am in no danger," she lied.

"There are many kinds of danger," Theresa reminded her. "Do you not recall what harm was done to Mabel's mother by the Greeks?"

"That happened a long time ago. Surely the new laws set forth to keep us under the thumb of Greek rule must now also give us protection from their tyranny. If any of them dare lay hands upon us in such a manner, we can use their own statutes against them." She managed a brief, deceptively brave smile before remarking in earnest, "you are a good friend, Theresa. I am grateful for your advice." She turned and swept purposefully out of the cottage.

"What am I to tell Langdon if you do not return?" Theresa called after her. But there was no answer.

Leah made her way quickly through the village and along the road to the bridge. Her eyes were drawn to the blue and white banner flying atop the palace. The sight of it fluttering in the light breeze made her courage waver as it had the first time she had come to the palace.

Fortifying herself with the thought that freedom was within her grasp if she would but remain strong, she crossed the drawbridge and entered the courtyard. It was a hive of activity, filled with both Greek and Turks alike. The men-at-arms had been pressed into duty making repairs, the elite busied themselves with the far more aristocratic pursuits of hunting and hawking. Some were enjoying the opportunity for leisure, but others had already grown nostalgic for the days of fighting.

Dozens of pairs of masculine eyes followed Leah as she crossed the bailey, but she was oblivious to the admiration and lust her beauty provoked. She headed straightaway for the keep, her bearing proud and regal, the single long braid hanging down her back swaying gently to-and-fro above the curve of her hips.

She saw no other women about—and wondered if either Mabel, Mildred, or Angela had returned to the palace's kitchen since the night she had tagged along. Theresa, she knew, had not yet been back. Nor *would* be, if her father had his way.

Her blood pounded in her ears as she climbed the steps and raised a hand to knock upon the great, iron-banded door. Suddenly a man inquired behind her, "you are the new laundress?"

Tensing, she turned to see one of the elite surveying her from the bottom step. He was very young, not much into his twenties, his black hair tumbling rakishly across his forehead and his expensive, brightly colored clothing molded to his slender form. His gray eyes were filled with a keen interest as they traveled over her.

She clasped here hands in front of her and fixed him with a chilling look "I am no laundress," she denied proudly.

"Ah, then a new cook, perhaps?"

"I have come at Sir Nicholas Constinos's bidding."

"Have you truly?" he drawled, setting his right foot on the step above and leaning a forearm upon his knee. The mocking amusement in his tone prompted her to lift her chin defensively.

"To be companion to his sister," she elaborated, then wondered why she should have done so.

"Lady Thalia has not yet arrived," he told her, his mouth curving into a smile that, while engaging enough, was undeniably predatory.

"All the more reason to make haste," Leah countered, with more than a touch of sarcasm.

She pivoted toward the door again, only to gasp in angry startlement when the elite hurried up the steps to detain her.

His hand closed about her arm.

"What is your name?" he demanded. "Are you from the village?"

"Release me at once!" Her diamond gaze kindled with fire, and it was difficult for her to resist the urge to slap him. "Would you keep Sir Nicholas waiting?"

"I would know you better." He pulled her closer, his smile broadening as his manner grew even more emboldened. He seemed not to care that they were being watched by others. "Sir Nicholas's taste is as impeccable as ever. I must remember to compliment him upon it."

"You speak nonsense. Unhand me, *Greek,* or I shall scream," she threatened, struggling furiously in his grasp. He pressed her back against the door.

"Why do you protest so?" He gave a soft, insolent laugh and raised his other hand to cup her chin. "I would but have a kiss. A sampling of the charms no doubt already being enjoyed by at least one able-bodied man in Karabey." He lowered his head toward hers.

She flung caution aside. Balling her free hand into a fist, she brought it smashing upward against his jaw. He rasped out a blistering curse and released her. She watched, wide-eyed and breathless, as he staggered backward and nearly lost his balance.

"By Zeus!" he growled, rubbing at his bruised flesh. Pain and surprise swiftly turned to a thirst for revenge. His eyes narrowed.

"You are in need of humbling, little Turkish vixen. Indeed, the flat of my hand upon your backside will soon enough teach you the folly of striking Sir Patrick Soppolous!"

Leah's throat constricted in alarm. Gathering up her skirts, she raced back down the steps. Patrick was hot on her heels, and caught up with her just as she rounded the corner of the kitchen. She cried out softly when she felt his fingers closing like a vise about her wrist. He yanked her back against him.

"You will learn—" he grounded out.

"*Release her.*"

They were both startled by the sound of that familiar, commanding voice. Leah's gaze flew to Nicholas. Tall and grim-faced, he stood only a short distance away. He had discarded his breast plate and cote-hardie; his long-sleeved white woolen undershirt was opened almost to his waist, and he carried an ax in one hand. His hair gleamed dark and gold-streaked in the morning sunlight.

"The wench raised her hand to me!" Patrick offered angrily. Instead of loosening, his grip tightened with punishing force. Leah's eyes met Nicholas's as she bit her lower lip to stifle another cry. She was surprised at the gleam of white-hot fury contained within their steady, piercing dark depths.

"Disobey at your own peril, Sir Patrick," he warned the younger man, his tone one of dangerous calm.

"Would you have us do nothing whenever we are ill-treated by these peasants?" Patrick challenged in disbelief.

"I would have you remember our purpose here."

Leah looked back to the man who held her captive. For a moment, she feared he would remain defiant. But, after a few further moments' hesitation, he reluctantly capitulated.

"She is not worth the quarrel," he remarked, with a forced chuckle. He released her and stepped away, then gave a nod to Nicholas. "I shall leave her to you, my lord. In truth, the whole thing was naught but a jest."

"Even so," Nicholas replied somberly, "it was lacking in humor."

Patrick paled a bit at that. He started to say more, but closed his mouth and took his leave, brushing past Leah with one last, dismissive glance.

Still seething, she lifted her head to a proud angle and looked to Nicholas. "It appears, Sir Nicholas Constinos," Leah charged, her color high and her gaze stormy, "the churlishness is a characteristic shared by all the Greek."

"He is young," Nicholas stated simply. His features betrayed none of the pleasure he felt at seeing her again—nor the lingering urge to retaliate against Patrick. "And far from home."

"You would use that to pardon him?" She caught her breath when he began slowly advancing upon her. Her own emotions had been thrown into utter chaos at the sight of him. But she stood her ground, folding her arms against her breasts and tilting her head back to face him squarely.

"No."

He stopped mere inches away. His eyes burned down into hers, his nearness making her heart race. She could feel the heat emanating from his body, could detect the not unpleasant scents of woodsmoke and leather about him Her gaze flickered briefly downward to where the unlaced opening of his shirt allowed a glimpse of the bronzed, muscular hardness of his chest.

"His behavior cannot be excused," he went on to assure her. "And you have my word that it will never be repeated."

"The word of a Greek?" she taunted.

"The word of a Constinos." he corrected, a ghost of a smile on his lips. Like her, he could still vividly recall each and every detail of their last encounter. Unlike her, he was not so certain that whatever was between them could be controlled. He was determined as she to resist temptation Perhaps even more so. But life had taught him to accept the inevitable, and that sometimes a battle can only be won by first accepting defeat.

Leah swallowed hard. Her gaze fell beneath his again; she was dismayed to realize that her courage, so resolutely drawn about her upon entering the palace gates, gave every sign of vanishing altogether. She fought the impulse to turn and flee—though she would have surrendered to it gladly if she had seen the warmth in Nicholas' eyes just then.

"Have you brought nothing with you?" he asked.

"No, nor shall I," she retorted, her anger giving her strength once more She glared up at him and snatched the letter from where she had tucked it into her belt. "I received your summons, my lord. Do you really think me the fool?" Before he could answer, she crumbled the paper and flung it to the ground. "Companion to your sister! By the gods, how can you ask it of me?"

"I thought you well-suited to the task."

"And what task is that?" Coloring hotly, she cast an anxious glance about the courtyard before admitting in a lowered tone, "I suspect you have other duties in mind. Duties that-that have little to do with your sister."

"You are mistaken," he replied, his own voice quite low and leveled.

"I think not!" She shook her head and tried, without a great measure of success, to ignore the way her pulse leapt at his nearness. Just as before, he made her feel incredibly small and vulnerable, and more aware of her femininity than any man had the right to do.

"Though I am loath to remember it," she continued, "I have not forgotten what occurred in the woods. Nor have I forgotten the accursed statutes that would brand the *both* of us traitors for it.

And so, I say to you now, Sir Nicholas Constinos, find someone else to do your bidding!"

"I have made my choice." He stepped even closer. The look he gave her was at once provocative and penetrating. "I do not ask this of you, Leah Baal," he pointed out, his authoritative tone laced with steel. "*I command it.*"

Her breath caught in her throat again. She felt a tremor of fear—and something else—as her gaze locked with his. "Why?" she demanded, her own voice little more than a whisper. "Can you not see the peril in this?"

"Yes." For a moment, his eyes glowed with ironic humor. "Still, the decision has been made. And I am not a man to change his mind."

"My foster father will never allow it," she proclaimed, now desperately trying another tactic.

"Then I will convince him."

"Do you truly hope to secure his blessing to dishonor me?" Her cheeks flamed anew, and she was dismayed to feel her heart give yet another wild flutter.

"I need no ruse to get you into my bed," replied Nicholas, his brow creasing into a somber frown. "If such were my intent, I would say so and be done with it."

"Sweet Hera, do you think me fool enough to trust you?" she countered feelingly. "Am I supposed to believe that you will not seek to accost me again while I am here? Will you give me the word of a Constinos in this manner as well then?"

"You will serve as companion to my sister. Unless you wish otherwise, your duties will include none save that."

Battling the damnable urge to draw her close, he tightened his grip upon the splintered handle of the ax. Another soft, fleeting smile touched his lips. "I believe you will prove more than worthy of the task I have set before you."

"I will not do it." Her eyes narrowed and flashed, then just as swiftly clouded with an apprehension that had nothing to do with the challenge he had raised. "I will not stay here."

The danger to her family, the threat of retaliation should she disobey his command—all were forgotten now as a voice deep within warned her to take flight. She closed her eyes. Before them rose a vision of startling clarity.

It was herself she saw. Or rather, a transparent, ghostly representation of herself, as though she had somehow become trapped between one world and the next. *He* was beside her, his arms about her. The two of them stood together in the midst of the forest glen, just as they had done only a few short days ago, save for one difference. This time, a crowd of villagers had gathered along the water's edge. Their eyes, full of rancor and reproach, were like daggers upon her. The blood drained from Leah's face. A sharp pang of dismay coursed through her. She gasped, her eyes flying wide. "No!" she cried brokenly. "*I cannot!*"

She turned to flee. Her skirts tangled about her legs and she stumbled. Nicholas's hand, strong and sure, was about her in an instant. He quickly steadied her, pulling her upright as his men looked on. Angrily conscious of their curious and amused gazes, he forced himself to release her. She trembled from the lingering warmth of his hand upon her, then nearly stumbled again as she stepped hastily away from him.

"I would not have thought you a coward," he said. His eyes gleamed almost harshly down into hers now.

"Coward?" She bristled once more, tilting her chin up to face him with the proud defiance he had already come to know so very well.

"I am a Baal—and therefore no coward!"

"Then prove it so." He lowered the ax to the ground, propped it blade down against the kitchen wall, and began striding purposefully toward the nearby stables. "Come."

"Where are we going?" asked Leah, following after him despite her resolve not to.

"To have a word with your foster father."

"You would go yourself?" Her tone was anxious, full of disbelief.

"I would."

"He-he is away." She stopped short and caught her breath when Nicholas turned to face her again. "He will not return till the morrow."

"Then you will not be missed this night."

"Will I not?" she countered, folding her arms beneath her breasts and giving an eloquent toss of her head. "Do you think, my lord, that there are no others to care if I am to be-to be imprisoned here?"

"I think, Leah Baal, that to hold you captive would render a man either mad or well content. Perhaps both."

Astonished, she stared speechlessly up at him. Somewhere in the vicinity of her lower abdomen, a traitorous heat was kindled. It frightened and confused her, so much so that she felt her knees growing weak again.

Nicholas took an instinctive step toward her.

"Lady Thalia approaches!"

Leah stared guiltily at the sound of the guard's announcement. His voice rang out within the bustling activity of the courtyard, eliciting an inward groan from Nicholas.

"My sister," he told Leah. His brow creased into another frown while his arm fell back to his side. "There is no time now, I will send someone to fetch your things."

"No," she protested weakly, but it was too late. She could do nothing more than stand, silent and wide-eyed and wracked by indecision, as he left her to offer a welcome to the three women and ten men who were fast approaching the palace walls.

Within moments, they had come into view. One of the riders in the lead held aloft the familiar blue and white standard, while another of the escorts, armed as were his comrades in the event of any unprovoked attack upon the travelers, officially proclaimed the arrival of the Lady Thalia Constinos.

The horses' hooves clattered, loud and thunderous, upon the muddied boards of the drawbridge as the group crossed through. In the center rode a woman whose aristocratic bearing and countenance lent immediate recognition of her status. She urged her mount impatiently forward into the bailey, reining to an abrupt halt the instant she caught sight of Nicholas.

"Nicholas!" Her face became wreathed in smiles of pure, impish delight. She could scarcely contain her excitement as he moved to greet her. With a faint, preoccupied smile of his own, he reached up to swing her down.

"Welcome to Karabey, Thalia."

"My dear brother, how I have missed you!" exclaimed Lady Thalia Constinos, laughing softly when her gold-slippered feet touched the ground. She proceeded to embrace him with an unladylike exuberance Leah was surprised to feel a sharp twinge of displeasure upon witnessing the brunette's obvious affection for her brother. Lady Thalia was prettier than she had imaged. And older. In truth, she was not a young woman at all, but a woman of perhaps thirty or thirty-five. Her figure, while slender, was beguilingly curvaceous. The fitted, dark velvet cote-hardie she wore, along with her bejeweled headdress and the delicately worked necklace of pearls about her neck, bespoke a level of affluence that none of the Turks (save for those who had prospered through their traitorous associations with the Greek) could ever hope to attain. Surely that alone was cause for resentment … was it not?

"Your journey was a pleasant one?" Nicholas queried, setting his sister firmly away from him yet keeping a hand about her arm. For a moment, his eyes strayed back to Leah.

"Pleasant enough," replied Thalia The corners of her mouth turned up again, and she cast a mischievous, conspiratorial glance back toward the dismounting members of her entourage "Though I fear the others may feel themselves ill-used."

"You were ever a trying person."

"That is unfair! It was only my haste to—"

"May I add my welcome to that of our liege, Lady Thalia." Patrick intruded at that point, stepping forward with all eagerness to capture her hand He gallantly raised it to his lips.

"Thank you, Sir Patrick." With an almost imperceptible coolness, she withdrew her hand from his grasp and transferred her sparkling, gaze to the two men who stood surveying her with a mixture of admiration and reverence from a short distance away. "I am very pleased to see you again, Sir Keith. And you as well, Sir John," she added, smiling at them both.

"It is a great honor indeed to have you here, Lady Thalia," murmured Keith, solemn and sincere.

"At your service, my lady," John offered, with a bow. "Zeus be praised! Light *has* come unto the darkness." His gaze moved with a warm significance toward the two young maidservants, who, alongside the gray-haired, rigidly maternal Dame Frances, stood blushing at the attention they were attracting.

"Are neither Sir David nor Sir Josh here to greet me?" Thalia asked Nicholas. Her eyes searched the area.

"They will appear soon enough." Tucking her hand within his arm, he gave instructions for the horses to be tended and the travelers settled. He then paused to bid a polite welcome to Dame Frances, who, upon seizing full advantage of her long-standing service to his family, did not hesitate to make known her displeasure of their al-tered circumstances.

"This a wretched place you have summoned us to," the old woman complained, scowling while her gaze darted critically about. "Cold and damp and dirty," she pronounced, with a shake of her wimpled head as the perusal only reinforced her first impression of Karabey Palace. "No doubt there will be an army of rats to plague us."

"Is this truly to be your home now?" asked Thalia. Her own features appeared a bit perplexed and disbelieving as she looked about.

"Yes," Nicholas answered curtly. He took her arm again and began leading her away, toward the spot where Leah stood watching.

"I fear father would not be pleased," Thalia remarked, with a sigh. Gracefully sweeping her skirts higher to avoid the dirt, she tried not to wrinkle her nose at the smells that filled the air.

"Father's pleasure, or lack of it, matters little to me."

"Perhaps Lord Ares could be persuaded—"

"Karabey is mine," he told her. His eyes darkened, then fastened with a meaningful intensity upon Leah. "And everything within its walls." The words had come of their own accord.

"Who is that woman?" Thalia demanded in a low tone, noting the direction of his gaze.

She frowned thoughtfully while conducting a swift appraisal of Leah's charms. "She is quite lovely, is she not? I do not believe I have ever seen hair that particular color of blonde. And there is so much *of* it as well," she murmured, thinking it odd that the woman had neither bound up her tresses nor covered them with a wimple. Also, she was wearing no cloak. Her figure was displayed to perfection in the red gown. She looked common enough ... yet there was something almost regal about her bearing. "Is she one of the women you brought from Greece, then?"

"We brought no women. She is one of the Turks." There was an underlying vibrancy to his tone. But Thalia was too preoccupied at the moment to detect it.

"Oh, I see. She is a cook or laundress then?"

"No." He spared her another brief half smile. "She is your companion."

"My companion?" Thalia echoed, glancing up at him in astonishment. She would have pressed for more, but they had drawn too close by now.

Leah stiffened at their approach. Fraught with anger and uncertainty, she could only stand and wait. Nicholas paid no heed to her predicament, in spite of the all too visible fire in her eyes.

"Mistress Baal," he said, giving her undue honor by addressing her first, "may I present my sister, Lady Thalia Constinos."

"Good day, Mistress Baal." Thalia put forth with a tentative little smile. When Leah did not offer an immediate response, she inquired bluntly, "Are you not cold?"

"No." It was a lie. She *was* cold. She was cold and confused and frightened of what would happen if she remained any longer. Why, oh why, did she not flee?

"My brother has told me you are to be my companion."

"Your brother has assumed too much." She met the other woman's gaze squarely, determinedly, yet not without a measure of kindness.

"I fear, my lady, that Sir Nicholas has made a grievous error. A misjudgment, if you will."

"Indeed?" Thalia gasped, both surprised and amused. Never before had she heard anyone dare to criticize her brother in such a bold manner. She looked instinctively to Nicholas.

"Mistress Baal has not yet realized the significance of her presence here," he declared quietly. With calm deliberation, he stepped closer to Leah. He did not touch her; there was no need. Their eyes locked.

"She shall serve as an example to her countrymen, to demonstrate that the Greek and Turks can live together in peace."

"You ask too much of me!" she protested.

"I think not."

"And the statutes? Will you truly set yourself above them?" For the moment, they had both forgotten Thalia.

"Such is not my intent," he assured her once more, his rugged features inscrutable. "I have sworn to serve Lord Ares and the glory of Sparta, charged with holding Karabey. And *that*, Leah Baal, I will do."

"Your vow rings false!" she cried hotly. The urge to take flight was greater than ever, as was the feeling, deep and redoubtable, that there was a great deal more at stake than either of them wanted to admit.

"If-if it please's you, my brother," an astonished Thalia now hastened to intervene, "I am impatient to see the palace." She turned to Leah and forced a winning smile to her lips. "Perhaps, Mistress Baal, you would be so kind as to provide an escort?"

Leah did not know what to say. Her head spun. She could not forget that Nicholas held the law in his hands.

He could force her to this ... and to anything else he wanted. *There are many kinds of danger,* Theresa had warned her. Dare she put him to the test?

"Lady Thalia!"

Dame Frances' voice, shrill and stern, heralded her progress across the courtyard. She descended upon the trio in a flurry of indignation, her white wimple quivering and her plum-colored woolen skirts swirling about her thin legs.

"You must come inside at once, my lady!" she urged. She shot Nicholas a speaking glare before firmly grasping her charge.

"You have already endured far enough of the morning's chill."

"Dame Frances, you must make the acquaintance of my new companion," insisted Thalia. To Leah, she murmured, "I can assure you, Mistress Baal, that she is not so much a monster as she sounds."

"It is to be *hoped,* Mistress Baal," the old woman said briskly, turning a critical eye upon Leah, "that you have some knowledge of housewifery."

"I am well convinced she can manage whatever task we set her," Thalia opened archly, looking back to Nicholas. "Or else, my brother would not have made the arrangement with her."

"Come," Dame Frances reiterated, tugging impatiently on Thalia's hand. "We must make haste if we are to see this accursed pile of stones habitable by nightfall!"

Thus was the matter settled? Leah found herself being compelled toward the keep along with the other woman. Although she offered little resistance, she made a silent promise to return home to Ponceel House before the day was through.

Her eyes searched out Nicholas one last time before she disappeared inside. He had retrieved the ax and was crossing back to the gates to have word with the newly returned Josh. His stride was full of masculine grace, sure and unhurried, and even without his soldiers tunic or armor it was apparent that here was a man born to command. But there was more to him than that. Much more. Blessed Zeus above, did she not know it?

I have made my choice. And so he had. Though the both of them might well be damned for it …

CHAPTER 6

▼

The day passed in a whirl of activity, better, Leah decided, than remaining idle with too much time to ponder her dilemma. Contrary to Thalia's faith in her abilities, she was not well-versed in the art of 'housewifery' and so had to rely upon Dame Frances' instructions as they cleaned and prepared the bedchambers.

The tasks were not at all the kind for which she had been summoned; indeed, her first inclination had been to offer a pointed reminder of that. In some strange way, however, the work gave her a sense of pride and satisfaction. The palace, belonging as it did among her childhood memories, was certainly deserving of better care. And though it had now been claimed by yet another invader from across the Aegean, it was nevertheless a part of Anatolia, a symbol of everything her people had once held and lost. No one, not even Sir Nicholas Constinos with all his stated intentions toward fairness and peace, could hope to change that.

In spite of her best efforts, thoughts of him rose in her mind with alarming frequency. How could they not? She knew him to be nearby. She knew that he would seek her out again. As the hours piled upon one another, so did her dread of the coming night.

The prospect of seeing him once more filled her with anxiety; She paled at the thought of his anger upon finding her gone. But she could not stay No matter what he threatened. No matter how strong the secret desire to remain near him.

With a long, ragged sigh, she smoothed the last of the beautifully embroidered quilts atop Lady Thalia's wool mattress. She knelt to arrange one corner of the brocade hanging that had been secured across the old, sadly lopsided bedframe. A fire burned across the room, the need for its warmth growing as the afternoon light faded.

Leah glanced toward the flames, only to groan in dismay when Nicholas's face swam before her eyes. Even without the trickery of her imagination, she could feel his presence everywhere.

"Remain calm," she whispered, her eyes sweeping closed while she prayed for guidance. She had been praying a great deal more than usual since he had come to Karabey ... Would the oracles mayhap tell her that his arrival was a mixed blessing? The thought made the corners of her mouth turn up briefly.

"We have worked no small miracle this day, Mistress Baal."

She started guiltily at the sound of Thalia's voice behind her. With visible haste, she climbed to her feet and shook out her creased, dusty skirts.

"It was wise of you to bring the furnishings with you," she remarked, with a deceptive insouciance. She tucked several wayward strands of hair back into the long plait that fell over her shoulder. A borrowed ribbon secured the plait; a borrowed apron covered the front of her gown.

"Dame Frances would have it no other way," replied Thalia. "She is ever determined to ensure our comfort when we are away from the known luxuries of court." She smiled and crossed to stand before the fire. Her headdress had long since been drawn off, revealing a matching pair of plaited and coiled lengths of golden-brown hair on either side of her face. Her features were heart-shaped, delicate, yet Leah sensed a strength in her that bellied her fragile looks, "You have toiled long and hard this day."

"No more so than you and the others," Leah murmured. In truth, Lady Thalia Constinos had proven to be nothing at all like the pampered, useless Greek woman she had expected. Possessed of a ready wit and surprising good humor, she had readily worked alongside her maidservants, and had offered not so much as a single word of complaint on her own behalf.

"Still, would you not agree that remarkable progress has been made?"

"I would indeed," Leah concurred, with a faint smile of her own. She cast a quick, appraising look about the room. Fine, thick tapestries hung on the walls, rushes covered the floor, and a carved wooden chest, full of elegant gowns and linen and the many accessories required for a well-bred lady, sat at the foot of the bed. An earlier survey of Dame Frances' bedchamber next door had offered further proof of transformation from sparse and filthy to clean and comfortable.

So long as the roof did not leak or the weather turn fierce—and so long as the villagers continued their wary association with those at the palace—there was every reason to believe that Lady Thalia's visit would be a pleasant one.

Zeus willing, it would not be a lengthy one, Leah mused while her pulse leapt in renewed disquiet. No doubt Sir Nicholas would insist upon her presence for the duration …

"I must confess," the palace is not at all what I had hoped it would be," Thalia said, with a frown.

"Yet this room is almost, I should think, as it was in days long ago," Leah remarked, drawn out of her unhappy reverie. "My foster father has spoken of the palace's former grandness. And I have heard many stories of its wicked past—though I daresay at least some of them are untrue."

"You are from Karabey then?"

"I am."

"I have never really known a Turkish woman before."

"Nor I a Greek one." Her mouth curved into a soft smile of irony.

"Are we so very different?" Thalia challenged amiably.

"It is too soon to be sure."

"I see. Well then, mayhap you will tell me how it was you were chosen to be my companion."

"It was ... Sir Nicholas decided I should come." She could feel her cheeks burning. Her gaze fell beneath the steady curiosity of the older woman's. She turned about and began smoothing the quilt again.

"I would not have thought it his usual custom to concern himself with such matters," Thalia reflected aloud, her brows knitting into a slight, pensive frown as she folded her arms beneath her breasts and watched Leah. "But then, I must confess that his usual customs are something of a mystery to me. He has been so rarely in Greece these many years past. On those rare occasions when I *did* see him, he was ever stern yet kind. I suppose, therefore, that I should count myself fortunate he was away so often," she concluded, with a soft laugh, her light brown eyes twinkling irrepressibly. "Else I would have been unable to conduct the many little flirtations I find so enjoyable. Mind you, they were nothing more than that. Naught but an amusing way to pass the time. Life at court can be very uneventful." She wandered across to the window and lifted a hand to the cold gray stones of the wall. For a fleeting instant, her gaze clouded and a wistful expression crossed her face.

"I would like to see the village tomorrow. Perhaps Sir Josh—" She broke off abruptly and forced herself back to the subject at hand.

"But, we were talking of Sir Nicholas, were we not?"

"Was he vigilant with his own daughters?" Leah queried, unable to restrain her own intense curiosity about the man who had forced his way into her life. The possibility that he was married, that he had a family tucked away back in Greece, brought a painful lump to her throat. *Sweet Hera, why should it matter?*

"He has no daughters. No, nor sons. At least none he has acknowledged," Thalia said, with a crooked, mischievous smile.

"One can never be certain of that, can one? And there is no wife to care if he should spend the remainder of his days here in Karabey."

"He has never been married then?" She moved to the opposite side of the bed and made another unnecessary adjustment to the quilt.

"No," said Thalia, returning to her stance before the fire. She watched Leah's face closely now. "Yet, I have heard there was a past betrothal that ended very badly. It seems his ladylove was untrue during one of his many absences. I cannot swear to it, of course, but Dame Frances once told me that a woman's betrayal was the reason he paid no heed to the ladies at court—and I can assure you there were scores—who sought to stir him to courtship. Why, it was said that the gods themselves have attempted to play matchmaker. Their efforts met with little success. I think my brother can be obstinate in the extreme" Her eyes drifted toward the flames again. "In truth, I cannot easily envision him as the long-suffering victim of a broken heart. He is much too stalwart and masterful to pine away for some foolish, unchaste woman who lacked the good sense to hold fast to such a man."

Stalwart and masterful, Leah echoed silently. Yes, he was certainly that. Unlike Thalia, however, it was not difficult for her to believe that he had once pledged his complete and utter devotion to a lady. She had sensed the longing in him, the need to cease his wanderings and rest his weary heart. But, to think that his betrothed had been false ... A sharp ache clutched at her own heart when she considered the pain he must have felt. Did he still yearn for that lost love? Could he ever learn to trust again?

It made no difference to her. It *must* not. Mentally shaking herself, she stepped away from the bed and faced Thalia. They had had little enough opportunity to talk throughout the day. But there was no time now ...

"I must go," she murmured. Her eyes strayed to the window. Night was fast approaching.

"And I as well," responded Thalia. "If you are to serve as my companion, it is only proper that we make your quarters as comfortable as Dame Frances'. I cannot think how Sir Nicholas and his elite have endured the cold and damp of this place." With a timely shiver, she swept across to catch up a blue woolen shawl draped across the top of the chest. She flung the shawl about her shoulders and headed purposefully for the doorway. "Once we have seen to your bedchamber, we will venture forth and discover if Dame Frances has wrought a similar miracle within the kitchen. I dared not intrude before, yet l am growing quite hungry and cannot help but wonder if—"

"I shall not be sleeping within the palace walls this night." Leah interrupted, with an assertiveness she was far from feeling.

"Shall you not?" Thalia countered, halting in surprise.

"I must return home."

"Home? Is it not customary for a lady's companion to remain close by?"

"Turkish customs are seldom the same as Greek ones."

"But what will Sir Nicholas say?"

"Sir Nicholas knows full well that I cannot stay." She hastened forward and declared earnestly, "I am sorry, Lady Thalia, but I cannot serve as your companion."

"If I have offered you offense in any way, Mistress Baal—" Thalia began in genuine perplexity.

"It is not that," Leah was quick to deny. She inhaled deeply, unevenly, searching for the right words with which to explain. "I do not belong here. I would not suit you as companion."

"Should we not reserve judgment upon that until we have become better acquainted?" suggested Thalia, her smile warm and persuasive.

"It was upon your brother's orders that I came!" Leah finally disclosed. Her blue eyes flashed at the memory, and she breathed an oath. "I would spare your feelings, yet you should know the truth. And the truth is that I-I ..." Her voice trailed away. She could not continue. How could she hope to explain the situation when she understood nothing herself?

While a startled Thalia looked on, she rushed from the bedchamber and fled back down the narrow corridor toward the stairwell. It had been her intent to wait until after darkness more fully cloaked the land, but the day had been so very long and tiring and she was suddenly quite desperate to escape. Now. Before it was too late. Before *he* sought her out again.

She gathered up her skirts as she prepared to descend the winding steps. And then, without warning, she found her arm caught in a strong, all too familiar grasp. A breathless cry escaped her lips. She whirled about to face Nicholas.

"What has happened?" he demanded curtly.

"Release me!" She gasped.

"*No.*"

There was scarcely enough time to struggle. With a silent and grim determination, and no gentle handling, he pulled her the short distance to his bedchamber. He thrust her inside, closed the door, and strode forward to confront her. She was certain he meant to seize her again, but he did not. She could not know the effort it was costing him to keep his hands from her. To him, in spite of her dirty clothing and tousled hair, she had never appeared more beguiling.

"I was on my way to find you," he confided, his tone low and res-onant as he towered above her in the firelit coolness of the room.

She inhaled upon a soft gasp and retreated a step, acutely con-scious of the fact that they were alone together. She gazed up at him in a chaotic tumble of thoughts and emotions. He had bathed and changed into a clean dark blue tunic, she noted. His hair waved damply across his forehead, while the pleasant aroma of soap hung about him. His eyes, far too penetrating and hypnotic, burned down into the stormy brightness of hers. The tension between them was as intense and palpable as ever … No, it had grown even stron-ger. Even more treacherous. *There are many kinds of danger.*

"Where were you going?" he asked her quietly.

"Home."

"This is your home now."

"I have told you that I will not stay!" With trembling hands, she angrily untied the apron and jerked it free. She flung it aside, then cried, "Find someone else to do your bidding, my lord, for I am not fool enough to tempt the fates."

"I never once thought you a fool. And the fates are not to be feared, Leah. Embraced or resisted, perhaps, but not feared." It was simple enough for him to block her path as she tried to push past him. Again, though he did not touch her, she felt scorched by his proximity.

"The matter has been settled," he decreed. "You will not leave this night. No, nor any other night until I give my consent to it."

Her gaze met his. "My foster father—"

"Will find a message waiting for him upon his return tomorrow. I am confident he will understand. You will find your things in the room at the far end of the corridor," he went on to reveal. A faint, sardonic smile briefly touched his lips. "My faithful steward per-formed the duty of riding to Ponceel House. It is to be hoped that the old serving woman he encountered there had the good sense to gather everything you will need."

Leah glimpsed the light of triumph in his eyes. Her heart sank as she reluctantly began to accept the inevitable. She would not be leaving after all. To defy him in this would create a great deal more trouble than she was prepared to face—she was certain of it. He had both the authority and the means with which to force her to his will. But even more alarmingly, he had the power to make her senses reel ...

Her gaze fell in defeat. She could not place her own welfare, her own selfish concern, above that of her foster parents. Langdon and Louise had been so very good to her these many years past. Could she now willingly bring misfortune upon them?

"Hera, μου δίνει τη δύναμη," she whispered, slowly shaking her head.

"Perhaps you would care to repeat that," said Nicholas. He stepped closer to her now. His features were deceptively impassive as the firelight played over them.

"I said that I have no choice." She tilted her head back to look up at him again. Her tone was bitter, her eyes gloriously ablaze when she warned him, "If it is my hatred you seek, Sir Nicholas Constinos, then—" She broke off with another gasp of startlement when he suddenly caught her up against him. His arm tightened like a band of iron about her waist. His smoldering dark gaze raked mercilessly over her countenance.

"Hate me if you will, Leah Baal," he grounded out, his own voice hoarse and edged with a fury she did not understand. "Yes, give me your hatred. Yet I will have something else as well. By Zeus or Hades, *I will have it!*"

Her hands came up to push against him, but it was useless. His other arm now encircled her with its hard, sinewy strength, and she could do nothing more than utter a strangled protest before his lips captured the parted softness of hers.

The kiss struck fear in her heart.

It was even more volatile than the first. Passion, hot and wild, flared between them as though renewed with the vengeance of Ares. Leah felt the traitorous kindling of her own desire, felt her heart pounding fiercely against Nicholas's. Trembling, and struggling for breath, she once again sought to push him away, only to moan when he gathered her closer. The kiss deepened. His mouth boldly ravished the sweetness of hers. His hand swept downward to curl about her well-rounded hips. Her legs grew weak. Her head spun dizzily. A delectable, frightening warmth spread throughout her entire body. She raised her hands to Nicholas' shoulders whether for support or in unspoken surrender, she could not have said. Her lips moved instinctively beneath the warm and demanding, yet remarkably tender, onslaught of his. Just as before, something deep within her offered the response she had told herself she must not give. And just as before, Nicholas found himself torn between a well-guarded sense of duty and a yearning so intense, so incredibly soul-stirring, that it transcended mere physical attraction. More than he would ever have thought possible. He yearned to possess her. He wanted her in his bed, in his presence each day and night. He needed her. She could still the battle raging within him and give him peace. He knew somehow that she possessed the ability to touch his heart like no other ...

I have sworn to serve Lord Ares and the glory of Sparta. His own words came back to haunt him with an ill-timed perversity. What hope of peace could there be in Karabey if he claimed Leah Baal as his own? She herself had asked him if he would set himself above Greece's laws. There could be only one right answer.

Only one.

He cursed both the fire in his blood and the intervention of his conscience. He cursed the circumstances that had led him to Anatolia in the first place, and even, albeit briefly, cursed the day he had been born. With considerable reluctance, he released Leah and set her firmly away from him. He stood gazing down at her with a fiery mixture of longing and anger. His resolve was very nearly shattered when his eyes traveled over her flushed, upturned coun-tenance. Her perplexity was obvious. And her own gaze was soft, still shining with a passion's glow.

"Forgive me," he told her in a voice that was gruff and measured. "I gave you my word." He did not wait for a reply, but pivoted about and moved to stand before the fire.

Shaken by the encounter—and the abrupt manner in which it had ended—Leah stared numbly at his back. Her pulse still raced erratically, while her breasts rose and fell rapidly beneath the tight bodice of her crimson gown. She was shocked to realize how very much she had wanted the kiss to continue, shocked at the memory of her own wanton response. *Why had he stopped?* For yet a second time, he had swept her up in a maelstrom of secret and forbidden passions. And once again she, like some weak-spirited young fool, had done shamelessly little to prevent it.

Her face flamed in mortification at the thought. Her gaze sparked and flashed as it flew about the room. Belatedly, it struck her full force that she was alone with her divinely handsome tor-mentor in the privacy of his bedchamber. No woman with any true measure of pride or decency would be found in such a predicament. No one worthy of the name Baal would allow herself to be touched—twice—as this Greek soldier had touched her.

"You cannot now command me to stay at the palace," she declared feelingly. "After what has happened—"

"Nothing has changed." Ah, but it had; his mind's inner voice gleefully pointed up the falsehood. Everything had changed.

He turned to face her again. His eyes, their unfathomable dark depths glinting dully now, met the liquid blue fire of hers.

"No doubt you are tired. It was never my intent that you should toil as a maidservant." He frowned at the image of her on her knees amid the damp and dirt. Had he not purposely absented himself from the keep all day, he would have learned of the injustice sooner and thus put a stop to it

"The work was not so arduous," murmured Leah, looking away.

"And-and Lady Thalia did not ask it." She felt so very awkward, wretchedly ill-at-ease, and yet *he* appeared to be suffering no such loss of composure. Sweet Hera, was the embrace so easily forgotten by him? The thought prompted a dull ache to spread about her heart.

"Nevertheless," he insisted, "I will speak to my sister. From this day forward, you will confine yourself to the duties of companion and nothing else." He turned half toward the fire once more and raised a hand to the splintered mantelpiece above. "You shall sit beside Lady Thalia at the table this night as well."

"My appetite has long since fled." Her breath caught in her throat as she took note of the way the flames spun gold in the rich darkness of his hair.

"Then it must be found." The merest hint of a smile played about his mouth. "The good women of Karabey have not passed across the drawbridge this day. We can only hope that Dame Frances' many skills extend to the kitchen."

"I warned you, my lord, that the Turks would not admit defeat so easily!" She raised her head in a gesture of spirited defiance, unaware that in so doing she only added fuel to the fire still simmering dangerously within him.

"And what of you, Leah Baal?" he challenged in a soft yet unnerving tone He advanced upon her again, his eyes lighting with a gleam that sent a shiver dancing down her spine. This time, however, she did not retreat. She was determined to stand firm and resolute against him, to show him that her brief, accursed moment of abandonment would never know a recurrence She could resist him. She had to. It did not matter that the very sight of him stirred her own soul. Nor that the sound of his voice was much the same as music to her ears.

"*I* obey for no other reason than to protect my foster parents from further ruin at the hands of the Greek!" she proclaimed vehemently, knowing full well that it was not the whole truth. "May Lord Hades have mercy upon your soul," she then choked out, "have you not made us suffer enough?" She did not wait to see how he would respond. Seeking escape at last, she spun about and wrenched open the door. Her feet raced along the shadowed corridor. Upon passing the newly cleaned and furnished bedchamber that was to have been Dame Frances', she glanced inside and spied the bundle of *clothing*— *her* clothing—atop the bed. She drew up short and stepped through the arched doorway. Seeking an explanation for the whirlwind that had caught her up. Her mother's face suddenly swam before her eyes. She was smiling. It was scarcely an hour later that she found herself facing the ordeal of a banquet in the great hall.

She had prepared herself for it as though sailing forth to face an inquest instead of a pleasant evening meal. Her creased and dusty gown had been exchanged for one of peacock green wool, laced down the front and trimmed with a delicate band of pearl embroidery about both the rounded neckline and the edges of the long, fitted sleeves. Underneath it, she wore a white silken shift and a pair of gartered, sheer wool stockings. A small leather belt, sporting a buckle of hammered gold, encircled her waist. Upon her feet were a pair of fine golden slippers. She had secured her long blonde hair into two plaits on either side of her face; they reached nearly to her hips. Spurning a proper headdress, she had settled for a slender band of matching green wool about her head, with a single pearl dangling from it to rest upon her forehead. And as a finishing touch, she had pinned a jeweled, star-shaped brooch to her bodice. It had belonged to her grandmother. She recalled how her father had once told her that it was a charm to bring good luck. She had not believed him, of course. Even as a child, she had never placed much faith in the like of fairies or ghosts or nymphs. Yet now, she found herself idly wondering if the brooch might perchance help her to ward against the dangers awaiting her below.

When she reluctantly descended the steps to the candlelit hall, she found Lady Thalia, Sir Nicholas, and his elite already seated at the table. They rose in unison at the sight of her. Thalia swept forth to bid her welcome. "Come, Mistress Baal," she said, smiling warmly. "You are much deserving of a meal."

"I would rather—" Leah tried to protest. Her eyes immediately strayed to Nicholas. He betrayed none of the intense pleasure he felt at seeing her again, though his own gaze glowed warmly across into hers.

"Have you yet made the acquaintance of everyone?" Thalia interrupted to inquire brightly. She was attired in a becoming gown of primrose, gold-trimmed wool, and looked at once, both young and elegant. Her pale brown eyes were shining with a secret delight.

"No," murmured Leah, clasping her hands together in front of her and forcing her gaze elsewhere.

"Then we shall not delay." Thalia led her forward to where the men, all bathed and dressed in their best tunics for the occasion, stood eyeing Leah with a wholly masculine admiration.

"Mistress Baal is to serve as my companion while I am here." Beginning with the slender, sharp-featured man at the nearest corner of the table, she announced, "This is Sir Keith Robards." He offered Leah a polite bow but said nothing. Thalia moved to the next man. "And Sir Patrick Soppolous" Leah stiffened, her eyes kindling at the sight of the young, raven-haired Greek man. He was the same elite who had accosted her earlier. She lifted her head proudly, acknowledging him with naught save a chilling look

"Mistress Baal and I have met," he muttered. His gaze was narrow and dismissive.

"Sir David Bandle," Thalia continued, gently urging Leah onward to meet the brawny, graying man who was the oldest of the elite.

"It is an honor, Mistress Baal," he told her. There was no sarcasm in his voice, nor animosity of any kind in his manner. Her mouth curved into a soft impulsive smile.

"Sir John Lanpolous," Thalia next proclaimed. "An honor *and* a privilege, Mistress Baal," John intoned smoothly.

Leah was startled when he caught her hand and raised it to his lips. His mouth lingered upon the smoothness of her skin. She grew uneasy and tugged her hand from his grasp. If she had ventured a glance at Nicholas then, she would have seen the way his eyes darkened.

"And Sir Josh Leonidas," Thalia finished, a telltale blush staining her cheeks when she paused before the attractive, golden-haired man to Nicholas's left. The smile he gave Leah was genuine and without rancor. "I am told it is your father's memory that is honored on the marble in the village square," he remarked, determinedly keeping his eyes from Thalia.

Leah tensed anew. She recalled all too vividly the day Josh and the other armed men had intruded upon the market in Karabey. And though she sensed in him a fair and decent man, she could not so easily forget that he had been the bearer of such ill-fated news.

"Yes. I am." She lifted her chin to an angrily defiant angle before charging. "It is surprising that you should remember such an insignificant thing, Sir Josh. I cannot but think our history and traditions hold little interest for you. But then, has it not always been the Greek tradition to trample all that lay behind, to conquer and then divide?"

Her stormy gaze moved to Nicholas. His features appeared quite grim now, and the piercing gleam in his eyes warned her against further impudence. Unrepentant, she looked back to Josh.

"Why, Leah!" Thalia gasped, visibly stunned. She was quick to rise to Josh's defense. "Surely you must—?"

"Mistress Baal is entirely correct," Josh said, with a faint smile of irony. When his gaze met Leah's again, she was disarmed to glimpse the hint of a twinkle.

"The traditions of which you speak is indeed both Greek and long-held. Yet, perhaps we can learn new ones. No doubt, there are those among us who would prove to be apt and willing pupils." He gave her a slight, gallant bow. His courtly response provoked more than a twinge of guilt within her.

"Are we not to dine this night?" snapped Patrick, making his impatience known.

A still annoyed Thalia led Leah to the empty seat to Nicholas's right. While Thalia resumed her own place beside Josh. Wanting nothing more than to leave, Leah fought the temptation and sank down into the high-backed wooden chair. The elite finally took their seats as well.

The meal that followed gave testament to Dame Frances' expertise in the kitchen. The two young maidservants, amid numerous blushes and sidelong winsome glances, carried forth wooden platters laden with roasted lamb, olives in herb sauce, wild fruits and nuts, and various other dishes concocted with surprising ingenuity on such short notice. Ambrosia was plentiful—the cups were never empty—and each course was fully appreciated by the men whose appetites had been whetted by a day of hunting and riding.

The formidable Dame Frances herself kept a watchful eye on the proceedings. Upon first taking note of Leah's presence at the table, she scowled darkly. Her resentment had already been sparked when she had learned that she had been cast out of the bedchamber next to Lady Thalia's chamber in order to make room for Leah. In her opinion, the Turkish woman was not in the least bit suitable as a companion for a high born Greek lady such as Thalia Constinos. And now, to see her sitting in a place of honor with the elite … Why, it was simply an outrage. Whatever had possessed Sir Nicholas Constinos to make the arrangement? Unaware of the animosity she had drawn from the old woman, Leah sat mostly in silence during the meal. She was relieved that she was seldom called upon to speak. Thalia was content to engage Josh in conversation, while the elite spoke among themselves All the while, however, she was painfully aware of Nicholas beside her. And of the looks directed her way by the other men as she toyed with her food and sipped at the ambrosia.

Her own gaze strayed frequently toward the fire blazing in the great stone fireplace. Candles burned brightly atop the table, torches flickered and smoked in sconces on the walls, while outside the wind howled with its usual vigor across the deep, cloud-choked night. The sound of it was a fitting match for Leah's mood. Her mind wandered back over the day's troubling events (particularly the fiery encounter of an hour ago,) and she became so lost in thought that she did not notice the involuntary shudder that gripped her.

"Are you cold?" Nicholas asked, his voice sounding close against her ear as he leaned toward her. She drew in a sharp breath and was dismayed at the way her pulse leapt.

"No." She swallowed hard and shook her head. "But, I-I would retire now."

"The night is still young." His gaze flickered briefly downward to her plate. "You have scarcely eaten."

"My appetite has not improved since …" Her voice trailed off and her eyes became downcast. A dull flush crept up to her face.

"Were you aware that we have a musician in our midst?" Thalia suddenly inquired of Nicholas. She smiled and confided, "I am but guilty of a moment's spying. It was a most unusual song I heard in Mistress Baal's bedchamber. "Did you learn from your mother?" she asked Leah.

"I did," Leah confirmed quietly. Her eyes flew back up to meet Nicholas'. She knew that, like her, he was remembering how the melody had drawn him to her in the woods.

"Perhaps you will consent to sing for us sometime," John drawled, leaning back in his chair while he negligently fingered his wine cup. His gaze narrowed with growing interest as it rested upon Leah again.

"Why not do so now?" Thalia suggested, pushing her plate away.

"In truth, a song would do much to improve the mood of so gloomy a night" She cast a swift, meaningful glance toward Josh.

"The laws forbid it," Patrick pointed out tersely. He frowned and looked to Nicholas. "Do they not say we are to have no association with musicians?"

"Surely, Patrick Soppolous, you do not fear corruption by so sweet a maid," John challenged, with a soft, derisive chuckle. "Her songs will do naught but stir your blood." His remark earned him a belligerent glare from the other man.

"We have been too much in one another's company of late," observed Josh, half to himself.

"What laws do you speak of, Sir Patrick?" Thalia demanded, her brow creasing in puzzlement.

"The statutes of Troy, my lady," he told her. Again, his gaze shifted to a solemn-faced Nicholas. "They are the new laws we are sworn to uphold."

"But another example of our Parliament's utter witlessness," David muttered in a low growl underscored with contempt. It was apparent to all that he had drunk far too much ambrosia. Though both Keith and Josh eyed him disapprovingly, neither of them offered him a rebuke.

"I have no *wish* to sing!" Leah declared, anxious to put an end to the quarrel. She sought to rise, but Nicholas's hand fell upon her arm to detain her. "And so you shall not," he decreed firmly, his eyes warn-

ing her against flight. "Yet we would not be deprived of your presence." She trembled at his touch and hastened to pull free. Flinging
him an angry, reproachful look, she settled back into the chair.

"If we but had music, we could dance," John pointed out, his
mouth curving into a mordant little smile. Patrick resisted the urge
to hurl a cup at his head.

"Do you play chess, Mistress Baal?" Keith queried.

"Yes," said Leah, "but—"

"By Zeus! I have not known many women with wits enough to
do so," David exclaimed loudly, raising the cup of ambrosia to his
lips again.

"I think it far better that Lady Thalia sing for us," Patrick put
forth. He smiled warmly at her, oblivious to the way Josh stiffened
in displeasure.

"I cannot sing without accompaniment," protested Thalia. Her
eyes were soft and pleading as they moved back to Leah. "May it
please you, Mistress Baal, can I not persuade you to sing with me?"
she appealed earnestly. "My voice is merely pleasant enough at best,
yet I am willing to expose it if you would but consent to help."

"It is forbidden," Leah murmured, though she found it difficult
to resist. Indignation took root within her. Why should *she* care if it
was forbidden? How absurd it was that the Greek were afraid of
something so beautiful and harmless as song. Perhaps she should
prove to them there was nothing to fear … Perhaps she should
prove the same to herself.

"Would it matter so much if we had a song or two this night?"
Thalia said with a rather childish exasperation. She suddenly rose
from the table and swept across the hall toward the stairs.

"Lady Thalia—" Josh tried to stop her, but to no avail. He and
the other elite stood as well. They were too gallant to give chase, and
too desperate for feminine company to risk incurring her wrath by

denying her the song. As was their custom, they looked to their liege to command them.

"The danger cannot be great," Nicholas said, while a faint, wry smile played about his lips, "so long as Greek and Turks join together." His eyes were splendidly aglow when they met Leah's.

"And would you cast aside the other laws so easily?" she ventured. Her soft, audacious tone was for his ears alone.

"I am but allowing a song," he replied, his expression growing quite sober. "Nothing more."

With one last speaking look of defiance for Nicholas, Leah left the table and moved forward to meet Thalia. She drew a chair in front of the fire, and sat down. "The song, Lady Thalia?"

"Whatever you choose," Thalia answered. "I shall listen awhile first."

Leah hesitated only briefly, then began to sing. She soon forgot the many eyes focused on her. She forgot that Nicholas was watching her and that she was, in essence, a prisoner among the Greek. Once again, the music transported her to another place, a place that held no danger, no treachery or confusion or secret yearnings that tore at her heart and would brand her disloyal.

The sweet, lilting strains filled the great hall and echoed throughout the keep. The elite—even Patrick—listened without stirring. A surge of homesickness rose up within them, for the music was plaintive, mournful. They found their thoughts drawn back to everything they had left behind on the far shores of Greece. They were reminded of mothers, of ladyloves, of too few years spent at home and far too many in the midst of battle. Most unhappily of all, perhaps, they were reminded that there were no women to warm their beds. Nor would there be any until they had achieved a greater degree of harmony in Karabey.

Equally touched by the song, Thalia drifted back to resume her seat beside Josh. She leaned as close to him as she dared. "Why have you offered me no proper welcome, Sir Joshua?" she whispered. Her face reflected her mingled hurt and disappointment.

"I ... thought it best this way." He tensed at her nearness. The scent of her perfume, and the warmth of her arm pressing against his, made him groan inwardly. She was even more lovely than he had remembered. *Even more dangerous.*

"Have you forgotten what I told you?" She cast a swift, cautious glance toward Nicholas before demanding again, "Have you?"

"I have not," he murmured, then frowned and offered up a silent oath. "Though I should have done so."

"How can you say that? When I—"

"The time is ill-chosen, my lady." He cut her off brusquely, his narrowed gaze flickering with significance toward Nicholas.

"I am not a child, Joshua!" she whispered angrily, her color high.

"Are you not?" His tone was one of condescending amusement. Wounded and angry, Thalia leapt to her feet again and swept loftily back to stand near Leah. Nicholas had overheard them. He intended to question Josh later; their exchange had sounded suspiciously intimate and would need an accounting. For now, however, his attention remained focused on Leah. His gaze burned as he watched her. His blood ran hotly in his veins. Her eyes had closed; her face appeared ethereal, mesmerizing, as the music swelled to a crescendo. The sound of it beckoned him to madness just as it had done the first time. His mouth twitched wryly at the thought. By the gods, he had never envisioned himself as prey to such wild flights of fancy. But the way his body ached for her was no mere product of his imagination. Nor was the way his heart turned over in his chest.

When Leah had finished the song, and the last vibrant tones had floated softly skyward, she opened her eyes. Though she was determined otherwise, her gaze sought Nicholas's.

What she saw therein filled her with dread. She suffered a sharp intake of breath, feeling at once light-headed and strangely feverish.

"That was most entertaining, Mistress Baal," Thalia stepped forward to declare, with a forced brightness. "Now, perhaps you—"

"I cannot," Leah murmured tremulously, even though she cursed herself yet again as a coward. *She had to get away.*

"Are you unwell?" Thalia asked, her brows turned into an earnest frown of concern.

"No. Yes, I-I ..." She folded her arms beneath her breasts while her eyes traveled across the faces of the elite. In that moment, they did not seem like enemies. But she would not have them witness her lack of composure.

"Leave the girl be!" David growled, drawing himself unsteadily upward from the table. He smiled at Leah through bloodshot eyes.

"She has sung. And by the grace of Apollo, we were not turned to treason!"

"Drink any more ambrosia, old man, and you may well find yourself tempted to it yet," noted John, with amiable irony. He, too, smiled at Leah, though his smile contained none of Sir David's guilelessness. "You have our gratitude, Mistress Baal, for a brief respite from a life too lacking in charm." Neither he nor the others wanted to admit how deeply they had been affected by Leah's magical voice.

"You were ever a smooth-tongued knave, John," Keith scolded idly.

"Ah, but an expert one," he parried.

"Will you not sing again for us now?" Thalia tried appealing to Leah again. Leah's eyes were full of an unspoken apology when she faced the older woman. Words failed her, and she looked helplessly to Nicholas one last time. He noted her distress. The sight of it provoked a surge of mingled guilt and protectiveness in him.

"Mistress Baal has already stated her wish to retire," he said, his voice quiet and full of authority. Thalia, all too familiar with the tone, ventured no further entreaties. She fell silent and wandered toward the fireplace.

Leah was both surprised and touched by Nicholas's response. She offered him no words of gratitude, however. Was *he* not the cause of her increasing turmoil?

"I bid you good night," she said, then set off toward the staircase. She did not look back.

"Good night, Mistress Baal." Nicholas spoke for them all. He and the other men resumed their seats once she had gone.

Thalia was not affronted by their waning gallantry, for she was deep in thought. She stared into the flames and fought against the urge to weep. Watching her, Josh battled perilous impulses of his own.

"The wench is pretty enough," Patrick opened nonchalantly. They each knew he referred to Leah. "It is a pity she is Turkish."

Every man at the table inwardly echoed his *sentiments—one more than the others.* A long silence rose in the hall. The crackle and hiss of the fire, the hammering of the wind against the marble keep, and the shadows dancing across the walls combined to evoke the same eerie, otherworldly atmosphere that had greeted them upon their arrival at Karabey. Only Nicholas remained unaffected by the tension in the room. His deep, gold-flecked dark gaze strayed upward, his pulse quickening at the thought of Leah in the bedchamber above.

For him, the night would be the longest yet.

CHAPTER 7

▼

Dawn broke all too soon.

Leah's eyelids fluttered reluctantly open at last. She heaved a sigh and stretched beneath the mountain of covers atop the bed. The fire had long since died. Clad in only her shift, she shivered in the cold as she pulled herself upright and impatiently swept the tangled mass of curls from her face. Her eyes traveled to the single narrow window, where the first determined light of the new day crept over the rolling countryside and promised (no doubt falsely) that there would be no rain that morning.

She frowned as her gaze now wandered about the room. Another sigh escaped her lips. Her slumber had been fitful at best. More than once during the night, she had been awakened by the wind's relentless howling. Though she was long accustomed to it, the sound had penetrated her sleep, causing her to toss and turn restlessly. And ever present; ever taunting, had been thoughts of Sir Nicholas Constinos. She had been keenly aware of the fact that he lay sleeping but a short distance away. And though she had taken the precaution of bolting the door, she had nonetheless half expected him to demand entrance. "And what would you have done if he *had?*" she challenged herself scornfully, her blue eyes flashing at her own weak-spiritedness. It was with vivid, damning clarity that she remembered the previous day's humiliations. Humiliations they had been, and she shared equal blame for them.

Muttering an oath, she now tumbled from the bed and hurried to dress. She poured water from the bucket into a bowl and leaned over it to wash her face. The cold, bracing liquid was precisely what she needed to clear her head. Donning the same gown she had worn the night before, and tugging on her stockings and slippers, she knelt before the hearth to coax the pile of softly glowing embers back to life. Once the flames began to dance amid the sticks and straw, she added a split log and then sank down upon the rush-covered marble floor to brush her hair.

Langdon and Louise would return from Troy this day, she recalled cheerlessly. What would her foster father's reaction be when he found her gone—and to the palace, no less? It mattered not, of course. Sir Nicholas would have his way. She frowned and dragged the brush through her thick, lustrous tresses with an ireful vengeance. Peatro Conrad's face suddenly rose before her. There was little doubt that *he* would receive the news badly, very badly indeed. In spite of her refusal of him, she knew that he considered her his betrothed. Yet … did he truly love her? The sudden, unbidden memory of his kiss only provoked more consternation within her It had certainly been nothing like *either* of Sir Nicholas's. Again, the comparison between the two was both inevitable and alarming.

She startled guiltily when a knock sounded at the door. Climbing to her feet, she moved slowly to answer it Her breath caught in her throat as she slid the bolt free, for she did not yet feel prepared to face Nicholas again. Profound relief flooded through her when she saw that it was Thalia who stood smiling across at her.

"My brother has invited us to ride with him this morning," the older Greek woman told her. She was wearing a beautiful cote-hardie of patterned sapphire velvet, her plaited golden-brown hair secured beneath a silver-threaded caul. If she was annoyed with Leah for deserting her the previous night, she gave no evidence of it.

"Surely my presence is not required," Leah demurred, her stomach knotting at the prospect.

"You are my companion, are you not?" She grasped Leah firmly, yet gently, by the hand. Her eyes danced with an irresistible measure of good humor "Come. It is early, I know. Sir Nicholas was ever regardless of anyone's desire to linger past first light. Someday, I would have him know the torment of being so discourteously roused from the warmth of his bed!"

Leah knew that further protests would prove futile. Pausing only to catch up her cloak, she accompanied Thalia from the bedchamber.

There was no one else about when the two of them sat down at the table in the hall below to break their fast. Afterward, they stepped outside into the crisp, sun-drenched morning air. The men, Greek and Turks alike, had already begun work; the warring sounds and smells filled the bailey as they had done for the past week.

Leah's eyes instinctively searched for Nicholas, but widened in surprise when they fell upon the buxom, dark-haired young woman who stood waiting for her at the foot of the steps. She murmured an excuse to Thalia, then hastily descended to speak to her friend.

"Theresa! What are you—"

"I have come with Angela and Mildred to work in the kitchen this day," Theresa declared in an undertone. "Yet in truth, I would speak with you." She cast a wary glance about—and frowned when she saw that Thalia watched them inquisitively from the steps above.

"What is it?" Leah demanded, her voice edged with anxiety as she forgot all else. Her hand curled about the other woman's arm. "Is something wrong?"

"Υπάρχει," Theresa said. "Peatro Conrad was away to Ponceel House to see you yesterday. Neither Margaret nor Marilyn would tell him anything, save that you were not at home. He stood upon my doorstep before sundown, demanding to know where you were and raising Hades own tempest while he was about it!"

"What did you tell him?"

"The truth," whispered Theresa. Then she amended, "well, a portion of it He thinks you are here willingly for a brief time, that you were seized with a strange curiosity and would learn the ways of a Greek woman. I cannot say that Peatro understood." She gave Leah a narrow, dubious look. "I did but wonder myself when you failed to return. Were you not vowing only yesterday morn that you would defy Sir Nicholas in this?"

"Yes, but ... I-I had no choice," stammered Leah, her gaze falling uncomfortably. "I took heed of your words. And of my own selfishness." Her eyes were full of an appeal for understanding when she looked at Theresa again. "As you said, Sir Nicholas Constinos has the power to bend us to his will. Sweet Hera, do I not know it?" she then murmured.

"*Mistress Baal?*" They tensed in unison at the sound of Thalia's voice. Leah pivoted about to witness her approach.

"I am but conversing with a friend, Lady Thalia," she proclaimed evenly. She and Theresa exchanged a swift, surreptitious glance.

"She is from the village then?" Thalia asked. She moved to stand beside Leah, her demeanor not at all the arrogant, superior one Theresa had anticipated. With a tentative smile, she told the young brunette, "you are welcome here. Though, I must confess, I had not expected visitors at such an early hour."

"I am called Theresa Unger, my lady. And I have come to cook." She raised her chin defensively.

"Oh. I am glad of it," Thalia replied. Her gaze returned to Leah.

"Dame Frances will be much pleased with the extra hands. Perhaps her temper will suffer an improvement." Catching sight of her guardian at last, she said, "we must go now. Good day to you, Mistress Unger."

"I will speak with you again, Theresa," promised Leah. She set off across the courtyard with Thalia. Her pulse leapt as it always had whenever she saw Nicholas. He was clad in a light mail shirt, his crimson tunic beneath it, and wore a pair of leather riding sandals. A sword rested in its scabbard at his side. It struck her once more that he had the look of a man ever prepared for trouble … the look of a man who had spent a lifetime amid struggle and strife.

"I bid you good morning, Mistress Baal," he declared, with only the ghost of a smile when she and Thalia approached. He stood near the drawbridge, holding the reins of two saddled horses who pawed and snorted impatiently in the sun's bright, benevolent warmth. His steady gaze belied his own restless night.

"I am told we are to ride," Leah responded. She glanced briefly at Josh. He, too, stood waiting with two horses. After granting Leah a polite nod, he turned his full attention to Thalia.

"My sister would see some of my holdings," offered Nicholas. "Sir Josh is to accompany us. No doubt it will soothe the farmers if you are seen with us this day. We have scarce been viewed with affection until now." His eyes glowed with irony.

"Is that why I am to come?" Leah challenged, concealing her sharp pang of disappointment at the thought. "To serve as your envoy among my people?"

"No." He gazed solemnly down at her. She grew warm and looked away.

"Are you-are you not afraid that I will seek escape once we are away from the palace?" she murmured.

"I would find you."

The quiet, vibrant tone of his voice set her heart pounding fiercely. She trembled at the touch of his hands about her waist, but she did not resist when he finally lifted her up to the horse's back. Josh assisted Thalia in mounting as well.

The four of them soon rode across the drawbridge, with Nicholas and Leah leading the way. Once they had left the palace behind, they allowed their horses to slow to a more leisurely pace. The breeze that swept across the land was sweet, scented with wildflowers, and there were as yet no storm clouds gathering in the sky above.

"Winter is almost upon us," Nicholas noted idly, grasping the reins with practiced ease as he turned his head toward Leah. A short distance behind them, Josh and Thalia had already entered into a private—and often discomfiting—conversation of their own.

"The feast of *Artemis will* take place in but three days," Leah mentioned on sudden impulse.

"*Artemis?*"

"It's November Eve. Ancient tradition demands that we celebrate it with a feast."

She sought to keep her voice calm and distant, but it followed its own rebellious course. Her eyes were equally willful, for they would not refrain from looking in his direction. *She* could not so easily forget that she had been in his arms but a few short hours ago. With an inward groan, she shifted in the saddle and tugged the front edges of her woolen cloak more closely together.

"I would hear more." Nicholas prompted her, his interest lying not so much in the story as in the telling of it. The sound of her voice filled him with pleasure.

"Do you truly wish to know?" she asked dubiously. It seemed quite extraordinary to be riding and speaking with him on such congenial terms. In spite of what had happened between them, he was still little more than a stranger. And yet … in some incredible, soul-stirring way, she felt as though she had always known him.

"Karabey is mine now. Should I not seek to learn all I can about its traditions?" His smile this time was both cryptic and disarming.

"Very well. So long as you are once again willing to risk the danger," she warned, casting him a saucy look. She was surprised to hear his quiet chuckle. Her heart fluttered at the sound of it, though she made a valiant attempt at normalcy. "In Anatolia, my lord," she continued, "there are but two seasons—summer and winter Cold and darkness will soon descend upon us. Cattle will be driven down from the safety of the summer pastures and slaughtered to provide sustenance for the bitter days ahead. Grain and vegetables will be gathered and stored. As much wood as can be cut will be set aside to keep the dreadful chill at bay. It is no more than others do to make ready."

"Tell me of the feast itself." He spared a cursory glance back over his shoulder, satisfied to note that Josh and Thalia were still deep within the midst of their own conversation.

"The entire village will assemble within the square just before nightfall. Sheep brack, feta rice, and baklava will be eaten. Wine will flow freely, music played, and there will be dancing. The feast is not only to mark the beginning of winter, but also to celebrate the one night when the boundaries between the living and the dead disappear."

"The dead?"

She nodded. "We are told that Lord Hades allows the spirits to roam the earth freely on November Eve. The nymphs as well. "Pausing, she gently cleared her throat and was dismayed to feel warm color staining her cheeks. Her gaze fell beneath his when she added, "It is also the night when young maids may find a new love, or even, perchance, be captured by a divine lover."

"And do you hold with these beliefs, Leah?" Her name upon his lips sounded like an endearment.

"I do not!" She shook her head in a vehement denial. "Even so, I will harbor no contempt for those who do."

"We face much the same dilemma, you and I," Nicholas observed ruefully. "I would keep to my sworn duty here, yet it is difficult to force ..." His voice trailed away, his brow creasing into a dark frown.

"Why did you come to Karabey?" Leah impulsively demanded. The question was as much of a surprise to herself as to him. Her eyes sparked with reproach when they met his again. "Why did you not remain in Sparta? Surely you would have found a far better welcome there than in Anatolia."

"Karabey was given as reward for my service to Lord Ares. I would offer no quarrel for his choice. And there was naught to keep me in Sparta."

"No family?" she persisted. "No duties at court, nor ladyloves?" Her breath caught in her throat while she waited for his reply. She remembered what Thalia had told her about the woman who had betrayed him.

"No." Along with the truth, his steady gaze held a disconcerting warmth. "Once, perhaps. But no longer." Indeed, he realized, thoughts of Lauren had not crossed his mind *since*—" *since he had met Leah.* "The fates led me to Anatolia. To Karabey."

"Are we not free to choose our own destiny?"

"Yes." His tone was a very low arid level, scarcely audible above the drone of the wind and the horses' hooves striking against the ground, "We are free to embrace it, or to deny it. Even then, the choice is fraught with peril." His eyes seared across into hers. "Yet it is a risk I will take."

Leah felt a sudden and alarming tremor seize her. She opened her mouth to offer a retort, only to find herself uncharacteristically bereft *of* words. Her gaze was shadowed by several conflicting emotions as it traveled across the fertile, rolling hills. She urged her mount a little ahead *of* Nicholas's, determined *to* put some distance between them. Determined, *too,* that he should not see *how* tempted she was to take the risk herself.

Josh and Thalia, meanwhile, were faring little better in their own efforts at harmony. Thalia's anger was all too visible, her eyes fairly snapping at the elite beside her.

"May Hades take *you,* Joshua Leonidas! Will *you* not at least admit that I speak the truth?" she entreated in a furious whisper.

"You have too long been granted your own way, Thalia." He frowned and breathed an oath, looking for all the world like a man in the company *of* an ill-favored shrew instead *of* a lovely and adoring woman. "It is time someone—"

"It is time someone reminded *you* that you are but flesh and blood!" She heaved a long, disgruntled sigh before braving caustically. "Perhaps I should henceforth refer *to* you as 'Divine Joshua.' You would allow your allegiance to my brother deny us both happiness? Why then not declare yourself immune to all pleasures *of* the flesh and join the oracles at Delphi?"

"If *I* were in charge," Josh countered menacingly, "I would teach *you* to curb your tongue." Indeed, he was at that moment *torn* between the desire to turn her across his knee and the far more agreeable urge to demonstrate just how nondivine he was.

His blue eyes darkened as he cursed the ache deep within his own heart. He possessed neither the wealth nor the family connections to count himself as suitor to Lady Thalia Constinos. And though he had not broached the subject with Nicholas, he knew that his liege would wish to see her wed to someone with much more to offer than simple love and devotion.

"I am no child!" Thalia reiterated, with a willful, thoroughly indignant toss of her head. "I have lived thirty years upon this earth, a more than adequate time to know my mind, to know that what I feel is not the passing infatuation of a mere crush!"

"Even so, my lady, I am not the man for you." His visage now took on the obstinate expression she had come to know too well. "You are the sister of Sir Nicholas Constinos. I will not seize advantage of your status or innocence."

"I can do naught to alter my status," she said angrily, provoked to rashness. "But mayhap I should seek to lose my innocence. Would you then consider me worthy of your regard?"

The look he turned upon her was positively thunderous. She inhaled upon a gasp, her pulse leaping in very real alarm. Hot, bitter tears of defeat stung against her eyelids, but she blinked them back. Quickly urging her horse forward to keep pace with Nicholas's, she kept her face averted from his—unaware that he saw far more than she would have wished.

Soon thereafter, the four riders came upon one *of* the outlying estates. It lay nestled within a serene valley, its large stone house, stables, and barns giving evidence of better days. Two men, both of them more than a few years past their prime, were harvesting wheat in the fields adjacent to the house. A much younger man stood chop-ping wood near one of the barns, while a dark-haired woman, carrying a bucketful of water in each hand, hurried toward the kitchen.

Leah's heart sank at the sight before her. Too late, she realized that they had arrived at the home of Peatro Conrad.

"May we not visit the farm?" Thalia asked Nicholas as they halted upon a rise just above the sun-warmed valley.

"No!" Leah blurted out. Dull color rose to her face. "They would not thank us for disturbing their work." The excuse sounded feeble, even to her own ears.

"We shall not tarry long," said Nicholas, silently noting her disquiet. He touched his heels to his horse's flanks and set off down the hill, with Josh and Thalia close behind. Leah hesitated, but in the end followed after them. They drew to a halt in front of the house and remained astride Thalia was to Leah's right, Nicholas to her left. Her gaze flew anxiously about, searching for Peatro. She tensed in the saddle and prayed silently that he would be away from home. But her hopes were dashed when she saw him emerge from the nearby stables. He headed straight toward her, his eyes widening in stunned disbelief.

"Leah?" he called out. His clothing was dirty, his sandals caked with several days worth of mud. But Leah noticed only how his gaze bridled with displeasure as it moved to Nicholas.

"You know the man?" Thalia questioned Leah, her own surprise evident.

Leah nodded mutely. Her eyes flew to meet Nicholas's. She paled before reluctantly turning back to acknowledge Peatro's approach.

"Good day to you, Peatro Conrad," she proclaimed, striving to conceal her trepidation.

He drew close to her. "Αυτόπου είναι εσείς που κάνετε?" he demanded in a harsh, accusatory tone. He spared only a disdainful glance for the others.

"I am but riding this morn with Sir Nicholas Constinos," she answered, her own voice underscored by a tell-tale edge. "And Lady Thalia Constinos. And Sir Josh Leonidas." Her eyes swept hastily across each of them as she revealed, "Peatro Conrad and I are old acquaintances."

"Acquaintances?" Peatro echoed. His face reddened with anger; his eyes narrowed malevolently. "I bid you no welcome, Sir Nicholas Constinos!"

"By the gods—" Josh grounded out, his hand moving to the hilt of his sword.

"Peatro!" Leah cried. Beside her, Thalia's eyes grew round with incredulity.

"Your manners need improving, Peatro Conrad," Nicholas remarked somberly Though his features remained impassive, his own gaze held a dangerous gleam. "We have not come to provoke you. Nor to suffer insult."

"Then I would see you off my lands!" snarled Peatro. Without waiting for a reply, he jerked his head about and told Leah, "I did not want to believe Theresa. I would not have thought it possible that you could be so foolish. You do not belong with them! How can you—?"

"Calm down!" she cautioned him. Her throat constricted tightly. "Please, Peatro. You must be silent!"

"These lands belong to the master of Karabey," Josh pointed out, with a foreboding grimness of his own. "And you will guard your tongue, Turkishman, or else risk losing it." His words earned him a shocked, open-mouthed look from Thalia.

"Do they know that we are to be wed?" Peatro asked Leah challengingly. He drew himself proudly erect and declared to the others, "Leah Baal is my betrothed. Soon she will become my wife!"

Leah inhaled upon an audible gasp. Dismayed, she looked to Nicholas.

"I-I am not …" she stammered breathlessly, her voice trailing away when it appeared that he took little notice of her.

"You have not yet sought my permission for the marriage," Nicholas advised Peatro. His tone was quiet, even, and his eyes were glinting dully. He gave no hint of the jealous, white-hot fury coursing through him. Nor of the fierce urge to dismount and beat Peatro Conrad until the man was bloodied and begging for mercy.

"It is the law," added Josh. "The lord must give his consent before anyone in Karabey may wed." Sensing Nicholas's inner struggle, he hastened to diffuse what he already knew to be a volatile situation. Thus, he instructed Peatro curtly, "Present yourself at the palace tomorrow. Sir Nicholas will hear your request then."

"But, surely you will grant them the right?" Thalia appealed to Nicholas "Why, if Mistress Baal and this man desire to marry—"

"No!" cried Leah. Desperate to put a stop to the travesty, she glared down at Peatro and threatened hotly, "If you value my regard at all, Peatro Conrad, you will say no more."

Filled with an inexplicable mortification, she suddenly reined about and took flight. Her eyes blazed as the animal beneath her thundered back the way it had come.

"Mistress Baal!" an astonished Thalia called after her. She looked helplessly to Josh, who shook his head in a silent warning against further interference.

"Leah will be my wife!" Peatro declared again, his rancorous gaze full of certain triumph as it momentarily locked with Nicholas's.

"She will not," vowed Nicholas. His features became a grim mask of determination as he now urged his horse about to give chase.

"Should we not go after them?" Thalia asked Josh, her head spinning as a result of all that had happened.

"No, my lady, we should not." He turned back to Peatro and said coldly, "You are a fool, Turkishman. Never again make the mistake of insulting Sir Nicholas Constinos as you have done this day. Better men than you have lost their lives for less." He looked to Thalia again and directed, "Come We shall return to the palace."

The two of them rode slowly away, leaving Peatro simmering in both vengeful rage and a pain-filled realization that Leah had once again denied him as her betrothed. Even worse, she had done so before the enemy. The memory of Sir Nicholas's eyes upon her was a bitter one … The thought of her beneath the same roof as the Greek man was even more so.

"I will yet send you to Hades, Sir Nicholas Constinos," he muttered, his gaze narrowing significantly toward the distant hills.

At that same moment, Leah discovered that she was being followed. She cast a quick glance behind her, and blanched in alarm when she saw that it was Nicholas who was giving chase. Instinct prompted her toward escape. Bending low in the saddle, she urged her horse to even greater speed across the green, undulating countryside.

But it was no use. Nicholas easily caught up with her. His hand shot out to grasp her reins. He forced her mount to a halt and subjected her to a fierce, hot-blooded look that increased her apprehension tenfold.

"Would you risk injury to yourself and the horse to avoid me?" he charged tersely.

"I would be left alone!" she flung back. She caught her breath as he dismounted and reached up for her. "Release me!" She resisted, her hands pushing at him, but he pulled her down and held her captive before him.

"Did he speak the truth?" he demanded, his eyes scorching down into hers

"No!" She renewed her struggles, then gasped when his fingers curled tightly about her waist.

"You were never betrothed to him?"

"I … The arrangement was made long ago, when we were but children," she confessed in a small and tremulous voice. Her sparkling, deeply troubled gaze fell beneath the smoldering intensity of his. "My foster father would wish it so."

"I will not give my consent," he decreed, his tone quiet and laced with steel.

"I do not seek it!" she exclaimed, shaking her head in a vigorous denial In the next instant, however, she regained her spirit of defiance. "Yet, if I *did* wish to become the wife of Peatro Conrad—or indeed, any other man—the lack of your blessing would not deter me." She looked away again and tried to ignore the way her flesh burned beneath his strong hands, the way her heart sang at the thought of his jealousy. "You play with me, my lord, as a cat with a mouse. I am only one of the Turks, a woman bound by the law to give you my *loyalty—but nothing else.* What should it matter to you if I were to find happiness with someone?"

"Would Peatro Conrad give you happiness?" he demanded, his fingers tensing with near bruising force upon her.

"I made no such claim!"

"You shall not be wed to him."

"You have no right to—"

"I have the right." He cut her off. His hands swept upward to her shoulders, and he drew her closer. "In truth, Leah Baal, I have the right. More than either of us would care to admit."

"The right?" she asked, a painful lump rising in her throat as she tilted her head back to face him squarely. "Why do you torment me so?"

He said nothing. The battle raged within him as he stared down at her, his eyes raking with bold possessiveness over her upturned countenance. The sweet-scented wind swept across them. It teased at the wayward tendrils of hair that had escaped Leah's long plait.

The sun beamed down, warm and golden. But the beauty of the day was lost to them. Lost in a tangle of heartache and confusion, and, still, a yearning so powerful that it threatened disaster at every turn.

"Would you truly cast aside all you have sworn to achieve?" Leah whispered brokenly. "Sweet Hera, would you place in jeopardy the peace you seek here?" Her eyes glistened with sudden tears. She raised her hands to Nicholas's chest. *"Please."*

The sound of her entreaty sent a sharp pain slicing through his heart. Though he longed to kiss her, to imprison her within his embrace and forget all else, he did not. This time, he let her go.

She spun away and hastened to mount again. Her hands were unsteady as she gathered up the reins, and she could not prevent her eyes from straying back to Nicholas's face. "You-you will not harm Peatro when he comes to the palace tomorrow?" she ventured.

"Does he mean so much to you then?" asked Nicholas, still fighting against the desire to make her stay.

"I would not see him hurt."

"By all the gods on Olympus, do you think me such a villain?" he grounded out. His voice held raw emotion, his gaze darkening.

"No," she answered in all honesty. "No, my lord, I do not." She left him then.

Later, after she had returned to the palace, she was grateful that Thalia did not immediately seek to question her about the morning's incident. It was obvious that the woman was filled with curiosity. Yet, she kept the tone of their conversation casual, speaking of books and music and life at court as the two of them strolled about the courtyard. They were surprised, pleasantly so, to discover how much they had in common. Indeed, mused Leah, if not for the many long years of political turmoil that stood between them, Lady Thalia Constinos might well have been a friend.

"Perhaps we are not so very different after all," Thalia remarked, as if reading Leah's thoughts. She lifted a hand to the low branch of a tree as they paused beneath it. Their privacy was assured, for work had yet to begin on that section of the bailey.

"Perhaps not," concurred Leah. "But I fear there are some differences that can never be overcome." Her eyes reflected her sadness. She closed them briefly, unable to deny the memory of what had happened that morning.

"Differences," Thalia murmured, her own gaze clouding. She released a disconsolate sigh and gazed back toward the nearby keep. "If only men and women were more alike."

"Would you truly have it so?" Leah asked.

"I suppose not." Thalia's mouth curved into a soft smile of irony, and her eyes sparkled mischievously. "At least not in the way that matters most." She quickly sobered again. With yet another sigh, she wandered away from the shadowing canopy of the tree and asked, "Have you ever lost your heart to anyone, Mistress Baal?"

"It is time you called me Leah."

"Then I am to be Thalia. But I would have an answer, if you please." She turned and observed the dull flush that crept up to Leah's face. "Is it Peatro Conrad who causes you such distress?"

"No," Leah denied in all honesty, shaking her head. "I do not return his affection."

"Then—?"

"No doubt there have been a great many gallants paying you tribute," Leah said, deliberately steering the conversation onto safer ground. She forced a smile to her lips. "Was there no one at court you would choose to wed?"

"There *was* a man, an elite, who captured my heart not so long ago But he will have none of me."

"Mayhap he fears your brother will not approve. Would Sir Nicholas consent to such a marriage?"

"I am not certain," Thalia admitted unhappily. "My brother's mind is difficult to know. Indeed, he is at times a most perplexing man."

A most perplexing man, Leah repeated silently. She had never known anyone more so.

They returned to the keep then. And later, once the noon meal had been taken, Leah busied herself by helping Theresa and the other village women in the kitchen. Thalia offered no complaint, apparently content to while away the afternoon in the company of Patrick and John. They offered her an escort into the village, and took great pleasure in regaling her with much embellished tales of their past braveries and adventures. She listened with all politeness, and secretly wished the entire time that she were in Josh's company. Though his rejection had angered and hurt her, she would not yet admit defeat.

It was nearing twilight when Leah emerged from the kitchen. She stepped outside, pulling her fine knitted shawl more closely about her shoulders as she inhaled deeply of the cool evening air.

And then she spied Langdon Fogus.

Her heart leapt in her throat as she watched him pass through the gates. He marched across the courtyard, his steps quickening when he caught sight of her.

"Hera help me!" she whispered. Certain that his visit would cause trouble, she hurried to intercept him. She drew him into the shadows behind the kitchen, anxious that their meeting should not be witnessed by Nicholas.

"We did but return from Troy an hour ago, only to discover that you had spent last night here among the Greek!" he told her angrily. "Zeus save you, girl! What are you about?"

"I shall only remain for a few days," she assured him with an admirable show of calm. Inwardly she was a mass of nerves. "I am but providing temporary companionship for Sir Nicholas's sister."

"I would speak with Sir Nicholas!" he pronounced, his wrath visibly increasing. "To command a Baal—"

"No! No, Langdon. You must not," insisted Leah, her hand closing about his arm. "I-I am here of my own free will, and would stay only a short time longer." Her voice wavered with the half true confession. She prayed that he would take no notice of it. "I was but seized with curiosity. I would know more of the Greek, else how can we be sure what they are about in Karabey?"

"You would spy upon them?"

"I would not call it that."

"Would you not?" He muttered an oath and demanded, "What of Peatro Conrad?"

"He has naught to do with this!"

"He would wed you at the feast," Langdon reminded her, with a paternal glow. "You must come home."

"I cannot. Not yet." She forced a smile to her lips, striving to keep her tone even as she promised, "I shall return before the celebration.

There can be no danger in staying until then. In truth, I am being treated with respect. Sir Nicholas-Sir Nicholas is not quite the heavy-handed rogue we judged him to be."

"You will become Peatro's wife then?"

"We cannot marry without Sir Nicholas's permission," she murmured. *I will not give my consent.* His words burned anew within her mind.

"Then Peatro must seek it at once." He heaved a sigh of angry resignation and shook his head. "Still, it matters not."

"But the law—"

"*Greek* law," he pointed out scornfully. "We will keep to our own ways. So long as they do not go against the new statutes, we are in no danger. A man such as Sir Nicholas Constinos can care little about the marriage."

"Have I not already given Peatro my answer?" She frowned and drew her hand away.

"You will not defy me in this, Leah!"

"Do my feelings not matter to you at all then?" she accused, her expression both wounded and mutinous.

"I love you as though you were my own," he declared earnestly, then shook his head again. "But you will keep to the promise that was made."

"It was none of my making," she retorted.

His only response was to compress his lips into a tight, thin line of displeasure and turned away. Leah stared after him as he strode back across the bailey. She cast a desperate glance skyward, then gathered up her skirts and made for the steps of the tower keep.

She shut herself away in the firelit solitude of her bedchamber after that, pleading a headache when Thalia sought to coax her downstairs for supper. She feared that Nicholas would disturb her, that he would command her presence at the table again, but he did not.

One of the maidservants, a slender girl named Jena, brought her hot water and offered to fetch the bathtub. Leah declined, and once Jena had gone, poured the water into the bowl. She stripped off all her clothing and hastened to wash before she became chilled to the bone. Once she had donned a clean white shift, she slipped beneath the covers of the bed and stared pensively up toward the heavy brocade covering draped above. Several long moments later, her gaze drifted to the bowl, which was set beside the fireplace. It was bathed in the soft golden glow put forth by the dancing, dwindling flames. For the first time in her life, she cursed the life she had been given.

CHAPTER 8

▼

The next two days were relatively uneventful—though filled with a strange disquiet felt by everyone within the palace walls. Peatro Conrad came to present his appeal as he had been instructed to do. He left without having gained the blessing he sought. And without having been granted the opportunity to speak with Leah. She knew that he had come, knew as well that the rejection would provoke even further ill-will toward the Greek. But she could not be sorry for it. Had there been no tall, brown-eyed elite to seduce her, she still would have resisted marriage to Peatro.

Life settled into a routine of sorts. She and Thalia passed away the hours with their sewing and reading, and with their many walks about the courtyard. Leah also paid several more visits to the kitchen, in order to talk with Theresa and help in whatever way she could. She even managed to win Dame Frances's begrudging approval by mastering the fine art of baking bread. The accomplishment, however small, was a source of pride to her; she had always regretted the fact that neither Louise nor her aunt in Troy had considered such skills necessary. Indeed, she recalled cheerlessly, it had always been expected that she would marry well and thus leave the housewifery to an array of capable servants.

The days passed pleasantly enough, but the evening meal continued to prove an ordeal to be endured. Leah was alternately puzzled, relieved, and disappointed that Nicholas spoke so little to her. She could only surmise that he thought it best to avoid her. In truth, she reasoned with herself, how else could they hope to extinguish the fiery, dangerous attraction that had sprung to life between them?

The elite, at least, seemed to have grown into an easier acceptance of her. Even Patrick Soppolous treated her with less hostility than before. Sir John's attentiveness was flattering yet discomfiting; And Sir David's nightly intoxication brought with it a barrage of compliments regarding both her beauty and her singing abilities.

Still, she was always keenly aware of Nicholas beside her. Always conscious of the fact that one unintentional brush of his arm against hers would send a shiver of mingled pleasure and alarm dancing down her spine. The tension between them increased daily. Her thoughts each day would not be kept from him. Her dreams each night were haunted by visions of him, of his voice and his smile and his eyes. Sweet Hera, how much longer could she bear it?

The feast of *Artemis* drew near.

Leah stood alone in the midst of her bedchamber, remembering her promise to Langdon. At sundown the following day, the celebration would begin.

"Hera help me," she whispered, her heart filling with dread at the prospect of what lay ahead. "Tomorrow."

She knew that both Peatro and her foster father would seek to force her into the marriage. She knew that few among the villagers would heed her protests, especially once they had begun to partake of the wine. And the oracles would offer her little enough assistance in the matter. For that one night of the year, they allowed the line between Zeus and Hades to be crossed without fear of condemnation. It was a popular indulgence on their part, one that led more often than not to twelve full months of fairly dutiful compliance with the oracles view toward guilt and penance. Besides, Leah recalled with a frown, an oracle's words were not required to make a marriage valid. In fact, no public ceremony was necessary at all—merely, the consent of both man and woman. The oracles recognized such unions, even if they did take place without their knowledge or blessing.

"'Doves shall fill the sky before an unwilling maid becomes a bride.'" A faint, humorless smile touched her lips as she repeated the old saying. Her blue eyes flashed in the next instant and strayed to the window. Darkness had long since fallen. The night was cold, the moon obscured by a thick churning of clouds. There would be storms before morning. Seized by a sudden, desperate need to escape the confines of the room, she whirled about and caught up her shawl. She flung it about her shoulders and stepped into her slippers as she crossed to the door. Slipping from the bedchamber, she crept cautiously along the narrow passageway. The palace was dark and quiet. Only a single torch burned softly high upon the wall.

Leah headed down the corridor toward the steps that led up to the battlements. She climbed them swiftly, her feet sure and her pulse racing. Once at the top, she eased open the door and stepped outside into the cold, rain-scented night air. She closed the door behind her.

The wind teased at her long hair, sending it into a glorious tumble of curls about her face and shoulders; She wore nothing save the shawl and her thin, white linen shift. It was madness to be here like this, and well she knew it, but the impulse had been too great to resist.

She moved to the outermost edge of the tower and pulled her shawl close about her. Her gaze swept across the darkened landscape, her heart soaring with the exhilarating sense of freedom she felt. Never mind that it was near to freezing, never mind that tomorrow would bring with it a host of troubles. At that moment, she felt at one with the world about her. She felt peace and contentment … and a sense of excitement that stirred her blood so wildly, so provocatively, that she struggled for breath.

"*Leah.*"

The peace was shattered. She startled violently at the sound of his voice Her eyes opened wide, her heart thundering as she spun about to face him. He had drawn off his tunic; his white shirt glowed softly against the background of stones.

"No!" She gasped. There was no mistaking the man who stood gazing across at her from a scant three feet away. Even in the darkness, she could make out the rugged perfection of his features. Even in the darkness, she could see the way his eyes, so incredibly dark and mesmerizing, burned with a desire that was well-matched within her. She turned to flee. But it was already too late.

He pulled her against him. His strong arms gathered her close, his body hard and warm and undeniably masculine as it pressed against the trembling softness of hers. She raised her hands to his chest and tried to push him away, frightened more by her own secret, tempestuous yearning than by his.

"Let me go!" she entreated, scarcely aware that she did so.

"*Never,*" he vowed huskily. His lips descended upon hers with a bold passion that conquered the last of her resistance. She moaned low in her throat and felt the now familiar heat spreading like wildfire throughout her body. Her hands clutched at his shoulders as her eyes closed. She swayed against him. The kiss deepened. Her mouth welcomed the hot, velvety invasion of his tongue. Her hands crept upward, curling about his neck while her head spun dizzily. She kissed him back with all the longing she had sought to deny, with all the fiery passion he had awakened within her.

His hand swept downward as he urged her even closer. She gasped when his strong fingers curled tightly, possessively, about the well-rounded firmness of her backside. His hand scorched her skin through the delicate white linen. The hard, throbbing evidence of his arousal pressed against her, reminding her with an inescapable clarity of the danger ahead. Her mind screamed a warning. Her conscience forbade her to continue. But still, she would not put an end to the sweet madness. If she were to suffer condemnation for something, then, Sweet Hera, let it be *this,* with *him* ...

His mouth left off its ravishment of hers now to roam feverishly across her face, then down along the silken column of her neck to where her pulse beat with such alarming swiftness in her throat.

His hand suddenly came up to the rounded neckline of her shift. He tugged at the fabric, ripping it in his impatience as he bared her breasts. Leah gasped anew when the night air swept across her naked flesh. Her eyes opened wide; she murmured something unintelligible, her hands pushing at Nicholas' shoulders in a feeble, half-hearted protest. But he would not be denied. His fingers jerked the torn edges of the linen aside. His lips branded her skin, then closed about one of the creamy, rose-tipped peaks. His mouth sucked greedily. His tongue swirled with a tantalizing vengeance.

Leah shivered, but it was from pleasure and not from cold. Her head fell back. Her eyes closed once more. She found herself straining upward, her fingers curling almost convulsively about the sinewy, hard-muscled warmth of Nicholas' arms. The shawl slipped from about her body to tumble into a forgotten heap upon the stones.

Their embrace was provoked by a furious, Hades-bent hunger that drove all other thought from their minds. The wind whipped about them. The heavy, boiling clouds in the sky above threatened to send a deluge upon the earth at any moment. Yet they were oblivious to the danger. From the very first kiss, the spark had been ignited. It burst into flames now. It fired their blood, and sent their very souls spiraling upward.

"You are mine, Leah," Nicholas decreed, raising his head to gaze deeply into her eyes. Her heart took flight at the sound of his deep-timbered voice. She thrilled to the intoxicating mixture of tenderness and desire within his gaze. And then, he suddenly swept her up in his arms and carried her to the far corner of the battlements.

Still holding her close, he sank down upon the stones. They were sheltered from the wind by the wall. He settled her atop his thighs. She entwined her arms about his neck and lifted her face to his, quivering when his mouth captured the willing softness of hers again. His hand moved boldly down her back, then he tugged the hem of her shift upward to her knees. Once more, she felt the rush of cold night air upon her exposed flesh. But she scarcely had time to notice it before his fingers stroked first her buttocks, then sought the moist, secret place between her thighs.

"Nicholas!" She gasped against his mouth. For but a brief moment, passion gave way to shock. Nicholas kissed her more deeply, his touch warm and sensuous and gentle in spite of the white-hot desire thundering through him. Another low moan rose in her throat. She squirmed atop the lean hardness of his thighs, unaware that in so doing she only served to make it all the harder for him to maintain any measure of self-control.

For Leah, the pleasure evoked by his caress was more intense than she ever would have thought possible. Her whole body was aflame. Her pulse raced, her heart pounded in her ears while an acute, exquisitely tortuous yearning built deep within her. She knew it was wicked. She knew it was still forbidden. Yet how could she resist any longer? How could she not respond to the melody in her heart?

Nicholas was equally torn. He burned to possess her. *Now.* With the storm inside them raging so wildly, with the darkness to keep them safe …

Whether by the fate's design or by the guiding hand of Lord Zeus, he was brought back to reality when the gods cast down the first, gentle drops of rain. They fell slowly, tauntingly, offering up but a promise of the deluge still to come. Yet they were all that was needed for Nicholas's conscience to be heard. Though he had tried to ignore it, his sense of honor would not be wholly cast aside. He had followed a strict adherence to duty—to fairness and loyalty and right over might—for too long.

It mattered not that Leah Baal was Turkish. It mattered not what any law set forth. *He could not take her.* Not yet. Not until he was certain that the bond between them was powerful enough to withstand the inevitable dangers. Not until he was sure her feelings for him were as strong and unwavering as his own. By all the gods on high, how could he find the peace he sought if he plunged them both into such jeopardy?

Leah sensed the change in him before his actions revealed it. Her eyelids fluttered open; she stared up at him with both surprise and bewilderment He said nothing. Yet she read the truth in his eyes— or at least what she thought to be the truth. Once again, humiliation washed over her. Catching her breath sharply, she pushed against him and scrambled free. Her legs were unsteady as she climbed to her feet and she felt hot, bitter tears welling up in her eyes as she clutched the torn edges of her shift to her breasts. It was only then that she became fully aware of the rain. The cold drops felt heavy and punishing against her fevered, thinly covered skin.

Nicholas drew himself up to his full height before her. "Leah, I—"

"*Damn you, Sir Nicholas!*" she choked out. "Yes, Sir Nicholas Constinos, may Hades take you and keep you far away from Karabey!"

"You do not understand," he said quietly. His blood was still a liquid fire within his veins. His gaze still smoldered as it traveled over the furious, upturned beauty of her countenance.

"Ah, but I do, my lord!" She swallowed a painful lump in her throat, trying to ignore the lingering ache within her own body. The ache within her heart, however, was the worst of it. Her eyes sparked and blazed reproachfully in the darkness when she declared, "I understand far more than you think! I am Turkish—and therefore worthy only of contempt. You would use me only as much as you dare and then cast me aside. How can you say I belong to you? How can you—?" She could face him no longer. With a strangled cry, she whirled and raced back to the doorway. Nicholas watched as she disappeared within the keep. He remained upon the battlements, muttering a vicious oath before turning his dark, fiery gaze upon the Turkish countryside below.

Leah flew back along the corridor to her bedchamber. Once inside, she bolted the door and crossed to stand before the fire. Her throat constricted as she struggled to regain control of her breathing. Her hands trembled violently as they tightened within the damp, tattered folds of white linen at her breast. "You are a fool, Leah Baal," she charged in a voice filled with scorn. She despised herself in that moment. "Naught but a wanton, weak-spirited fool!" She closed her eyes against the highly disturbing memory of Nicholas's hands and lips upon her—and of her own shameless response. Twice before, she had fallen into the trap. Twice before, she had thrown both pride and caution to the wind. But the madness had gone too far this time. Hera help her, she could bear no more! Her crystal blue gaze lit with a sudden determination. She spun about and hurried to dress. Once she had donned her cote-hardie, stockings, shoes, and cloak, she gathered her other things into a bundle. Her heart felt even heavier than before as she headed for the doorway, but she would not turn back. *She had to get away!* She slipped from the room again, and was soon there after emerging into the rain-swept darkness outside the keep. The gates had not yet been closed for the night, nor the drawbridge raised. Unaware that a courier had only moments ago arrived with an urgent message for the master of Karabey, Leah gave silent thanks for the fact that she was allowed to pass through the gates without interference. She could only assume that the man who stood watch above believed her to be one of the village women who had stayed late to work in the kitchen. Filled as she was with the desperate need to escape, she would have found a way to leave no matter what—or who—stood in her way. Bending her head against the rain, she hastened across the drawbridge and toward the river. And only when she was safely away from the palace, her near-panicked steps leading her to Theresa's cottage and the horse she had left there so many hours before, did she finally allow herself the luxury of tears.

Langdon and Louise were startled by her sudden appearance in the middle of the night, but seemed to accept her terse, breathless explanation about a sudden need to be at home again. She tumbled into the sanctuary of her own bed and listened to the wind and rain lashing against the house. But it was the sound of her own heart thundering in her ears, that finally chased her into the mercy of a deep and dreamless sleep.

Throughout the following day, her emotions remained quite raw. She feared that Nicholas would come to take her back. Her nerves were strung tight as a bowstring at the prospect, her troubled gaze continually scanning the horizon whenever she ventured outside. But he did not come. Nor did he send any message. His lack of action, his silence, both surprised and perplexed her. She could not believe that he would release her from his command so easily. And what of Lady Thalia? Would she not seek an explanation for her 'companion's' abrupt departure?

The thoughts raced chaotically within her mind until her head throbbed. Still wracked by guilt and embarrassment and a longing she dared not name, she tried her best to pretend that her life could continue as it had been before the Greek had come to Karabey. But she failed dismally. In truth, she felt caught in an awful sort of limbo. She did not know how to break free of it.

And then, November Eve arrived.

The night promised to be appropriately clear and moonlit. A soft morning mist had soon enough given way to the pleasure of blue skies once more. The air smelled fresh and clean after the previous night's storms; the ground was still moist. Now, as darkness began to fall, Leah joined her foster father at the wagon in front of the house. "It's time we were away," said Langdon. He cast a quick glance toward his wife, who stood eyeing them fondly from the doorway. She had professed herself unwell, and would not be accompanying them to the celebration.

"I am of a mind to stay behind with Louise," Leah confided to Langdon. Frowning, she tied the strings of her cloak and pulled the hood over her plaited blonde tresses.

"You must come." He drew a nonchalant air about him before reminding her unnecessarily, "Peatro awaits."

"I shall not wed him at the feast tonight!" she reasserted, her eyes kindling anew.

"Have you not yet come to your senses, girl?" he demanded angrily. "Peatro Conrad is a good man!"

"I know." She looked away before murmuring, "And perhaps— perhaps if I cared but a little more for him, we could be wed."

"What of your mother? What of her promise?"

"Please, Langdon. Do not plague me so," she entreated, a telltale catch in her voice. "My mind is set upon refusing him."

"Then you must change it." He hoisted himself up to the wagon seat and reached a hand down for her. Hesitating only briefly, she took it and climbed up beside him.

"We will not tarry long at the feast?" She was reluctant to go at all, for her heart was heavy and she knew she would find little joy in the festivities. Still, the music and dancing might offer her a respite, however brief, from the thoughts that tormented her so.

"Have we not always remained until the final toast is drunk?" replied Langdon, his brow darkening in annoyance again.

"Yes, but—"

"Do not *be difficult*, Leah." He snapped the reins together above the horse's head. The wagon lurched forward as they set off toward the village.

Falling silent, Leah clutched at the seat for support and heaved a sigh as her eyes strayed downward to her plain, gray wool gown. In truth, it belonged to Theresa. She had chosen it at random from the midst of her own clothing. Its sober simplicity suited her mood far better than any jewels or finery would have done. Yet … Was it not the same gown she had been wearing when she had first encountered Sir Nicholas Constinos?

She gave an inward groan, her eyes clouding at the sudden memory. She tried to settle herself more comfortably beside Langdon. All about them, there was a distinct, pervasive atmosphere of expectation. It wasn't long before they were joined by other celebrants along the road, some in wagons like their own, some on horseback. Greetings were exchanged. Boasts were made regarding which man could drink enough to see Pan, yet not so much that he would awaken among the livestock. A wizened old oracle offered up a prediction that some poor maid would be captured by an otherworldly lover that night. Or perhaps spirited away by a god. Her narrow, baleful gaze lingered upon Leah as she said it.

Leah's mouth twitched briefly. The same prediction was made every year—and employed by more than one young woman as an excuse for her disappearance from the feast. The villagers never considered it necessary to conduct a search for the abducted girl. She always reappeared at home the following morning looking suspiciously content about her ordeal. Because the incident occurred during *Artemis,* none ever thought to offer a rebuke. And whenever a child was born of one of these 'mystical' unions, it was more often than not claimed by a man who was undeniably (and unsurprisingly) human.

The journey was a short one. The group of travelers soon neared the outskirts of Karabey. The sounds of music and laughter drifted to them on the wind. The village was ablaze with the light of a dozen bonfires, the square itself already crowded with the men, women, and children who would forget their troubles and responsibilities for that one night. Too soon, the bleakness of winter would be upon them. Leah caught her lower lip between her teeth and looked toward the palace, which rose against the sky on the other side of the river. Nicholas's face swam before her eyes. His voice echoed once again within her mind.

You are mine, Leah.

By the gods above, what was she to do? She had spent these many hours waging a furious battle within herself, reflecting with a growing despair upon all that had happened. Things could not go on as they were. Whatever she felt for Sir Nicholas Constinos, whatever he felt for her, did not matter. They could never be together.

Her thoughts turned to Peatro then. She knew she did not love him as she should. It was not possible that she could feel for him what she felt for Nicholas. Yet, she *was* bound by duty to marry him.

As Langdon had so recently reminded her, it had all been arranged long ago. To break her mother's promise would be to bring dishonor on the name of Baal. She had come so close to that already.

She could leave Karabey, of course She could return to Troy and seek asylum with her aunt. But, the thought of never seeing Nicholas again provoked such a painful twisting of her heart that she knew she could not go. At least Peatro Conrad wanted her for his wife. That *he* cared for her, she did not doubt. Perhaps, if she married him, she could find some small measure of contentment herself. Contentment and redemption …

"Leah?"

She tensed at the sound of Peatro's voice. Her wide, sparkling gaze traveled to where he stood waiting in the bend of the road just ahead. As soon as Langdon drew the wagon to a halt beside the old village wall, Peatro, hurried to her side.

"I feared you would not come," he remarked, his hands clasping her firmly about the waist. He swung her down and subjected her to a hard, close scrutiny. "After what happened yesterday—"

"It is *Artemis.*" She cut him off. Forcing a carefree smile to her lips, she eased the hood of her cloak back to rest upon her shoulders. "I have never yet missed the feast."

"And did you then find it so easy to leave your 'friends' at the palace?" His tone was bitter, laced with reproach. Stung by the memory of her rejection, he vowed that she would regret it. Before the night was through, she would beg his forgiveness. Yes, and would learn that a Conrad was not to be treated with so little respect.

"We will not speak of it, Peatro," Leah replied curtly, her eyes flashing up at him. "Else I shall not stay."

"Will you not lend me a hand, Peatro Conrad?" Langdon intervened at that point. He strode to the rear of the wagon and reached inside for the things he had earlier placed in the bed.

"Louise has sent along a goodly portion of her sheep brack in addition to the wine." The aroma from the traditional baklava hung sweetly in the air as he flung back a cloth to reveal it.

Peatro wavered. Finally, and reluctantly, he moved *to* help Langdon. Leah was left to wander away. The music beckoned her onward to the village square, the harp and flute and fiddle joining together to produce a lively, infectious tune that had already set a convivial mood. Immersing herself within the crowd that flanked the ancient common, she paused and took in the sights before her. Her eyes lit brightly. Couples were already dancing in the center of the square, their feet flying gaily above the stones. Men were raising their cups in a toast to days long past and the years ahead. Women exchanged their own hopes and dreams—and smiled together at the prospect of the new romances that would spring to life before dawn. As ever, children seized advantage of their mothers' inattention to snatch handfuls of candy and race wildly about. The largest bonfire of all blazed high in one corner, its smoke joining with the strong, pleasing scents of the food and the wine and the perfumes—fashioned at home with crushed wildflowers—worn by the women only on special occasions such as this. Leah could not help but smile. For a moment, her spirits lifted. Her heart swelled with both pride and affection, and she cast aside all that had been troubling her. At this moment, there were no worries. There were no Greek, no laws, no uneasy truces to be coaxed along. On November Eve, there was only the night and the magic it held.

"Leah!" Theresa called from nearby. Leah turned her head, watching as the buxom brunette, clad in a simple yet pretty new gown of forest green wool, made her way swiftly through the crowd.

"I did not think to see you here this night!"

"I am at the palace no more, Theresa," Leah disclosed. The two of them warmly clasped hands. "Nor shall I return to it."

"But what of Sir Nicholas? Will he not—?"

"He-he has set me free." *Free.* Would she ever truly be free of him?

"It is said that Peatro Conrad will claim you this night," Theresa remarked soberly.

"He will not," Leah said, quick to deny, a shadow falling across her face now. Her brow cleared again in the next instant and she smiled.

"But come, Theresa Unger, are we not here to celebrate? We must join in the festivities. Mayhap you have already promised a dance to someone."

"I have," Theresa admitted. Her eyes twinkled, while her cheeks grew rosy. "Ronald Cayden will be searching for me soon enough. Yet, I will not be so easily found. If *I* am to be claimed before the harpies crow, then it must be by a man who can keep his wits about him." She gave a soft laugh and linked her arm companionably with Leah's.

The two of them set off through the crowd.

They were soon enough hailed by other friends and spent a pleasant time in their midst before Ronald Cayden finally captured his willing prey. Watching as Theresa was swung into the dance by the powerfully built, blonde-headed young blacksmith, Leah drifted back to stand near the crackling warmth of the bonfire. She amiably declined the many offers to join the dancers. She knew that Peatro would seek her out eventually. Her brows knitted into a frown at the prospect.

"You have dined with Hades, Leah Baal."

Startled, Leah whirled to face Margaret Hellyer. The old woman was surveying her closely in the firelight. There was no doubt that she referred to Sir Nicholas Constinos.

"Not Hades, Margaret," Leah replied quickly, a dull, guilty flush staining her cheeks as her gaze fell. "In truth, the master of Karabey is naught but a man."

"Has he bewitched you then, girl?" Margaret suddenly demanded, stepping closer. Her hand curled tightly about Leah's arm while her eyes narrowed and filled with suspicion. "Perchance he has cast a spell upon you! Did you not heed the warning I gave at the very first?"

"No!" cried Leah. She pulled free and shook her head. Her hand fluttered up to her throat when her gaze met Margaret's once more.

"I am not bewitched. It is not possible for a man to—"

"*It is,*" the old woman insisted. "Are you truly so simple that you do not know of the evils such a man can do? Viggo Baal would not be pleased to know his daughter had grown to such a fool. No, nor would he smile upon you for your treason!"

"Treason?" Leah echoed in disbelief. Her eyes sparked with anger. "I have committed no treason, Margaret Hellyer!"

"Did you not deny Peatro Conrad before the Greek? Did you not—?"

"I will hear no more!" With Margaret's words still burning in her ears, she spun about and made her way back through the crowd to where the food lay spread upon makeshift tables beneath the stars.

The rousing strains of the Turkish music swelled to a crescendo, the villagers laughing and talking and drinking with increasing abandonment as the night deepened. Yet Leah took little notice of it all. The magic had faded away. She wanted nothing more at that moment than to go home. It was with some relief that she spied Langdon striding toward her. She hastened to meet him.

"Louise has come," he told her.

"Louise?" Her eyes grew round with astonishment. "But she-she is unwell!"

"No longer." Without offering an explanation, he took her by the arm and led her purposefully to the opposite side of the square.

Louise awaited them there. She smiled brightly at Leah and held aloft the garment she had brought with her.

"Do you not recognize it, Leah?" she asked. Petite, with chestnut-colored hair still unstreaked by gray, she was as good-natured as her husband was sour. "I did but tarry so that I could surprise you with it."

The color drained from Leah's face. Her eyes filled with dismay as they traveled over the faded blue gown.

It had been her mother's. "She wore it when she was wed to your father," Louise reminded her, though it was not necessary. "And if she were still upon this earth, she would—"

"No," whispered Leah, numbly shaking her head while the awful truth began to sink in.

"It is time, Leah," Langdon decreed. "Peatro has the right to claim you now."

"Sir Nicholas Constinos withheld his permission!" she pointed out in growing horror.

"I told you we would not be bound by Greek law in this," her foster father growled. "Nor will any others who would be wed this night. Now come. You must put on the gown. Peatro would have the ceremony witnessed by the whole village. And if the oracles will but give their blessing, so much the better for it."

"I cannot!" Unable to believe what was happening, she shook her head again and rounded on Langdon with eyes that were furiously ablaze. "Have I not made my distaste for this marriage known to you?"

"Is it not said that a fortunate maid shall find a new love upon November Eve?" Louise remarked in a more gentle persuasion. She grasped Leah's hand and smiled again. "You and Peatro have known each other since you were babes together. I am well convinced that he will be good to you. In truth, many marriages begin with far less affection than what you already share with him."

"It is not the right *sort* of affection!" Leah avowed desperately. Her head spun; she felt panic rise within her. "Do not press me to do this, Louise. My heart-my heart is untouched by Peatro and will remain so!" All of a sudden, Nicholas's face swam before her eyes.

She caught her breath upon a sharp gasp. "Sweet Hera, I cannot marry him!"

"The matter is settled," said Langdon. His brow cleared somewhat when he spied Peatro in the crowd. "You will be convinced soon enough."

Noting the direction of his gaze, Leah turned and caught sight of Peatro as well. He moved forward to join them. The look on his face confirmed Leah's worst fears.

"You must not do this, Peatro!" she entreated, backing away when he would have touched her.

"If I truly believed you unwilling, Leah Baal, I would not take you as my wife," he said stiffly. His expression grew more stubborn. "We will become husband and wife. And forget all that would have kept us apart."

"Have you no pride? Would you force me—?"

"Force?" He gave a short, humorless laugh. His eyes were bitter and accusing upon her. "I have been patient enough. We should have been joined together long ago."

"Do you not fear Sir Nicholas's wrath then?" she asked, her tone laced with contempt. "He will see you punished for your disobedience!"

You shall not be wed to him. The memory of his words, and the way in which he had uttered them, filled her with even more dread than did Peatro's angry, covetous gaze.

"Speak of the Greek no more!" Langdon snapped, his voice rising above the music. He snatched the gown from Louise and thrust it at Leah. "You shall go and put it on!"

Simmering with indignation, she gazed at him wrathfully, then looked at Louise, and then at Peatro again. Their betrayal hurt her deeply. And betrayal it was—of her feelings, of her future, of all that mattered most.

"So be it," she murmured, her voice low and quavering with barely controlled emotion. She took the gown from Langdon and gathered it close to her breast. "You have made the choice for me, have you not?"

"I will await you here," said Peatro. His triumph assured, he relented enough to promise, "You will find only happiness this night, Leah."

She did not answer. Threading her fingers within the soft folds of her mother's wedding gown, she pivoted slowly, deliberately, and walked away. She crossed to the edge of the square, leaving behind the crowd and the fire and the celebration as she was enveloped by the shadows. Her feet led her farther into the cold darkness of the alleyway. She would not wed Peatro. She would not be forced into a marriage that would bring naught but disaster to them both. And what of Sir Nicholas Constinos? her mind's inner voice put forth. If *he* had been the one to claim her, she would not have resisted …

A sob rose in her throat. Sudden tears threatened to blind her. Clutching the gown as if to still the painful thudding of her heart, she began to run. The shops and cottages she fled past were empty, for everyone was at the celebration. Her skirts tangled about her legs as she raced along. She did not know where she was going. She did not know how she could hope to escape. Shaken and breathless, she burst into a clearing at the edge of the village. She paused and looked about in indecision, certain that she would be found if she dared to return to Ponceel House. Without warning, a dark figure suddenly loomed before her in the moonlight. A loud gasp broke from her lips. Her gaze widened when she saw that it was a man upon a pale horse. *"Nicholas!"* She stared up at him in wonderment. His handsome features were set in a grim mask of determination. His eyes burned down into hers. Her heart leapt wildly, her body flooding with a joy and relief such as she had never known before. Without a word, he reached down and swept her up before him. She closed her eyes, leaning gratefully against him as the horse carried them toward the palace.

CHAPTER 9

▼

He carried her quickly up the winding turret stairs and into the fire-lit warmth of his bedchamber, kicking the door closed behind him. Leah struggled to catch her breath as he lowered her to her feet beside the bed. She swept several wayward strands of gold-colored hair from her face and tilted her head back to look up at him.

"Why did you come for me?" she demanded tremulously.

"Did you wed him?" he grounded out, his hands closing about her shoulders with such force that she winced. His gaze was dark and thunderous, searing relentlessly down into hers. She had never seen him so angry.

"No!" She shook her head in a vehement denial. "But how did you know—?"

"Do you think me so easily deceived?" He cut her off brusquely. "I know far more of your customs than you think. Yet, I did not …" His voice trailed away; he muttered an oath before suddenly releasing her. Stunned, she watched as he strode across to the window and gazed outward. "Would you have agreed to the marriage if I had not come?"

"I would never have become Peatro Conrad's wife," she told him earnestly "In truth, my lord, I was running away when you found me."

"Why did you leave?"

"Because I do not love him."

"That's not what I meant." He turned back to face her again. "Why did you run away last night?"

"You know why," she murmured, her gaze falling beneath the steady, piercing intensity of his. "I could stay no longer." Her voice held both pain and reproach when she remarked, "It cannot have troubled you so very much You sent no word, you—"

"I thought to give you time. To give us both time." He slowly closed the distance between them. "Did you truly think I would ever let you go?"

"It matters not what I think!" She dashed impatiently at the tears that filled her eyes once more. "We are from different worlds. We are forbidden to-to care for each other."

"And do you care, Leah Baal?"

"I must not!"

"Have I not told myself the same these many nights past?" he quietly confessed, towering above her. His eyes softened a bit as they raked over the flushed, proud beauty of her face. The jealous fury raging through him was tempered now by the regard he felt for her. "Yes, have I not fought against it from the very beginning? And still, my heart will not be silenced."

"Is it your heart then; Sir Nicholas Constinos, that led you to treat me so ill?" she asked, with bitter irony. "Was it your heart that caused you to try and steal my womanhood last night?" She paled at the way his deep, gold-flecked dark gaze smoldered anew.

"I could have allowed the marriage to take place," he advised her in a tone that was low and brimming with raw emotion. "I could well have claimed the *rights by seizure.* As the lord, it would have been my right to take you on your wedding night. No statutes would have been broken, no harm done to either Turkish tradition or Greek law." He moved even closer, the fierce gleam in his eyes making her pale when he said, "Yet I could not see you wed to

Peatro Conrad. By the blood of the gods, no other man shall have you!"

"And why not, my lord?" she retorted hotly, retreating a step as she struggled to understand what was happening. "Why should I not accept a husband? You have said that I belong to you. But that can never be!"

"It *shall* be."

"No!" Though her heart inexplicably soared at his words, her stomach knotted with very real alarm. "What you want is forbidden. Would you brand yourself a traitor? If you were judged guilty of treason, you could lose all that you have been given. You could lose your very life!"

"You can say nothing I have not already said to myself, Leah Baal," he answered. "It matters not. You are mine. You have been so from the very beginning. And before this night is through, I will hear you admit it as well."

"You are mad," she said, breathing harshly, her eyes widening in disbelief.

"Perhaps." The merest hint of a smile touched his lips. "Yet it is a madness I welcome." His hands reached for her again, closing gently about her arms while his gaze bored deeply into hers. "I am no young, untried gallant. I have spent these many years past in the midst of battle serving Sparta. For too long, I have yearned for peace. And now, for the first time in my life, I have found a woman to touch my heart, my soul, to make me forget all else. Though it be called treason, I will not deny it. I would be naught but a traitor to myself if I did so."

"Would you risk your very life for but a moment's pleasure?" she asked, her own hands lifting to his chest. His heart beat strong and sure beneath her fingers.

"Yes. But I will have more than that. Much more."

"What do you mean?"

"I will have you for my wife."

"Your wife?" Incredulous, she pulled away. "We-we cannot marry!"

"We can and will." He frowned, reminding her, "No ceremony is required. Nor blessings from the oracles. We have only to agree upon it. Is that not true?"

"Under Turkish law, yes!" she conceded dazedly. "But you are Greek, bound by—"

"Yes, bound by duty and honor. Bound by statutes that I have sworn to enforce yet cannot now resist casting aside." Again, the grim, determined look in his eyes filled her with trepidation. "It may well be an affront to the gods. I may well find it necessary to defend myself against charges of treason when the news of our marriage reaches Sparta." Or Troy, he added silently, recalling the message he had received the night before. In but a week's time, the prince would be in Anatolia. Was it possible that the prince would understand. *It made no difference.* "But still," he vowed anew, "I will have you."

"No!" she cried in a strangled voice. Spinning about, her hands trembled with the force of her desperation, with the force of her own secret desires. Could it be that he spoke the truth?

"It is too late, Leah," Nicholas decreed, his voice low and splendidly resonant in the silence of the room. He moved toward her. She lifted a hand to the hard, splintered surface of the door and rested her head upon it She closed her eyes, tears coursing down her face. "It cannot be too late," she whispered brokenly.

"It has been so from the first time I saw you." He drew close behind her She could feel the heat emanating from his body, and though he did not touch her, she felt scorched by his nearness.

"I shall not let you do this," she suddenly vowed, rounding on him in a renewed flash of spirit. She had to be resolute. Hera help her, she had to save him from himself! "Do you think to coax me into your bed with such words? Do you think me so easily swayed by—?"

"*It is already done,*" he murmured huskily. His powerful arms gathered her close then, his lips claiming hers in a kiss that was deep and compelling and sweetly savage. Leah felt the familiar, liquid warmth streaking throughout her body. She moaned and swayed against him. Her arms crept willfully upward to entwine about the corded muscles of his neck, while her mouth beckoned him to greater passion. Still, there was some small part of her brain that would make her flee from disaster. "We cannot," she cried, tearing her lips from his.

"Dear Hera, *we must not!*" She pulled free again and stumbled across to stand before the fireplace. Her breasts rose and fell rapidly beneath the low, tight-fitting bodice of her gown, while her glistening eyes held a silent appeal for mercy and reason.

"While I cannot deny there is something strong, some mysterious force between us, my lord, I beg you to remember that we are from two different worlds. I am a Baal, a descendant of the high kings of Anatolia, and you are yet another invader, an elite come at the bidding of Lord Ares to subdue the Turks. Even if we—if I— wished it so, it could never be."

He crossed the room in two long strides, masterfully catching her up against him once more. She drew in a sharp breath and tilted her head back to meet his gaze. The firelight played softly over the somber, rugged perfection of his features.

"We are man and woman this night," he told her. "Nothing more."

"But desire alone cannot sustain a marriage."

"Do you not hold more than desire within your heart?"

"I-I do not know what I feel," she exclaimed, pushing weakly at his chest.

"Do you not?" He gave her a faint, tender smile—and declared with a vibrancy that made her legs threaten to give way beneath her, "I love you, Leah. Though I fought against it, my heart was well and truly captured by you. You shall yet know the depth of my feeling."

"You love—?" she started to say, her eyes growing enormous within the delicate oval of her face.

"It is neither desire nor honor alone that would bind me to you forever. I want all of you. Body and soul." He drew her even closer and vowed, "I take you as my wife this night, Leah Baal."

"No!" she said, though her conviction was fastly wavering.

I love you, Leah. Her senses reeled as his words burned within her mind. Sweet Hera, was it possible? Could he care so much for her that he would give her his name, that he would risk his very life? Her heart leapt wildly, and she clutched at his arms for support.

"All that remains is for you to say it," he said firmly.

"Lord Zeus himself shall bless our union. And none shall break it." He kissed her again, his arms tightening about her until she could scarcely breathe.

"Say it," he commanded when he raised his head a few moments later.

"My lord," she whispered in protest, still recalcitrant.

Growing impatient, he scooped her up in his arms and carried her to the bed. He lowered her to the feather mattress, then placed his body atop hers. His lips captured the softness of hers once more.

Leah found herself returning his kiss with all the fire of her own passion. Forgotten was the feast of *Artemis,* forgotten were Langdon and Louise and Peatro Conrad. There was only Nicholas—only the man whose very touch set her aflame. As before, something deep within called her to this wild, reckless abandonment. And though she told herself it was only the sounds of the celebration drifting along on the wind, she could have sworn she heard one of the old songs being sung just as her mother had once done ...

She was already light-headed with desire when Nicholas's hand suddenly entangled within her skirts. His warm, strong fingers glided across the pale smoothness of her naked thighs, then moved to the triangle of silky blonde curls between. At the same time, his mouth trailed a fiery path downward to where her full breasts swelled above the neckline of her bodice.

"Nicholas!" she cried out softly. Her hands curled upon his shoulders, her eyelids fluttering open as his lips roamed boldly—hungrily—across the upper curve of her breasts. He tugged the neckline of her gown farther downward, baring more of her delectable flesh. And all the while, his fingers caressed her with such skill and tenderness and sensuous persuasion that the yearning built to a fever pitch within her. She was certain she could bear no more of the exquisite torment. Her back arched instinctively, her breath nothing but a series of gasps as her thighs parted wider of their own accord.

"Say it, Leah," Nicholas commanded hoarsely, his lips moving close to hers once more.

"Please," she moaned. "I—"

"Say it!" His own self-control was slipping away. He yearned to possess her, to make her accept what had been inevitable from the very first time he saw her.

Leah gazed up at him. The certainty of defeat rose before her. Yet, it was a sweet surrender and well she knew it. Far sweeter than the prospect of denying what the fates had decreed.

"*Sweet Hera,*" she finally capitulated, her voice scarcely more than a whisper in the firelit darkness. "I-I take you as my husband."

And so it was done.

Nicholas's magnificent brown eyes glowed with mingled love and triumph, his heart thundering joyfully. He would wait no longer. His other hand came down to slip beneath Leah's hips. He lifted her slightly, and positioned himself between her thighs. He was determined that she should know as little pain as possible. He eased himself slowly, gently forward. She gasped, frightened at the heat, certain that she would be torn asunder. In spite of the ache still begging to be eased, she pushed feebly against him. But it was too late. There could be no turning back. His lips claimed hers once more, swallowing her gasp of mingled pain and startlement as his manhood now sheathed fully within the tight, moist warmth of her feminine passage.

The pain quickly faded. In its place came a yearning even more profound than before. Her eyes swept closed. She was surprised at the pleasure gathering within her, surprised at the way her body seemed to fit so perfectly against Nicholas's. His hips tutored hers in the age-old rhythm of love, his thrusts becoming deeper and faster. Her head tossed restlessly upon the mattress while his lips branded the satiny fullness of her breasts again. She grasped at his shoulders. Her heart soared skyward, her very soul taking flight with his as their mutual passion blazed hot and wild and all consuming.

And then … *release.* It was as though she had been touched by lightning. A soft, breathless cry broke from her lips. Her eyes opened wide. Trembling, she felt Nicholas tense above her. In the next instant, he flooded her with his potent, life-giving warmth. She gasped anew while her head spun dizzily.

The final blending of their bodies, fiery and tempestuous as it had been, left them both shaken. Nicholas rolled to his back upon the bed and pulled Leah's pliant, well-rounded curves against him. She offered no resistance. Truly wonderstruck by what had just occurred, she heaved a long, uneven sigh and closed her eyes. She felt as though she had been taken out of herself … as though she had, indeed, been spirited away by something otherworldly. Never would she have thought it possible to experience the strange, wickedly pleasurable sensations her new husband had created within her.

Husband. She had become the wife of Sir Nicholas Constinos. In every sense of the word, she belonged to him now. She had joined with the enemy. She had betrayed her people.

"Leah." The sound of her name upon his lips drew her out of her troubling reverie. She shivered as his deep-timbered voice washed over her. It only served to remind her of her disloyalty. Of her thorough, eagerly embraced defeat at the hands of the master of Karabey. "The gods be merciful, what have I done?" she whispered, tensing now as sharp pains of guilt began to slice through her.

"Langdon—"

"Must accept what has come to pass," said Nicholas. "I will send word to him. At once, if you like."

"No!" She abruptly drew away and sat upright in the bed. Her cloak lay twisted beneath her. Shaking her head, she exclaimed, "Not now! Not tonight!"

"Will they not wonder at your disappearance?" he asked quietly. His eyes glowed anew while they traveled over her. Never would he have thought it possible to love a woman as he loved her. The prospect of her in his bed each night, in his presence each day, filled him with a deep happiness. Yes, he mused with an inward smile, and with the peace he had sought for so long.

"It matters not," she murmured, coloring warmly beneath his tender, penetrating gaze. "It is *Artemis.* Others will go missing. No doubt, my foster parents will think I have fled to a safe place. But, tomorrow …"

"You are my wife now, Leah. Once that is known, none will dare to offer you reproach."

"You have little understanding of the Turks, my lord."

"Do you not think it time you called me Nicholas?" he suggested, the vibrancy of his tone disarming.

"I think it time I regained my wits!" she retorted.

Swinging her legs over the edge of the bed, she scrambled down and crossed hastily to take up a stance before the fireplace. Her hair was tousled, the plait down her back sadly askew. Her breasts threatened to spill from the creased bodice of Theresa's gown.

"And what of your own men?" she demanded, her eyes gloriously ablaze as she turned to confront Nicholas again. "Will they accept me—one of the *accursed* Turks—as the lord's lady? Will they defend your right to set yourself above Sparta's glory?"

"Each man must choose his own path." He climbed from the bed now as well "Yet I am convinced of their loyalty." With movements that were both purposeful and unhurried, he unbuckled the thick leather belt about his waist and pulled it free. He tossed it atop the massive chest at the foot of the bed, then sat down and began taking off his sandals.

Watching him, Leah felt her pulse leaping again. She moved closer to the fire. Though she would have looked away, her eyes would not obey. "I must go," she declared, her voice unsteady as alarm filled her once more. "If I but return to the feast before—"

"You will not leave." He stood and drew off his scarlet tunic.

"But no harm has yet been done." Her breath caught in her throat; she was dismayed to feel her face flaming at the memory of his lovemaking. While she did not consider herself harmed, something had most assuredly changed. "I ... No one will know of what has happened between us."

"I will never let you go, Leah." Taking off his long, white linen shirt, he remained clad in nothing but his woolen braies. The tightly woven fabric molded his lower body to perfection. "We are wed, remember?"

"The marriage can be dissolved." Her color deepened as her gaze roamed in fascination across his bronzed, half-naked body. His chest was broad, covered with a light curling of dark hair. His arms were sinewy and powerful, his trim waist tapering down into a pair of lean hips and hard-muscled thighs. As she had noted before, he looked every inch the fierce, battle-hardened soldier that he was. But she had known his gentleness as well. She had known his passion and his love. *His love.* Her heart stirred again.

"Indeed, we-we have only to agree upon it," she stammered, her eyes growing very wide as he began slowly advancing upon her.

"No."

"There are many reasons from which we may choose." She swallowed hard, her mind racing as it filled with thoughts of the ancient Byzantine laws. If a woman were to prove barren, if either she or her husband were to be unfaithful, or if they were to live apart for a length of time, then they could set aside the marriage as though it had never taken place.

There was another reason, of course, one that had been used more frequently than any of the others. Her whole body grew warm. She could attest with a certainty that Sir Nicholas Constinos had not come to the marriage bed 'unarmed.' It was impossible to imagine that he would ever be unable to perform his husbandly duties.

"*You* are mine, Leah. Now and forever." He paused before her, his hand caressing her cheek.

"We shall both yet be damned for this," she whispered.

"No." He smiled down at her in the soft golden glow that filled the room "We shall both thank Lord Zeus for it."

He gently turned her about. With a skill that surprised her, he loosened the plait and thereby freed the luxuriant blonde tresses that caught the firelight. His hands moved to the lacings on the back of her gown.

"But surely we have already—?" She protested weakly, her own hands trembling as she clutched at the front of the bodice.

"I would see what manner of woman I have married," he remarked in a tone laced with both amusement and desire. "And are men in Anatolia so easily wearied then?"

"I have little knowledge of such matters, my lord!" She gasped when he suddenly sent her gown tumbling to the floor.

"Nor shall you learn of them," he vowed. He urged her to face him again. "Save with me."

In spite of the flames behind her, she shivered. Her thin white shift and black woolen stockings were all that remained to shield her from his smoldering, highly appreciative gaze. She folded her arms across her breasts and tilted her head back to a proud, defiant angle.

"If I *were* to seek this knowledge elsewhere, would you release me then? Would you—?" She broke off with yet another sharp intake of breath when his fingers clenched about her arms.

"Never think to try me," he warned, his voice low and his handsome features dangerously grim. "Though I love you well, I would not allow betrayal to go unpunished. No, nor would the man who dared to touch you live to see another day."

With that, he carried her back to the bed. She struggled as best she could, but it was a battle already lost and she knew it. She soon found herself stripped of her stockings and her shift. Embarrassed to have her body bared to him, she rolled to her side, her arms seeking to cover her breasts once more. But Nicholas would not be denied the pleasure for which he had longed since the night she had crept inside the palace.

His hands closed about her wrists and forced her arms above her head as he pushed her back upon the mattress. His eyes gleamed hotly as they explored, with a bold intimacy, every sweet curve and valley. Her breasts were full and rose-tipped, her waist and thighs slender, her bottom saucy and well-rounded. She was every bit as beautiful as he had expected. And every bit as passionate as he had hoped.

"I believe, my lady, that we are well-matched," he murmured huskily. His brown eyes caught and held the crystal blue fire of hers.

"For how long will that be so?" she parried, once again torn between wisdom and desire. "Until the dawn breaks? Until my foster father comes to demand my release?" She squirmed beneath him, only to cease abruptly when his masculine hardness pressed against the softness of her naked hips.

"Think only of this night, Leah." Releasing her wrists, he left her momentarily in order to take off his braies. She tugged her cloak across her, then grew still as she watched Nicholas cast aside the last of his clothing. He knelt beside her again. Her eyes strayed to the cluster of dark, tightly ringed curls at the apex of his hard-muscled thighs … and to what lay between. She had seen the bodies of men before. The male inhabitants of Karabey had made little attempt to conceal themselves whenever bathing in the nearest spring or pond on a fine summer's day. Yet, she had never seen a man such as the one before her. Whereas the others had aroused only a mild curiosity within her, the sight of *this* one caused her heart to quicken and her body to warm.

He snatched the cloak away and lowered his body atop hers. She gasped when naked flesh met naked flesh. It was a wickedly pleasurable sensation. Even so, she could not refrain from making one last attempt to save them both.

"When morning comes, I shall be gone," she proclaimed, struggling to keep her voice even as his hand moved possessively over the curve of her hip Her fingers curled upon his shoulders.

"I would find you." He had said it before. This time, however, his voice held so much conviction that she trembled.

"Sweet Hera!" she cried in exasperation. "Why will you not listen to reason?"

"You are mine," he said, then entangled a hand gently within the silken, blonde-colored thickness of her hair.

Startled to hear him declare his love for her in the Kurdish language, Leah blinked up at him in amazement.

"How-how is it you know that?"

"It was not so difficult to learn." For a moment, she glimpsed a teasing light in his eyes. But he quickly sobered again.

"I would know everything about you, Leah. About your ways, your family, and all that has gone before. And if that is called treason as well, then so be it."

"You shall yet rue the day the fates brought us together," she told him, with a telltale catch in her voice.

"Never," he declared, and set about to prove it. Even if they were to share only this one night, *he would make it last a lifetime.*

With infinite skill and patience, he made love to her a second time, his hands and lips joining together to prove that she belonged to him alone. He kissed her until the sweet madness had come upon her again, until passion chased away doubt. His caresses were tender, demanding, fiercely provocative. And when her body entwined with his in the ultimate, soul-stirring embrace once more, there was no pain, only a pleasure so deep and wondrous that she was certain she had been changed forever.

In the village just across the river, the feast continued. Music played and couples danced. Food was eaten and wine drunk to excess, while the revelers laughed and gossiped and tried to forget that winter's harshness would soon descend upon them. If the nymphs and spirits were about then so were Turks who would gladly believe in them. The clear, magical night wore on, carrying along with it the promise of love.

For Leah, however, the outside world had receded. And by the time the first soft light of the new day crept upon the horizon, she slept peacefully in her new husband's arms, her captive heart beating in unison with his.

CHAPTER 10

▼

Morning had not been long broken when a knock sounded at the door. Jolted awake by the sound of it, Leah pushed herself upright in the bed and instinctively clutched the covers to her breasts. She looked toward Nicholas, who had been sleeping beside her. *He was gone.*

"Leah?" It was Thalia's voice.

"Yes?" she called back hastily. Her fingers strayed with a will of their own to the indentation, now grown cold, where her husband's tall, powerfully muscled body had lain. The memories of the night returned to her with a sudden and pleasurable vengeance.

But now tomorrow had come. "Leah?"

"I ... Just a moment!" She flung back the covers and scrambled from the bed. There was a slight, lingering soreness between her thighs, but she had no time to think of it. Snatching up her cloak, she tossed it about her shoulders and pulled the front edges together in order to cover her nakedness. Her face was flushed when she opened the door, her long hair tumbling riotously downward to her hips.

"Sir Nicholas commands your presence in the hall below," Thalia related a bit stiffly. Her gaze widened as she observed Leah's dishabille. Though her brother had presented her with the news of his marriage but a short while ago, she was nevertheless shocked at the evidence before her. Shocked, and yet at the same time delighted. "You are to come at once."

"Am I indeed?" said Leah. Her color deepened guiltily, and she battled the impulse to offer an explanation of her own for her presence in Nicholas's bedchamber. How could she possibly explain what had happened, when she understood so little of it herself?

"I must dress," she murmured, looking away in embarrassment.

"Oh, Leah. Please make haste!" the older woman exhorted with a sudden vehemence. "I fear there is a great trouble brewing!" She said no more, but whirled about and swept back down the corridor.

Leah frowned at the startling, enigmatic words. They echoed within her mind as she closed the door and hurried to prepare. She washed first, wishing for all the world that she could have a proper bath, and donned her shift. There was nothing else to wear save the same plain woolen gown of Theresa's. Heaving a sigh, she tugged it on and searched for her stockings and slippers. She found them, and also happened upon the knitted shawl she had left behind on the battlements. It lay draped across the single lopsided table near the fireplace. Strangely stirred by the sight of it, she drew it on as well. Her hair was a tangled mass of curls, but she did her best to tame it into a plait before leaving the room. She descended the turret steps slowly. Nervous at the prospect of facing her new husband in the light of day, she wondered what had prompted his summons. It pained her to think that he could treat her as little more than a servant after what they had shared. Could he have already forgotten what they had shared throughout the night? No, she realized in the next moment, her eyes glowing softly as she shook her head. In her heart, she knew he had not. Tugging the shawl more closely about her, she reached the coolness of the great hall and proceeded toward the fireplace. Her eyes opened wide in astonishment when she discovered that both Langdon Fogus and Peatro Conrad were already waiting to confront her. One look at their faces filled her with dread. She paled and drew to an abrupt halt beside the table. Her gaze instinctively sought Nicholas. He stood tall and silent and dangerously solemn a few feet away, his dark hair gleaming in the sunlight that streamed through the high-arched window. Her pulse leapt wildly as her eyes met his. She was tempted to race forward, to cast herself upon his chest and forget all else, but she could not. The moment of reckoning had arrived. And Hera help her, she must now accept the consequences of her misdeed.

"Margaret Hellyer waited until dawn to tell us what she had seen, Leah Baal," Langdon said. "Were it not for the fact that she was witness to your going, we might have feared you dead! Did you not think we would search for you? Did you not think you would be found?" His tone was harsh, edged with a bitter and angry censure. He scowled darkly, and might well have set hands upon her there and then if not for the presence of the lord. "We have come to take you home."

"Her home is here now," decreed Nicholas. He spoke with a calm, quiet authority, but his gaze held danger.

"Tell me he took your innocence by force, Leah!" Peatro demanded hotly. "*Tell me you are his prisoner!*"

"No!" she said softly, her hand moving to her throat. She crimsoned while her gaze fell. "I-I gave myself freely."

"The Greek man claims you as his bride," said Langdon, eyeing her narrowly from the other side of the table. "Do you deny it?"

She opened her mouth to reply, but no words would come. Her apprehensive gaze shot back to Nicholas—and she was thrown into even more of a quandary by his grim expression. If she denied what had passed between them, then there was yet a chance that disaster could be averted. If she did not, the course would be set.

It is too late, Leah. She closed her eyes for a moment, recalling again the night's enchantment.

"Mayhap, my lord, you meant only to seek the lord's right to claim the bride on the eve of her wedding." Langdon appealed to Nicholas in a vain, ultimately foolish attempt to turn things about. "If that be so, then release her now and all will be forgotten."

"Suggest that at your peril, Langdon Fogus," Nicholas warned, his voice laced with steel while his gaze darkened. "Leah is my wife. I will never release her. Nor will I ever again hear it said that she is less than the lord's lady."

"You have betrayed us, Leah Baal!" Peatro charged furiously, closing the distance between them now. His features were ugly, suffused with a vengeful anger. Though he did not touch her, she felt stung by the look in his eyes.

"You have betrayed yourself as well! How could you so easily bring dishonor upon your father's name? How could you join with the Greek against—?"

"Enough," Nicholas grounded out.

Leah caught her breath upon a gasp. She looked to him again, dismayed to note that his hand had moved to the hilt of his sword.

"I beg of you, Peatro, to try and understand!" she entreated. Her fingers closed upon his arm, but he jerked away as if the contact had burned him.

"Understand?" he repeated, with biting sarcasm. "You were betrothed to *me!*"

"Did I not tell you the marriage would never take place?" she reminded him. "Even if Sir Nicholas—even if he had not come for me last night, I would not have wed you."

"She has made her choice, Peatro Conrad," Nicholas stated, calling upon his strongest will to refrain from violence against the man.

"What of the statutes, my lord?" Langdon demanded of him. "The Greek are forbidden to marry with the Turks. What honor can there be in this? By damn, would you make my foster daughter a part of your treason then?"

"Langdon, please," cried Leah.

"If I am indeed guilty of treason, then no blame lies with the woman I have taken to wife," Nicholas asserted evenly. "She will not suffer for it But my loyalty to Lord Ares and the glory of Sparta is unchanged. As is my duty here. Peace shall yet reign in Karabey."

"What peace can there be if you would steal another man's bride?" Peatro flung at him, then blanched inwardly at the simmering heat of the other man's gaze.

"Leah is mine." Nicholas's eyes moved back to her; she felt her heart give an almost painful flutter. "It has always been so."

"Will you not come with us, Leah?" Langdon prompted in one last futile attempt to sway her. "Will you not deny the Greek man and return to live among your own people?"

Meeting his gaze, a great sadness welled within her. Yet there was joy as well. Dear Hera, she lamented silently, nothing made sense any longer ... There was no right or wrong, nothing to light her way through this terrible, swirling darkness of confusion save for the memory of what she and Nicholas had shared. Though she was still uncertain of her own feelings, and, in truth, of how constant his would remain, she knew she was a willing captive.

"I *cannot*," she finally answered, scarcely aware of the moment when the words fell from her lips.

"Ambrosia is sweet, but paying for it is bitter," Peatro sneered, his rage all too visible. "You have been bewitched by this man, Leah Baal. And I pray Lord Zeus will but help you when you awaken to your own falseness!"

"Think not that we will forget what you have done, Sir Nicholas Constinos," Langdon added. "Like you, I once held hopes for peace between us. I would have urged others to tread softly about the truce, however uneasy it was. But now, you would destroy it with your own lust." He rounded slowly on Leah once more, his eyes full of mingled anguish and wrath and dismay. "It is dangerous for you here, Leah."

Her throat constricted tightly. She wanted to offer yet another plea for understanding, to confess her bewilderment about all that had happened, but she knew he would not listen. Her luminous, sorrow-filled gaze followed him as he turned, and, without looking at Nicholas again, strode across the hall to the doorway. Peatro did the same. But he paused before leaving, his own eyes glinting with a murderous intensity.

"I will be avenged, Sir Nicholas," he promised. "I will be avenged—and see you in Hades for your treachery!"

"Peatro, no!" Leah gasped in horror. He cast her one last reproachful glare before disappearing.

"They speak in anger, Leah," Nicholas reassured her, his tone quite low and level in the highly charged silence of the room.

"I-I must go with them!" She impulsively gathered up her skirts and started forward, but Nicholas moved to intercept her.

"It is too late," he told her softly, his hands closing with a gentle firmness about her arms.

"No!" She looked up at him and shook her head in a fervent denial. "Naught has happened yet. We can still avoid—"

"Last night cannot be forgotten." He frowned, his brown eyes searing down into the troubled crystal blue depths of hers. "We are joined forever, Leah. You must not waver because of their rashly spoken threats."

"I have never yet chosen a clear path," she declared in a choked voice. She pulled away from him and walked over to the table. Her hand touched its rough surface, her gaze fixing upon the flames that danced and crackled within the great stone fireplace. "I do not know how this has happened, or why, but I-I could not deny you before them." She released a long, ragged sigh and suddenly whirled to face him again. "*Why?*" she asked in genuine perplexity. "Why was I disloyal? Why am I so weak-spirited that I could offer so little resistance last night?"

"I have never known a woman with a spirit stronger than yours," he avowed, with a faint smile of irony. Then he added seriously, "You could not deny me because your feelings run as deep as my own."

"That cannot be!" She crossed her arms tightly against her breasts and tried to ignore the way her heart beat faster at his words.

"Perhaps, as Peatro said, I am bewitched."

"I have cast no spells upon you." He moved toward her, his steps unhurried yet purposeful.

"Have you not?" she retorted. Her cheeks flamed anew as she cast him a narrow look. "You are knowledgeable in the ways of women, my lord. So much so that I can scarcely believe you have not worked the same magic across all of Greece." She was surprised, and secretly warmed by the sound of his quiet chuckle.

"I have not lived as an oracle these many years past." He stood before her now. "But, I am well content to spend the remainder of my years with no other woman save one. Indeed, I give you my promise that it will be so."

"The madness cannot last forever," she whispered, trembling at the potent combination of tenderness and desire contained within his steady, dark, gold-flecked gaze.

"Not madness, Leah," he said, his voice splendidly low and resonant. "A love that will defy the hatred and intrigue of others."

His strong arms came about her. His head lowered, his warm lips capturing the sweetness of hers in a kiss that served as a vivid, intoxicating reminder of their wedding night. Leah moaned softly. Her hands drifted upward to cling to him, her body swaying closer to his while her head spun dizzily. When he finally released her, she was flushed and breathless, and had, at least for the moment, forgotten about the recent ordeal with Langdon and Peatro. Nicholas might well have surrendered to the temptation to carry her upstairs, if not for the untimely appearance of Josh. He came striding into the hall with a preoccupied frown creasing his brow. As soon as he realized his blunder, he stopped short and watched in obvious embarrassment while Nicholas reluctantly allowed Leah to pull free.

"I most humbly beg your pardon," Josh murmured. Leah tugged the shawl back across her breasts. She cursed the hot color flooding her face, but lifted her head proudly and announced with admirable composure, "I must return upstairs." She fled then, her heart pounding fiercely as she climbed the steps. It was with some surprise that she opened the door to Nicholas's bedchamber and discovered Thalia within.

"What—?" she started to query, only to stop when her gaze fell upon the carved marble bathtub sitting before the fireplace. It was already filled with steaming hot water. A length of thick toweling lay folded on the table beside it, with a bar of lavender-scented soap in evidence as well.

"I would gladly have offered the use of it before now if I had but known of your need," said Thalia. She smiled, her eyes twinkling with their usual good humor. "I cannot think you would wish to bathe in the cold waters of the river. Nor in the stables as the elite have done. I have brought you a fresh cote-hardie and undergarments as well, though I fear I am not as tall as you."

"It is very kind of you," Leah replied in all sincerity.

"We are sisters now, are we not?" Her long velvet skirts swayed gently as she crossed the room and took Leah's hand in a warm, affectionate grasp that proved her eagerness to strengthen their friendship. "Perhaps, sometime, you will consent to tell me how it came about. Mind you, I do not doubt that Sir Nicholas was an impatient bridegroom!" She gave a soft laugh and watched as sun color rose to Leah's face.

"Indeed, it-it was all quite sudden."

"So sudden that you could not have confided in me?" Thalia asked, without any trace of anger.

"In truth, I had not planned to wed anyone at all," Leah confided, her gaze clouding. "What was between us could not have been foretold."

"It matters not. You are wed now. And I am glad of it."

"Are you, Thalia?" Leah asked, both surprised and pleased by her response.

"Yes." She nodded, and gave an eloquent wave of her hand before adding, "Oh, I am well aware of the perils of such a match. My brother thinks me ignorant of such matters, but I am not. I know that the law would keep Greek and Turks apart. Yet I cannot believe Lord Ares will deny Sir Nicholas Constinos this one concession. He has served his name *too* long and too well to be punished for it."

"Do you truly believe he will not face judgment?" Her voice held a desperate plea for hope.

"He has many friends in Sparta. And it is said that Prince Michael would never hear ill of him. How can he *not* have you when he has asked for little else these many years past?"

"I pray you are right," murmured Leah, half to herself. "I pray that, long after reason has returned, he will not suffer for it."

"What a strange remark, Leah," Thalia said, her brows knitting into a slight frown of bemusement. "Why, one would think you had gained naught but unhappiness from your marriage. Can it be that Sir Nicholas is not all that you desired in a husband?"

"He is all that any woman could desire," she replied, without thinking. Upon noting Thalia's smile, she groaned inwardly and averted her gaze.

"I am curious to know more. But I shall leave you to your bath now." Moving to the door, she opened it and tarried for a moment longer.

"Truly, Leah," she remarked earnestly, "I am much pleased by your marriage to my brother. I would see him happy at last." She left then, pulling the heavy, iron-banded door closed behind her. Once she had gone, Leah hastened to undress. She stripped off all her clothing and climbed into the bathtub. Her eyes closed, her long tresses swirling about her naked body as she lay back and delighted in the feel of the hot, soothing liquid upon her skin. For a brief time, she would seek to forget all that troubled her.

Downstairs, meanwhile, Nicholas had summoned his elite before him in the hall. They knew of his marriage already. They knew that Langdon Fogus and Peatro Conrad had come to demand Leah's return. And, even more significantly, they knew that their lord would never let her go.

"We have sworn our loyalty to you," David proclaimed gravely. Along with the others, he stood facing Nicholas across the table.

"I know," said Nicholas, the hint of a smile tugging briefly at his lips His gaze was both solemn and perceptive as it moved from one man to another. "But I would have you consider the danger you may now face as a result of my actions. I have defied one of the statutes. The decision was mine and mine alone. I would not see you—"

"If any man would try and take her, he shall answer to … *me!*" vowed Brian, surprising everyone save himself.

"And to me as well," Patrick seconded. In spite of his distrust of the Turks, and his initial lack of respect toward Leah, he nevertheless remained devoted to the man who had given him the chance to prove himself many times over.

"While I cannot deny that I am uneasy with this alliance, my lord," John confided, "I will defend your right to wed where you will." A slow, wry smile spread across his face. "I have seen women in the village who would tempt even *me* to matrimony."

"There is every chance that Lord Ares will allow the union," Josh remarked pensively. "Perhaps, given your family's noble connections, it will be seen as an encouragement toward peace. In truth, how can we ever hope to conquer the Turks if we must forever keep ourselves distant from them?"

"Those weak-livered fools in court are to blame," David complained, with a gesture of disgust. "They would call it treason, and yet not a man among them would dare to face the enemy with sword in hand!"

"We have sworn to uphold the laws they set forth," Nicholas reminded him His features were impassive, but his eyes gleamed with a fierce, unrepentant determination. "I offer no excuses ... I have willingly married one of the Turks, and I cannot now release her. Nor will I allow her to be taken from me."

"It is scant enough reward for the battles you have won," Patrick opinioned.

"It is more reward than I could ever have hoped for," Nicholas declared, his voice underscored by a vibrancy that none could mistake.

"Then so be it," said Josh. His gaze flickered collectively over the other men. "We shall await the prince's arrival. And if the Turks dare to seek either retaliation or rebellion, we shall use force to subdue them."

"They are ill-prepared to offer any sort of defense against us," David asserted.

"I fear you underestimate them," Nicholas warned. Again, his gaze lit briefly with ironic amusement. "They possess a pride, a strength or spirit, which can prove far more dangerous than any other weapon."

The elite dispersed soon thereafter, each one renewed in his resolve to endure whatever lay ahead. Only Josh remained behind with Nicholas, the two of them wandering toward the fireplace while the warmth of the morning sun became obscured by clouds.

"They love you well, my lord," Josh remarked quietly.

"And yet I repay them with a danger that is none of their making," replied Nicholas. He lifted a hand to the mantelpiece and frowned, his gaze darkening again. "They will not suffer for it, Josh. When I speak with the prince, I—"

"Has not every man among us made the choice freely?" Josh cut him off with the ease of an old friend. "We *will* defend your right to the marriage. We would do so even if we held any belief at all in the accursed statutes."

"Do you echo David's treasonous talk then?"

"He speaks naught but the truth."

"Does he?" Nicholas folded his arms across his chest and frowned again before announcing, "I must send Thalia back to Sparta."

"She will not thank you for it," Josh insisted, his mouth twitching at the thought.

"Perhaps you will be sorry to see her go," Nicholas suggested, his gaze far too penetrating.

"I, my lord?" replied Josh. He shook his head and remarked with a nonchalance that exposed the true extent of his feelings, "She is an engaging woman. But she does not belong here. She is-she is far too delicate a rose to thrive outside the rich dazzle of court." With that, he excused himself and beat a hasty retreat. Nicholas stared thoughtfully after him for several long moments, then allowed his gaze to drift upward.

Unaware of the fateful decision that had just been made in the hall below, Leah rinsed the last of the soap from her body—and leaned forward to wash her hair. It was difficult, but she managed it well enough. Once she was done, she stood and climbed from the tub. She grasped the toweling, wrapped it about herself, and bent her head to squeeze the water from the golden blonde thickness of her hair.

Suddenly the door swung open behind her.

A loud gasp of startlement broke from her lips. She tensed and spun about, her eyes opening wide when she saw that Nicholas stood surveying her from the doorway. "I-I thought you outside!" she stammered breathlessly.

"It was never my intent to abandon you so soon," he remarked, his eyes glowing hotly as he closed the door. In two long strides, he crossed the room and caught her up against him.

"But, it's midmorning!" protested Leah. Though she raised her hands to push at his chest, she felt her legs weaken beneath her.

"All the better to see what I have wed." His brief, teasing smile quickly gave way to an earnestness that made her pulse race. "Night or day, it matters little to me. I would have you with me always, Leah."

"There is work to be done," she said, though without a great deal of conviction. For the first time, she noticed that he, too, had washed and donned fresh clothing. Her gaze traveled slowly over his face—and sparkled when it was captured by the loving intensity of his.

"None will come today. I have no doubt that last night's celebration will keep many of the villagers long abed. Or filled with regret for what they have done in these few hours past."

"And do you have such regret, my lord?" She offered it archly, but they both knew she was quite serious.

"None." He kissed her then, his lips branding hers with a fiery tenderness that sparked passion once more. Before Leah quite knew what was happening, the toweling had been pulled free and she was naked. Nicholas drew her down with him to the soft woolen rug in front of the fire. His hands boldly explored her sweet curves, his mouth ravishing hers before roaming hungrily downward to her breasts. She clutched at his shoulders, catching her lower lip between her teeth while liquid heat coursed through her body. The flames on the other side of the hearth kept the chill away, but it was Nicholas's ardent, tantalizing caresses that truly warmed her. She strained upward beneath him, secretly wishing that he were naked as well. Her eyelids fluttered open when his lips trailed purposefully downward, across the smoothness of her stomach to the triangle of soft, silken blonde curls between her thighs.

"Nicholas!" she said breathlessly, shocked at what he meant to do She squirmed in an effort to stop him, but he would not be denied. Her fingers threaded within the rich darkness of his hair, her eyes closing again as she was caught up in a veritable whirlwind of desire. Her breath became a series of gasps. She moaned and trembled, and in so doing sent his own white-hot passion flaring near the uppermost limits of control. When he finally plunged within her honeyed warmth, she met his thrusts with an equal fire. The sweet fulfillment was soon upon them. And in the afterglow of their fiercely pleasurable union, Leah remembered something Margaret Hellyer had said to her the night before. *You have dined with Hades, Leah Baal.* If that be so, she mused with a faint, inward smile of irony, then she was truly damned. For she could not resist this Greek man's touch. Her very heart and soul delighted in his words of love; in his vow to hold her forever. At that moment, not even the memory of Langdon's anger or Peatro's threats could diminish her contentment.

"Will your men not wonder at your prolonged absence?" she asked Nicholas softly, her head cradled upon his chest. The blaze within the fireplace had dwindled; a chill began to fill the corners of the room.

"It is likely that my men will guess at the reason." He smiled and gently smoothed the damp tresses from her forehead. "We are but newlywed. None could blame me for lingering."

"In Anatolia, my lord, we do not 'linger' when the sun is so high in the sky."

"Then I am glad I have brought Greek customs with me."

"And is it a Greek custom to spirit women away under cover of darkness?" she challenged saucily. She raised her head in order to meet his gaze.

"I would have killed anyone who tried to stop me," he declared, his tone quiet and solemn. His arms tightened about her, and she trembled anew.

"What if the wedding had already taken place?"

"Then you would have been made a widow before morning."

"You cannot mean that," she exclaimed in disbelief, drawing away and into a sitting position beside him. She caught up the length of toweling and quickly draped it across her body. "You would have taken the life of a man simply because—?"

"At the very least, Leah Constinos, I would have punished him for his defiance and declared the marriage invalid."

Leah Constinos. She felt her heart stir at the sound of it. Her eyes grew very round as she watched him climb to his feet.

"I-I have heard it said that you were once betrothed to a lady," she murmured on sudden impulse.

"Yes. It was a long time ago." Frowning, he adjusted his clothing and placed another log on the fire.

"Why did you not marry her?" She stood and watched as he moved across to the window.

"She was untrue," he stated simply, his eyes clouding at the memory.

"And yet, you must have loved her," Leah persisted, surprised to realize how much the thought pained her. She swallowed hard and looked away.

"I thought I did," he acknowledged. "I was mistaken."

"How can you then be certain that you have not made the mistake a second time?"

He closed the distance between them again, his hands closing about her waist. She caught her breath at the look in his eyes.

"I am no longer easily deceived. But even if that were not so, I would still know that I love you. And that you are like no other." He emphasized his words with another deep, provocative kiss. When he reluctantly took himself off to see to his duties as lord, Leah sank down upon the softness of the bed and stared after him for a long time.

Outside, within the courtyard, Josh found his own morning routine shattered. He had intended to oversee the repairs to yet another section of the stables. Though the repairs would have to be made by the men-at-arms in the absence of any of the Turks, he was determined that the work should take place. A purposeful Thalia, however, intercepted him on his way across the bailey.

"I must have a word with you," she insisted, her manner all that was proper but her eyes imploring him to a familiarity he could not offer.

"What is it, my lady?" he queried stiffly.

"Alone if you please, Sir Joshua." She gathered up her green, silk-embroidered velvet skirts and swept with an inborn gracefulness toward the far side of the town—Josh hesitated, knowing full well the danger of a private conversation with her. Yet he could not prevent himself from following. She stopped beneath the canopy of a tree and clasped her hands together in front of her. Josh drew as close as he dared, his eyes traveling with a will of their own over her pretty, heart-shaped face and slender curves. *I am sending Thalia home.* By all the gods on high, did he not know it?

"What can you have to say to me that demands this seclusion?" he asked. His brusqueness was in direct contrast to his true feelings, but he would not reveal them.

"I would speak with you of my brother's marriage," replied Thalia. She looked away for a moment—and appeared to be searching for words.

"What can my opinion of it matter?"

"Oh, Joshua. You do not truly believe him to be in peril of losing his holdings here, do you?" she asked for reassurance.

"I believe him to be entirely capable of defeating anyone who would try and take what is his," Josh replied, a wry smile playing about his lips.

"Can you not be serious?" Her light brown eyes bridled with irritation.

"What would you have me say, my lady?" His own steady, blue gaze held a passion that simmered just below the surface.

"I would have you say that you love me!"

"*That,* I cannot say. And if we are no longer to discuss Sir Nicholas's marriage, then I must be—"

"Do you not desire me at all, Joshua?" she asked tremulously. Sudden tears gathered in her eyes; she looked saddened, so forlorn and yet softly beguiling, that it was all he could do to refrain from sweeping her into his arms. "Am I so unattractive to you then?"

"No, my lady." He cursed the fire she had set to burning within him. More than anything in the world, he wanted to tell her of his love, to carry her off as his lord had done with the Turkishwoman. But he could not. "Never that," he added in a voice that was little more than an undertone. Schooling his features to impassivity, he prepared to take his leave.

"I could not believe it so!" Thalia said in triumph. Her eyes dancing brightly, she flew toward him. She cast herself upon his chest and entwined her arms about his neck. His hands immediately came up to close about her wrists, to set her firmly away from him, but she held fast.

"You see? I am not so much a grand, well-bred lady of the court that I will let you keep me at arm's length any longer!"

"By damn, Thalia! You must stop this!" he scolded furiously.

Her petite size exposed both her strength and her determination, and he was anxious not to hurt her. Most troublesome of all, however, was his own reluctance to put an end to the embrace. The feel of her body pressing against his, the beckoning nearness of her sweet lips, made him clench his teeth as desire raced through him. Still, it was his responsibility to bring them both back to reason. The irony of it was not lost upon him, for years, he had been a willing participant to scores of dalliances and flirtations. He had believed himself immune to any true engagement of the heart. But now, this mere slip of a woman threatened to bring him to his knees.

"Have you not yet learned the hazards of such impetuous behavior?" he grounded out.

"I would behave thus with no other save you," she parried, doing so without an ounce of contrition. "And if you will not kiss me, Joshua Leonidas, then you are less of a man than I had hoped."

The battle was lost then, and he knew it. With an inward groan of defeat, he allowed his arms to come down about her. He lowered his head and captured her lips with his own. The kiss was both tender and demanding, and so gloriously compelling that Josh knew he could never settle for only one Thalia thrilled to his ardor—and returned it with the long-denied force of her own. She swayed even closer, unmindful of any who might witness her heartfelt surrender.

When Josh finally let her go, she was quite flushed and breathless.

She smiled, her eyes still aglow with passion as she stepped back and primly smoothed her clothing.

"I would say, Sir Joshua, that you are every bit as much a man as I had hoped."

"Sir Nicholas should turn you across his knee," Josh told her, though the sensuous enchantment still lingered in him as well.

"You may have the privilege yourself once we are wed," Thalia countered sweetly.

"I have not proposed marriage." Yet he now realized that it had been on his mind from the first time he had set eyes on her two years ago in Sparta. She had matured a great deal since then—a fact for which he could not be sorry.

"You must first seek permission from my brother. Only then shall I—"

"No, Thalia." He shook his head, quickly sobering. "I cannot do so now."

"Because you still fear he will not consider you a suitable husband for me?"

"It is not that alone. There is yet another reason. Things are too unsettled as a result of his marriage. He means to send you back to Sparta."

"I will not go," she declared, lifting her head to a rebellious angle.

"You will do as you are told," he commanded sternly. "If there is danger to be faced, neither I nor Sir Nicholas would see you in the midst of it"

"But Leah shall remain. Why can I not—?"

"Leah is Turkish. And she is wed to the master of Karabey. Her place is at his side."

"My place is at yours," argued Thalia, her countenance stormy. She folded her arms angrily across her chest and presented her back to him. "Though I love my brother dearly, it is *you* I journeyed so far to see. Surely you cannot want me gone?"

"Though I have no right to say it," Josh conceded as he lifted his hands to her arms and pressed his cheek against the fragrant, chestnut gold softness of her hair, "I want you with me always." He was rewarded for his honesty when she turned about and presented him with a smile that would have melted the last of his resistance if he had not already cast it aside.

"I love you, Joshua," she proclaimed softly. "I have done so since that day you accompanied Sir Nicholas to visit me in the oracle's temple at Delphi. I vowed then that I would wed no other. I know you think me too delicate, but—"

"You *are* too delicate." He cut her off with a frown, then heaved an audible sigh of resignation. "It would be better if you were to choose a husband from among the young men at court, a man who can give you the sort of life to which you are accustomed. I have neither wealth nor a particularly well-favored family. But I can deny my love for you no longer."

"Do you not understand? I would rather be the wife of a man who offered me his heart than one who married me to gain naught but a decoration or a-a brood mare. In truth, I am not the spoiled little fool you have sometimes thought me!"

"Are you not?" His mouth curved into a brief, crooked smile, and he could not resist drawing her close one more time. His eyes twinkled down at her. "You bear little resemblance to a brood mare, Lady Thalia Constinos."

"Does that mean you will not consent to father my children?" she challenged winsomely, her arms stealing back up about his neck.

"I shall perform the honor as often as you like." He kissed her again, his heart thundering at the prospect of sharing his life with such a woman For the first time, he dared to hope that she would be his.

From a window in the tower above, Nicholas watched the two lovers embrace. A faint smile touched his lips—and his eyes glowed with a satisfaction that would have surprised even the man who had been his friend for many years time.

CHAPTER 11

▼

It was the following day before Leah gathered enough courage to venture into Karabey. Thalia and Dame Frances announced their intention to go as well, though Nicholas insisted upon providing them with an escort. He would have willingly performed the duty himself, but Leah professed the desire to be apart from him for awhile. She was unable to consider things in a truly rational manner whenever they were together. And she longed to share a private conversation with Theresa.

"We will ride later," Nicholas decreed as she prepared to leave. "The fresh air will do you good."

"Do you mean to say, my lord, that I am looking ill?" she parried, drawing on her cloak.

"Far from it."

She colored warmly beneath his bold, loving gaze. The second night of their marriage had proven every bit as magical as the first. Indeed, she reflected with an inward sigh, she had taken even *more* pleasure in it. As always, however, that pleasure was tempered by confusion. She hoped that a visit to Theresa's would serve to clear her mind.

A short time later, she crossed the bridge with Thalia and Dame Frances at her side. Josh, Keith, and John followed closely behind, their swords buckled on in readiness and their gazes vigilant against any sign of trouble. The day had dawned cold and overcast. The wind swept with chilling mercilessness across the countryside.

Leah's stomach knotted in apprehension as she pulled the cloak more closely about her. She wore a beautiful, primrose silk cote-hardie borrowed from Thalia. Though it was a trifle too short and snug-fitting across her breasts, she was grateful for the loan of it. She carried Theresa's neatly folded gown in her hands. Her gaze traveled about, searching for a friendly response as she and the others entered the village. The people were carrying on with their work as usual, the sounds and smells the same as every day. The market square was crowded with the makeshift stalls and the many fruits, vegetables, and other goods that had been put forth to tempt anyone with money to spend. Leah made her way slowly through the crowd. Each of the faces she saw was familiar to her. Some of the men offered a polite greeting, or even a tentative smile and nod. Yet none of the women spoke to her. They looked away, their expressions closed and distant. She could hear their whispers and murmurs follow her as she passed. In truth, she had expected their judgment, but her heart still ached at the reality of it.

"Are we not to stop and make any purchases, my lady?" Dame Frances asked Thalia as they paused before a table laden with apples. She had addressed no more than half a dozen words to Leah in the past two days—not because of any real disapproval, but rather because she felt awkward as a result of her own initial hostility toward the young woman who was now the lord's lady. She had never before been faced with such a dilemma.

"Of course we are," Thalia replied, with a smile. "Leah, will you not join us?" she called to her.

"I shall return shortly," Leah answered from where she had stopped a short distance away. She hesitated only briefly, then turned and continued on toward Theresa's cottage.

"We should not let her—" Josh stepped forward to protest.

"She would have but a few moments alone with her friend, Sir Joshua," Thalia advised him. Her eyes glowed softly up into his.

"Sir Nicholas instructed us to keep watch over her," he said, frowning in spite of the way his pulse leapt.

"Surely she will come to no harm here," remarked John. His gaze made a broad, encompassing sweep of the square. "These are her people, are they not?"

"Perhaps Josh is right," Keith unexpectedly seconded. "Perhaps I should follow her. Sir Nicholas will have our heads if anything should happen."

"Go then, if you must," Thalia told him, with a mild sigh of exasperation. "But I pray you, Sir Keith, tarry outside in order to allow her at least a small measure of privacy."

Keith nodded mutely and set off through the crowd. He soon caught sight of Leah, and watched from a vantage point nearby as she approached Theresa's cottage.

Leah kicked at the door. She was relieved when it was opened by Theresa, and stepped quickly inside. The other members of the family were at the market. Theresa, as usual, had been left behind with the cooking.

"Leah!" she said, her eyes growing very round. "Why, it is a surprise to see you here. I had not thought—"

"Are you not wed to Ronald Cayden then, Theresa Unger?" Leah interrupted, with a teasing smile.

A telltale blush stained her cheeks, and she responded with a smile of her own while closing the door. "Before the new year, if I can but convince him of it." She grew serious then, her eyes filling with worriment as she asked in a tumble of words. "But what are you doing here? You should not have come! Not yet. It is too soon after your marriage to Sir Nicholas. There are some in the village who call you a traitor. They cannot understand how you could choose the Spartan over Peatro Conrad!"

"I understand little of it myself," Leah confessed shaking her head. She wandered across to the table, lowered the gown to its surface, and sank wearily down into a chair. "I would not have wed Peatro. And when Sir Nicholas came for me, I could not resist the urge to go with him. Oh, Theresa. He is like no man I have ever known!"

"He broke the law, Leah."

"I know."

"Peatro has sworn revenge."

"I know that, too." She released a long, ragged sigh. "I am sorry for the pain I have caused him. And Langdon as well."

"No one will return to work at the palace," Theresa warned, taking a seat opposite Leah. "Even should force be threatened, none will come now." Glimpsing the distress in Leah's eyes, she reached out and grasped her hand in a comforting gesture. "There is talk of appealing to the Greek court in Troy to have the marriage declared invalid. Even the oracles have spoken out against it—all save Oracle Victoria. *She* says that the law is a bad one and must be cast aside." She paused and leaned forward before confiding in a low, wary tone, "But it is not the Greek law that troubles the people of Karabey. They cannot forgive Sir Nicholas for stealing a Turkish bride."

"He did not steal me! I was never Peatro's. Never—"

"Was there not an agreement made between your families? It is a matter of honor. And now, some are speaking of a rebellion."

"A rebellion?" echoed Leah, her gaze widening in mingled startlement and dismay.

"There have always been those among us who would drive the Greek from Karabey."

"Yes, but many years have passed since any dared to try!"

"Mayhap now is the time to do so."

"Theresa, no!" Leah cried, horrified at the thought. She leapt to her feet and began pacing anxiously to-and-fro. "How can any think to defeat Sir Nicholas and his elite? They are seasoned warriors; they have the whole of Greece behind them!"

"The whole of Greece is not within the palace walls," Theresa pointed out gravely.

"It would take but a day for them to receive reinforcements from Troy!" She moved to the window, her face paling as she murmured, "Hera help me, what have I done?"

"Why did you go with him, Leah Baal?" Theresa demanded, her eyes seeing a great deal more than Leah would have wished. "It was not to escape Peatro. You could have fled elsewhere. You could have waited until after the madness of *Artemis* had passed. Surely Langdon Fogus would not have forced you into the marriage once you made your distaste of it so publicly known." She stood and swiftly joined Leah at the window, her expression both knowing and reproachful. "Is it only the pleasure of sharing his bed that makes you stay? Or do you care so much for him that you would risk all, that you would betray everything you have been taught to believe?"

Leah caught her breath at the sudden, powerful tremor that shook her. The truth came to her then … like a blinding flash in the darkness. *She loved him.* "Sweet Hera!" she said, the confusion falling away at long last. She understood now why her very heart and soul took flight at his touch. And why she had allowed him to carry her away. It was just as he had said—the fates had decreed their union. How could she not have known it? How could she have been so blind? *I love you.* Her eyes swept closed at the memory of his words of love.

"If you truly love him, you must leave him," urged Theresa.

"Leave him?" Leah clutched a hand to her chest and shook her head in a vehement denial. "He will never let me go!"

"Leave now. Before it is too late!"

"But how? How can I—?"

"Langdon sent your things to me this morning," said Theresa. She hastened over to the far corner of the room, retrieving the bundle of clothing placed near the hearth for safekeeping. She returned to thrust them at Leah. "I was to tell you that he awaits your return. He would forgive you. He would forget your betrayal and start anew. And Peatro—"

"No!" Leah choked out. "I will never wed Peatro. I am wed to Nicholas!"

"Yes, and could become a widow for it!" Theresa countered impatiently. "Do you not see, Leah? You place your husband in jeopardy if you stay. And the lives of others as well. Leave now, and perhaps, when the talk of vengeance has passed, you may yet return to him. Once you are gone, there is a chance that the peace will not be shattered. Now, you must delay no longer!"

"But how can I—" She still resisted, her voice hoarse with emotion.

"How can you *not?* Langdon will know what to do. Once you are home—"

"Nicholas will search for me at Ponceel House," Leah remarked numbly. Her head spun at Theresa's vigorous prompting. It was all happening so fast ... She had no time to think, no time to consider the wisdom of such action. Sweet Hera, could she really leave the man she loved more than life itself? The prospect sent a sharp pain slicing through her heart.

"Then you must take my father's horse and ride to Troy," said Theresa. "A friend of my mother lives there. She is related to a tavern keeper, a man named Tyke. They live but a stone's throw from Colossus Gate. If I could but write—But wait! Give her this." She lifted her hands to the small, hammered silver brooch she wore, unfastened it, and offered it to Leah. "She will know it is mine."

With trembling fingers, Leah took the brooch. She hugged the bundle of clothing beneath one arm and carried the brooch with her other hand. Her legs felt heavy as she moved toward the doorway. A painful lump rose in her throat; she felt herself plagued by a keen, terrible doubt.

"Theresa, I—" she said, her reluctance visible.

"Do you not wish to save your husband?"

Nicholas. Yes, she told herself, for that reason alone she could be strong. Loving him as she did, she must try and protect him. Nothing else mattered. She opened the door and started to leave, only to hastily draw back when she spied Keith waiting for her in the narrow lane outside Her throat tightened with alarm, her mind racing to think of a way to evade him. "He will never allow me to pass," she whispered.

"Give me your cloak."

Leah removed it at once. Theresa flung it about her own shoulders and drew the hood over her head. "Hera be with you, Leah Baal," she murmured, before slipping outside. She kept her head down and her steps measured as she headed toward the square. Keith, deceived at least for the moment, followed after her.

Leah waited until they had disappeared, then hurried outside and to the rear of the cottage. Her hands shook as she saddled the horse there. She tied the clothing behind the saddle, mounted up, and reined about. The cold wind punished her for the lack of a cloak, but she paid little heed to it as she urged the horse down the lane and away from the cottage. Her disconsolate gaze strayed toward the palace. She felt a sob well up in her throat, felt so weighed down by doubt and sorrow that she very nearly surrendered to the urge to turn back. But she fought it, reminding herself that it was only by fleeing that she could hope to prevent true disaster. Greek and Turks alike would suffer if she remained. Though she loved Sir Nicholas Constinos with all her heart, *she had to leave him.* She tore her gaze from the palace and gathered her courage about her once more. Her heels pressed gently against the horse's flanks. Following

the river, she soon left Karabey behind. The ride took her north-
ward across the wild, undulating beauty of hills that were still green
in spite of winter's touch. She kept away from the road, hoping to
avoid anyone she knew, and set a course near the trees. Though the
journey would take longer as a result, it would in the end prove
safer.

The day wore on. Leah lost all track of time as she rode. Her
muscles ached from the many hours she spent in the saddle, but it
was nothing compared to the ache deep within her heart. She
stopped only to rest the horse; she had brought no food with her,
yet knew that her stomach would have rejected anything with which
she might have tempted it with. Never in her life had she felt so mis-
erable. Nicholas's face rose in her mind at every turn ... When she
finally reached the outskirts of Troy she drew her wearied mount to
a halt and paused to survey the city before her. Her eyes were drawn
first to the palace, standing massive and well-favored alongside the
river. She allowed her gaze to travel farther then, over the stone and
half-timbered buildings lining the narrow streets, the arched byways
and slips, the round tower that had reached skyward for hundreds of
years' time. With the abbey and priory and temple testifying to its
importance—indeed, it was second only to Athens. Troy was both a
symbol of pride for the Turks and a convenient political base for the
Greek. Her father had often brought her here. She had returned but
seldom since his death. She urged the horse down the hill now,
riding across the wide bridge and through the gates of the old wall.
The beautiful, marble-columned Temple Square rose against the sky
before her. She frowned at the sight of it, for she knew it stood
opposite the buildings occupied by the Greek lawmakers. These
were the men who had set forth the statutes. The men who could, if
they chose, exact a swift and deadly punishment for Nicholas's disobedience. Her eyes clouded anew. Drawing in a deep, ragged
breath, she continued onward. As always, the city was crowded with

all manner of people. Some had traveled far to conduct their business; others merely followed their everyday routine of visiting shops that offered a vast, impressive array of goods. The air was heavy, filled with smoke, the smell of animals and food, and a familiar, inescapable stench rising from the streets. Human voices joined with the creak of wagons and clatter of hooves to create a din that was carried along by the cold November wind.

After pausing to ask a kind-looking woman for directions, Leah drew her mount to a halt before Tyke's tavern and swung down from the saddle. She looped the reins about the post in front of the narrow, three-storied building and swept inside. The large room in which she found herself was dark and smoky, and smelled little better than the street outside. There were only a handful of men seated at the rough-hewn tables. The ceiling was low, supported by thick wooden beams, while the marble walls were crumbling and blackened by years of undisturbed grime. But it was warm inside, and Leah felt a sharp pain of hunger as she caught the scent of freshly baked bread.

"Here now, girl! We shall have none of your kind in here!" a stout, dark-haired woman suddenly exclaimed. Her eyes took in the sight of Leah's pallor, windswept hair, and travel-worn clothing. She bustled forward to confront her, her features disapproving but not rancorous.

"You must—"

"Are you the mistress of the tavern?" asked Leah, unmindful of the fact that she had been mistaken for a harlot.

"I am," the woman replied warily, her eyes narrowing as she wiped her hands on her apron. "I am called Dame Regina. And who is it that wishes to know?"

"My name is Leah Baal." *Leah Constinos,* an inner voice taunted. Trying her best to ignore it, she drew Theresa's brooch from the pocket of her gown and displayed it within her palm. "I have come from Karabey. Theresa Unger told me that I may seek refuge here."

"Refuge?" Dame Regina echoed. Her concern was genuine when she asked, "You are in trouble, child?"

"Yes." She nodded and battled a surge of fresh tears. "It is a serious trouble, though none that would place you in peril. I would but remain for a few days ..." Her voice trailed away, and it was a moment before she lifted her head determinedly and announced, "I ask for no charity, Dame Regina. I shall gladly work for you."

"And have you ever before worked in a tavern, Leah Baal?" the older woman challenged, with an ironic smile.

"No. But I would learn quickly," Leah promised. Her eyes held a heartfelt appeal as well as sadness.

"Then you shall stay," agreed Dame Regina, with a surprising lack of hesitation. She smiled again and led the way to the wooden staircase. "My daughter's bedchamber will do well enough for you, I think. She has but recently wed." She stopped and turned back to inquire, "You have brought nothing with you then?"

"I have a few things outside ..." She would have gone then to fetch them, but Dame Regina's hand upon her arm detained her.

"Tyke!" the woman called in a tone that resounded throughout the smoke-filled warmth of the room. Her cousin, a giant of a man who would have rivaled Ronald Cayden in size, dutifully presented himself before them. "Mistress Baal will be staying with us for a time," Dame Regina told him. "Mind you, she wishes no one to know she is here." Her eyes twinkled when she asked Leah, "Would it please you to be called Mistress Jimaal? It was the name of the woman who owned the tavern long ago. In truth, I have heard it said that she poisoned three husbands. Surely you have murdered no husbands of your own?"

"No," Leah murmured, her eyes falling as Nicholas's face swam before them once more. Not murdered, she added silently, but plunged into certain danger. "I shall be Mistress Jimaal then." Though grateful for the other woman's attempts at levity, she could not be a willing participant in them.

"Whatever your reason for coming to us, Mistress Jimaal," Tyke remarked, grinning in appreciation for her beauty, "I cannot deny that you will much improve my custom. By Zeus, once the men of Troy know that you are here, Turks *and* Greek, naught will keep them from my door!"

"Cease your blathering, Tyke Sorilos, and fetch her things from outside!" snapped his wife, casting him a severe look. Her brow cleared again before she began escorting Leah up the stairs. "In good time, I would hear of your trouble. Till then, you must rest. Come nightfall, the tavern will be filled. And then, Mistress Jimaal, you may well have cause to think ill of my generosity."

Leah was to remember those cryptic words. For the moment, however, she was grateful for a place in which to rest from her journey. The room at the very top of the building, which Dame Regina assigned her, was small yet comfortable, and it was there upon the bed that she allowed the tears to flow freely once she was alone. Again and again, she agonized over her decision to leave Nicholas. And prayed fervently that it would not be long until she was reunited with him. There had to be a way for them to be together. There had to be! Surely the fates could not be so cruel as to grant them such a love and then wrench them apart with no true hope of deliverance. *You are mine, Leah. Now and forever.* Sweet Hera, her heart was breaking in two …

Later, once the storm of weeping had passed, she washed and exchanged Thalia's gown for a soft blue woolen one of her own. She returned downstairs, drawn there by the sounds of raucous laughter and the lively, distinct strains of song. Her crystal blue gaze clouded with trepidation as it made a broad, encompassing sweep of the room. She was sorely tempted to flee back upstairs, but told herself that she could not repay kindness with cowardice. Just as Dame Regina had predicted, the night had brought with it a crowd of masculine revelers. They talked and drank, and drank some more, each apparently determined to forget his troubles for at least a few hours' time. Though the tavern had long been a favorite among the Turks, several of the Greek had taken to frequenting it as well. Men-at-arms from the palace, and even heavy-pocketed travelers newly arrived upon Anatolia's borders, would often drift inside. Tensions always ran high whenever any Greek men put in an appearance. But Tyke Sorilos, ever mindful that he could well lose his livelihood if too many insults were offered, did his best to keep the atmosphere convivial. It was a delicate balance, one that had been upset on more than one occasion in spite of his efforts.

Dame Regina had mentioned to Leah that there were two other women who worked in the tavern. Delivering the tankards of ambrosia and food to the tables, they flirted with the customers and responded with only a laugh or saucy retort whenever a hand strayed across their ample backsides. Both were some years older than Leah. One was a sharp-featured brunette named Melissa, while the other, a blonde named Anne, would have been pretty if not for the hard look about her eyes. They glared jealously at Leah when she appeared at the *foot of* the staircase.

"I sense a restlessness within the crowd this night," Dame Regina cautioned, hastening toward her now. She was forced *to* raise her voice above the clamor. "No doubt it is because *Artemis* has *come* and gone. Keep near the tables at the front," she instructed, with an accompanying nod. "Tyke will make certain *you come* to no harm."

"I thank you, Dame Regina," Leah replied in earnest. Wishing *more* than anything that she were back at the palace in Nicholas' arms, she *took* a deep, steadying breath and started through the crowd. Immediately she was seized upon by a coarse, bearded man who smelled as though he had not bathed in many weeks' time.

"I have not seen *you* before!" he exclaimed, his bloodshot eyes lighting with pleasure as he slipped an unsteady arm about her shoulders.

"Release me, sir!" she demanded indignantly. Her gaze searched *for* Tyke, but he was not in sight.

"I will have but a kiss first!" the man insisted. He stood and yanked her close. She pushed at him with all her might—and succeeded in sending him crashing backward against the table. Laughter, oaths, and derisive comments erupted from the onlookers. Leah whirled and continued on *to* where Tyke stood filling tankards *from* a row *of* kegs behind a tall wooden counter.

"You fool, would *you* bring the law down upon us?" Melissa hissed, materializing at her side now. "Treat them gently, or none *of* us shall have a roof above our heads!"

"Is it expected then that I should allow myself to be accosted?" Leah countered angrily.

"Take care, Mistress Jimaal," Tyke told her, a good deal more compassionately than Melissa. "It is best to parry with words if you can."

"I shall try," she promised. She took the tray he pushed her way and set off toward the table he indicated. It was difficult to move through the crowd. Other men grasped boldly at her as she tried to pass. The ambrosia spilled over the tops of the four cups on the tray, prompting a string of complaints and curses from those it wet. The noise, the smoke, the stench of unwashed bodies, all combined to make Leah's stomach churn. When she had at last reached the table, she was greeted with yet another assault.

"Why, it is a Turkish Nymph!" jeered the lithe, fair-haired man who suddenly leapt to his feet and snaked an arm about her waist. Both his clothing and his manner of speaking identified him as one of the men from the palace.

"Would that she were a Greek one instead." The younger man seated beside him spoke morosely, raising his cup to his lips again.

"Like the others in this accursed place, she is forbidden to us."

"Ah, but is not forbidden fruit the sweetest?" The first man laughed. Leah, attempting at once to lower the tray to the table and pull away, watched in dismay as the tankards fell and clattered to the floor.

"Release me at once" she said furiously, her eyes ablaze. She would have jerked free, but his other arm came up about her as well. Struggling within his grasp, she grew increasingly frightened. "Let go of me!"

"Perhaps you should sweeten the request," he suggested, with a malevolent chuckle. His hand swept downward to close about her buttocks.

"No!" She managed to lift an arm—and did not hesitate before bringing her hand against his cheek in a stinging slap. He swore, his features ugly and suffused with angry red color as his arms tightened about her with punishing force. She cried out, her gaze once again searching for Tyke. He was already making his way toward her, but the crowd was fast closing in about them.

"Release her, Jason." Another man at the table sought now to intervene. He rose to his feet and glanced nervously about, tensing in alarm at the hatred that was visible on the faces of the surrounding Turkishmen. There were rumblings of vengeance now. The music had stopped. A dangerous, highly charged atmosphere began to fill the room. "Release her, else we—"

"Keep quiet!" Leah's captor growled. She cried out again before his mouth swooped cruelly down upon hers. Bile rose in her throat. *Nicholas!* her mind screamed. She could not believe what was happening. The nightmare had worsened. And then suddenly she was free. Stumbling back against the table, she pressed a hand to her bruised lips and watched in astonishment as her assailant scrambled up from the floor. His chin bore the mark of a well-placed blow, his gaze narrowing in murderous rage.

"You disgrace yourself, sir," the man who had hit him advised dispassionately. "Yes, and bring shame upon the rest of us as well."

There was something in his voice that made Leah gaze at him in wonderment He was quite tall, blonde, and handsome in a thoroughly noble Greek way His clothing, however, was in direct contrast to his regal bearing, for he wore a simple gray tunic and coarse woolen braies. His eyes were clear and blue and almost hypnotic. He reminded her of Nicholas.

"I shall send you to Hades for that, you bastard!" The man named Jason sneered. Made reckless by both anger and an overabundance of ambrosia, he pulled his sword from the scabbard at his side.

"Take care!" Leah gasped out a warning. She caught her breath, her eyes growing wide with horror. Her rescuer merely smiled faintly and shook his head.

"I am well-versed in the art of swordplay," he declared, his gaze never wavering from the other man's face. "Strike me at your own peril."

Jason would have lunged at him, but was prevented from doing so by his fellow men-at-arms. They each seized one of his arms and hastily pulled him back. The rumblings of the crowd intensified. Leah's pulse leapt in alarm, and she was only dimly aware of the fact that Tyke had reached her side.

"Death to all Greek!" someone bellowed.

"Hold your tongue, you fool!" Tyke shot back. His own concern mounting, he grasped Leah's arm and started to lead her to the stairs. Their path was blocked. The Turkishmen, provoked not only by the ambrosia but by two centuries' worth of oppression, offered up other traitorous talk. Tyke released Leah and turned back in an effort to diffuse the volatile situation. Leah's eyes widened when she caught sight of Dame Regina, who stood with Melissa and Anne on the otherside of the room. Their faces reflected their fear.

"Have they not taken enough then?" another man suddenly exclaimed from behind Leah. "Will we now stand idle and let them take the best of our women as well?"

"I fear even Hades would reject them!"

"Enough!" roared Tyke, towering above the heads of most every other man there. "Would you bring the soldiers upon us this night? If you will but sit and drink—"

"Drink?" Jason repeated scornfully. "By all the gods, I will drink to the death of those who speak treason!" He jerked free and raised his sword above his head. Leah inhaled upon a sharp gasp and suddenly found herself being propelled forward by the crowd.

The whole room erupted then. Jason and his friends were immediately surrounded. Other swords were drawn, only to be wrenched away and cast aside Threats and curses and fists flew, while Turks fought Greek—and one another. Tyke Sorilos still towered in the very midst of the fight, still trying in vain to restore order. Dame Regina and Melissa managed to make their way to the relative safety of the counter, while Anne raced outside to summon help. Leah struggled to extricate herself from the melee, but was forced against the wall with little hope of escape. The Greek man who had only minutes earlier come to her aid now did so again. She felt someone grasp her hand, felt herself being pulled none too gently along to a door at the rear of the tavern. Her skirts tangled about her legs, and she was forced to twist aside in order to avoid the bodies of several combatants who were sent reeling from blows, but in the end she was outside in the shadows of the alleyway. She inhaled deeply of the cold night air. Her eyes, wide and luminous in the moonlit darkness, lifted to the face of her twice-proven champion. "My gratitude, sir, for your assistance," she offered breathlessly. The bodice of her gown was torn, revealing a goodly portion of her shift, and her hair was half tumbling from what had been a neat, single plait.

"Is it your habit, fair maid, to incite your admirers to such violence?" the man asked, his tone both soft and ironic as he smiled down at her.

She colored, yet raised her head proudly. "I have never yet provoked a tavern brawl. And it is *not* my custom to see myself besieged by either compliments or assaults."

"I thought as much. You do not have the look of the others. In truth, any man with wits could see that you do not belong here."

She grew uncomfortable beneath his steady, indulgent gaze. It struck her then that she was alone with him in the darkness. And though she sensed no threat from him, she hastened to break their intimacy. "I thank you once again," she murmured, her voice still quavering a bit. "I must go."

"Mayhap you share the opinion of those inside?" he suddenly demanded. His aristocratic visage had taken on a solemn expression; he urged her farther away from the door when the roar from within the tavern swelled menacingly.

"I am not certain as to your meaning." She gazed up at him in bemusement.

"'Death to all Greek'?" he clarified, repeating the cry heard inside.

"No," she was quick to deny. She shook her head, her own expression unmistakably sincere. "I, least of all, would share such loathsome sentiments My husband is—" She broke off and quickly looked away.

"You are married?" he queried, with an equanimity that exposed his acute disappointment.

"I am indeed." A shadow of pain crossed her face. She folded her arms across her chest, tensing at the ache within her heart.

Nicholas.

"The marriage brings you little pleasure, I see."

"On the contrary," she corrected, while her eyes met his once more, "it brings me more pleasure than I can say." Her color deepened and she swallowed hard. "Whoever you may be, sir, I pray that Lord Zeus will reward you for your kindness this night." With that, she finally turned and hurried down the alleyway. The tall Greek man hesitated only briefly before following after her. He was close upon her heels when she reached the street, but she was unaware of his presence behind her as she drew to an abrupt halt before the tavern. Though the fight still raged within, it had by this time also spilled out into the street. Greek soldiers, alerted by Anne's cries for help, had descended from the palace. They numbered more than twenty in all—and dismounted with swords already drawn in an effort to quell the fracas. But many were immediately drawn into it as well, so that the situation only worsened. One of the men rode back to appeal for reinforcements. A small crowd of onlookers gathered in the darkness. Leah's gaze filled with dismay when she saw that Jason stood a short distance away. The light streaming from the tavern made his features all too visible. He had recovered his sword and looked more dangerous than ever. His eyes narrowed vengefully when he caught sight of her.

"Sweet Hera!" she whispered, her pulse leaping in alarm. He started toward her. She whirled to flee, only to very nearly collide with the man who had kept watch over her. He steadied her, his mouth curving into another faint smile while his eyes glinted like cold steel.

"Stand aside, good lady," he commanded quietly. He drew his sword and prepared to confront Jason. Leah watched in horrified disbelief as the two Greek men approached each other.

"Traitorous bastard!" Jason growled. "You would stand with the Turks against your own countrymen, and so you will die for your infamy!"

"You are worse for drink, sir, and speak rashly," the other man cautioned. Poised in defensive readiness, he nonetheless made one last attempt to avert a battle between them. "I would but appeal to you to see reason, to—"

"Coward!" Jason lunged forward, fully intent upon running his opponent through, but the blow was parried with an almost effortless skill. "Retreat, Jason, or else you will die this night."

"It is *you* who will rest in the river Styx!"

Again, an attack was launched and easily deflected. Leah's rescuer had as yet to make any offensive moves. She could see that he was, indeed, the far superior of the two, and she began to hope that the conflict would end without tragedy. It was obvious to her that he was reluctant to draw blood. She eyed him in admiration—and found herself musing that he would have much in common with Nicholas.

But her hope was short-lived. Five other men-at-arms suddenly came forth to add their support to their comrade. They closed in on the tall, fair-haired Greek man, gripping their swords and daring him to offer further resistance.

"Arrest this bastard!" Jason shouted, his voice heavy with fury. "By all the gods, he shall be hanged for treason!"

"No!" cried Leah. She impulsively raced forward and planted herself in front of the man whose name she still did not know. Lifting her chin to a proud, defiant angle, she faced the six men-at-arms bravely. "He has done naught but seek to restore peace!" She raised her arm, pointing to indicate Jason. "*This* man bears the blame for what has come about. In truth, he—" She was prevented from saying more when her champion grasped her arm and forced her behind him once more. "I will hide behind no woman's skirt," he told her gruffly.

"Seize him!" Jason reiterated. He and the other five men-at-arms started forward again, but their prey made it clear that he would not surrender. He held his sword with a steady hand, his face a grim mask of determination. Leah gasped when the first man ventured an attack. Though it proved in vain, another and yet another was to follow. Panic rose within her as she watched the tall Greek man parry each blow. Out-numbered as he was, it could be only a matter of time before he tired, no matter how skilled a swordsman he was. She was tempted to call out for assistance from the crowd, yet knew that none would stand with him against the others. They were all Greek. Even though the man she so desperately wanted to save had proven himself decent and kind, the fact that he was one of the enemy would take precedence over all else. Her eyes closed; she offered up a swift prayer for guidance. She opened her eyes again and made for the tavern, intent upon finding Tyke Sorilos.

Suddenly a pale horseman rode through the crowd toward her. She caught her breath upon a gasp, her eyes widening with incredulity as she watched him swing down from the saddle and draw his sword.

"Nicholas!" she said. Her heart soared, her whole body flooding with happiness in spite of the danger. She would have embraced him, but he spared her no more than a furious, speaking glare as he moved past.

"Stay here!" he grounded out. He wasted little time in joining the man who had helped her. Within moments, he was fighting alongside the other Greek man. The harsh, echoing sound of steel against steel rose above the din. Leah's gaze filled with mingled bewilderment and dread. She clasped a hand to her throat and watched as Nicholas showed himself every bit as proficient at swordplay as the man he aided. He held his own against three of the assailants, while his well-matched partner did the same with the remaining three. With dizzying swiftness, the two of them emerged victorious. Jason lay sprawled upon the cobblestones, bleeding from a wound to his shoulder. Three of the other men-at-arms had been injured as well, though none of them mortally so. The last two, upon realizing the futility of their efforts, had disappeared within the crowd.

Leah could scarcely believe it was over. With a strangled cry, she sprang forward to cast herself upon Nicholas's chest.

"Thank Zeus you are safe!" she murmured, then was surprised when, frowning, he moved her firmly away from him. She longed to ask him how he had found her, and to explain why she had run away. But he would not yet allow it.

"We must be away from here," he said, his gaze flickering briefly toward the continuing skirmish at the tavern. More soldiers had arrived, and it seemed that the hostilities were easing, but danger was still present.

"To the palace then," the other man decreed.

"The palace?" echoed Leah, her brow creasing into another frown of puzzlement. She had no time to argue, however, for Nicholas took her arm in a firm, almost punishing grasp and propelled her along with him to retrieve his horse. He said nothing else to her as they quickly accompanied the stranger up the hill. They left the horse secured beside the river. The fair-haired Greek man led the way through a secret underground passage, lit by torches, that took them beneath the palace gates. When they emerged from the tunnel, they were standing in the midst of a candlelit bedchamber. It was quite large, furnished with all the elegance and taste one would expect to find in a palace built by a wealthy Greek nobleman.

"How is it you—?" Leah started to question the man who had brought them here. Her head spun as a result of all that had happened. *Nicholas had come for her.*

"You have the great honor, my lady, to be addressing Michael Gill, Prince of Thrace," Nicholas revealed at last. He slipped an arm about her waist and drew her to his side. It was all he could do to refrain from sweeping her up in his arms there and then. In truth, he was torn between the desire to kiss her and the urge to offer a fitting retribution for her disobedience. His eyes burned down into hers when she blinked up at him in stunned astonishment.

"Prince Michael?" Her round, sparkling gaze moved from him to the prince and back again. "But he-he was at the tavern!" she stammered, at once realizing that she had been deceived.

"An infrequent pleasure," Michael told her, his mouth twitching. "It is far easier to move among the people as a common man than as a royal prince." He sobered and extended his hand toward Nicholas, who clasped it firmly. "Once again, Sir Nicholas Constinos, you have proven yourself a good friend." More than a friend, of course, if it were ever proved true that the same blood ran in their veins. He smiled, negligently folding his arms across his chest as he regarded Leah again. "Now, perhaps you will enlighten me as to your acquaintance with this fair maid."

"Leah is my wife," Nicholas declared without hesitation.

"You jest, Sir Nicholas." Michael chuckled disbelievingly.

"No, sire. It is true." He drew his arm from about Leah's waist and captured her hand with the strong warmth of his own. She trembled, and felt her heart give another wild flutter. "We were wed but three days ago."

"But she is Turkish, is she not?"

"Yes." He gave a curt nod, and stated in a low, even tone, "You were not expected until the week's end. It was my intention to ride henceforth with the news of my marriage. I would have you hear it from no other save myself."

"By all the gods on high, man, what have you done?" demanded Michael, his gaze darkening. There was no trace of amusement upon his features now. He looked quite angry, and his own voice was underscored by an ill-boding edge when he charged, "What of the statutes? You know such a marriage is forbidden! How could you willingly break one of the very laws you have sworn to uphold?"

Breathing an oath, he spun about and moved to the writing table in the far corner of the room. He clenched his hand into a fist and brought it smashing down upon the table's surface, then rounded furiously on Nicholas again. "I would not have thought to find such a flaw within your character You have always been a man of honor, a trusted soldier and friend. Have you then changed so much in but a few months' time?"

"I have changed," Nicholas admitted, his gaze unflinching.

"And you would now cast aside all you hold dear for the sake of such an ill-favored alliance?"

"I would."

"Do you not know that you could be judged guilty of treason as a result?" Michael persisted, closing the distance between them. His eyes searched Nicholas's face and held an erstwhile appeal for contrition. "For the love of Zeus, do you not know that death could be your reward for such?"

"I beg of you, sire. The fault is mine alone," Leah exclaimed.

Horrified at the prince's words, she could be silent no more. "I-I have bewitched him!"

"Leah," warned Nicholas, scowling down at her.

"It is true," she cried. Pulling away from him, she pleaded with Michael to believe the lie.

"He was powerless to resist. Have you not heard of the magic we practice? It is said that some of us possess the ability to—"

"Damn it, Leah! *Enough!*" Nicholas ordered tersely.

"Even if it were not true, even if we did but fall in love as other men and women have done," she continued while tears of desperation gathered in her eyes, "then surely you must be merciful. Have you never loved a lady? Have you never cared so much for another? We have harmed no one. We have done naught but seek the happiness that has been granted us, for however brief a time. And yet, the law—a cruel, unjust law—would tear us apart! Your father has expressed his wish for peace between us. But how can there be peace when there are statutes to prevent any hope of it? May Zeus help us all, how can there be peace when we are forever denied the freedom to follow our hearts?"

"Do you love him so much then, my lady, that you would trade your life for his own?" Michael put to her gravely. In that moment, he understood his friend's transgression—and would gladly have changed places with him.

"Yes," Leah was quick to affirm.

"No," Nicholas grounded out. He thrust her behind him, his handsome face thunderous and his eyes smoldering hotly. "I was the one who forced the marriage. And by the blood of the gods, I would do so again!"

"Would you indeed?" murmured Michael. His anger visibly diminishing, he heaved a sigh of resignation and promised, "I shall seek to intervene with Lord Ares. It is safe to assume, I think, that no heads will tumble. I could not see your many years of loyal service repaid thusly. Besides, have you not saved me again this night?" He allowed a faint smile of irony to touch his lips before warning, "But the charge of treason may still be unavoidable. You may yet lose your holdings at Karabey."

"I would forfeit them willingly," Nicholas replied.

"Pray that it will not come to that." Their gazes, each incredibly fathomless, met in a look of silent understanding.

"Do you-do you mean that my husband no longer faces the possibility of death?" asked Leah, still not daring to hope that the worst had passed.

"You have my word upon it, my lady," the prince responded earnestly. The ghost of a smile touched his lips again. "I should very much like to know how the bride of Sir Nicholas Constinos came to be within that tavern."

"I but sought refuge there," she told him.

"Refuge? Perchance you are ill-treated by your husband then?" His gaze was filled with an unholy light as it traveled over her.

"No. No, sire. I am not." She ventured a glance at Nicholas, only to pale at the way his mouth tightened grimly once more. "I felt it necessary to leave Karabey, in order to spare my husband both the charge of treason and the threat of a rebellion."

"You shall remain here this night," Michael decreed. Reluctantly he turned away. "I will leave you to your privacy now, and will see that your horse is cared for. We shall speak more of this tomorrow. No doubt the brawl will have ended soon enough, but I must make certain of it. Jason and his cohorts will have ample cause to regret that I am not the simple traveler I seemed." He crossed to the doorway, then paused and looked back at Nicholas. "I fear your marriage may well bring the rebellion your wife speaks of. Do your men stand with you?"

"Yes," Nicholas confirmed, his voice steady and sure. "As always, they have granted me their loyalty."

"And so they should." The prince met Leah's gaze one last time before leaving. The door closed softly behind him.

Leah looked up at Nicholas. Without a word, he gathered her against him. She closed her eyes, a long sigh escaping her lips as his strong, loving arms came about her.

CHAPTER 12

▼

They remained clasped to each other for several long moments. Finally, Nicholas's hands swept upward to close about Leah's arms. He moved her away from him a bit, frowning down at her while his eyes glowed dully.

"Why did you leave, Leah?" he asked. His deep-timbered voice was laced with both anger and tenderness.

"I could not remain and see you lose everything because of me. I could not watch my own countrymen seek revenge because of—because of my selfishness." She drew in a ragged breath and pressed her hands to the hard breadth of his chest. "How did you know where to find me?"

"Theresa Unger," he answered simply.

"I cannot believe it," she protested. "Theresa would not tell—"

"She did so reluctantly." A momentary glimmer of amusement appeared within his gaze when he told her, "It is my understanding that, when neither Josh's nor Keith's threats would coax the truth from her, John tried his hand. He has long possessed the ability to charm a good deal more than information from women."

"Sweet Hera, do you mean to say that he *seduced* a confession from her?"

"Not quite." The merest hint of a smile played about his lips before he suddenly released her and turned away. Battling his temper, he moved to the window and braced a hand against the stones. "You gained naught by running away, Leah. The harm, if it would be called harm, had already been done."

"Perhaps," she allowed, releasing another audible sigh as she sank wearily down upon the foot of the massive four-poster bed.

"Still, I could not help but feel the peril was made worse by my presence at the palace. Theresa warned that a rebellion was fast brewing. And the main provocation for it is my betrayal of Peatro Conrad. It was treachery enough that I rejected him, that I failed to honor the agreement made so many years ago, but that I then chose to wed a Greek man is unforgivable." Her tone was fraught with emotion when she appealed, "Do you not see? I *had* to leave."

"I see only that you disobeyed me," he replied harshly, rounding on her again. "By Zeus and Hades, do you not realize what you have put me through? When I discovered you gone—" He broke off, muttered an oath beneath his breath, and crossed the room in two long, angry strides. He stood towering ominously above her, all the while fighting against the urge to lay hands upon her. "Did you not consider the dangers of traveling such a distance alone?"

"I was in no danger!"

"The evidence before me suggests otherwise." His eyes raked boldly—furiously—over her torn gown and disheveled curls. "What by Hades possessed you to seek refuge within a tavern?"

"It was safe enough," she insisted, though her gaze fell uncomfortably beneath the piercing intensity of his.

"Next, perhaps, you will deny that I arrived to find you in the midst of a brawl." His temper flared perilously at the memory.

"Is it my fault then, my lord, that men would fight?" In spite of her brave words, she felt a warm, guilty color staining her cheeks.

"The sight of you would entice even the purest soul to violence," he remarked, his tone caustic.

"Unfair," she retorted, rising abruptly to her feet before him now.

"I sought to entice no one!"

"It is done all the same." The storm within him finally eased somewhat, and it was with gentleness that his hands closed about her waist. "Never again leave me, Leah," he commanded, his voice splendidly low and vibrant. His eyes caught and held the softening fire of hers.

"But what of the rebellion? What if—"

"We will endure whatever comes." His mouth curved into a disarming half smile when he said, "At least, my lady, you are not soon to be a widow."

"How can you tease me about such a thing?" she scolded, her heart twisting anew. "You cannot imagine the dread I have suffered. To think that I might have been responsible ..." She shuddered at the thought.

"Were there not two of us involved?"

"Yes, but it was *I* who began the madness when I came to the palace."

"Not madness," he asserted quietly. He pulled her closer, his tone scarcely more than a whisper when he pointed out, "You have never yet said that you loved me, Leah."

"Have I not?" She was surprised to feel a shyness then.

"No. But did you not proclaim to the prince that you would give your life for my own?"

"I-I suppose that I did."

"Though we have been wed but three days, it seems an eternity that I have waited for you to admit that your feelings run as deep as my own." He gently ran a hand through the gold-colored thickness of her hair. "Say it, my love," he bade her. "I would hear it from your own lips."

She complied, with a sweetness and sincerity that stirred his very soul. "I love you, Nicholas. I have done so from the very beginning."

His eyes gleamed with an irresistible combination of triumph, love, and desire. He drew her close once more. "Will you still do so if I lose my holdings? Will you love a penniless elite with only his heart to offer?"

"I will indeed. And shall follow him to the very ends of the earth." She smiled softly up at him, her own beautiful eyes holding the truth.

"Though, I must confess, I would have the earth end at Karabey."

"As luck would have it, lady wife, I have it in mind to make my home in Anatolia. If we can but have some measure of peace, I would happily remain upon this lush and mysterious land for the many years left to us."

"Oh, Nicholas," Leah sighed, her gaze involuntarily clouding again at the unbidden memories of Theresa's words and the recent brawl.

"How can we hope for peace when tensions between Turks and Greek still run so high? We are enemies yet. It is as if these few hundred years past have taught us little ... Our differences are still far too many to be overcome."

"So long as we have each other, all things are possible," he vowed, with so much authority that she dared to believe it. His arms tightened possessively about her—and his features were heart-stirringly solemn as he said, "The fates brought me to Anatolia, Leah. And to you. I cannot believe we have found each other for but a brief time. Lord Zeus *shall* bless our union." His lips claimed hers then. She moaned in an eager, passionate surrender and strained closer to him. Though they had been parted for only a day, they ached for each other. Soon they were entwined beneath the brocade canopy of the four-poster, their lovemaking fierce and wondrous, and, for Leah, no longer bound by the fear that the marriage would bring the severest retribution of all. She gave herself fully, secure in her love for him and his for her. Emboldened by this knowledge, she assumed an active role, her hands and mouth setting him afire as his had done to her. When he could endure no more of the delectable torment, he gave a low groan and rolled so that she was astride him. Her eyes opened wide, for she was shocked at the position. But she was soon enough past caring when he brought her down upon his manhood. She rode atop him, her whole body atremble as she met his thrusts, her loosened silken tresses swirling about her body while his fingers grasped at the firm roundness of her backside. Once the storm of desire had given way to a soft, lingering ecstasy, they lay together and watched the candles burn low. Leah urged Nicholas to tell her of his childhood, of his family and his life before he had come to Anatolia. He was reluctant to do so at first, but finally capitulated with a long sigh. "When I was very young," he began, his warm hand trailing downward to rest in its preferred spot upon the naked curve of her hip, "my life was content enough. My father was a nobleman, descended—so it is said from a bastard son of Dinukos the Conqueror. My mother was the daughter of an elite whose own antecedents lay within Athens."

"And have you any other brothers or sisters?" she asked. Her own fingers traced a light, tantalizing pattern upon the bronzed hardness of his chest.

"I have naught but a sister, Thalia is my elder by some three years. Upon our grandfather's death, she inherited both the title and the estates near Sparta."

"What of your mother? Does she live in Greece still?"

"No. She has been dead these five years past." He frowned and gathered her closer to his virile, lithely-muscled warmth. "Though she was much opposed to the practice, I was sent away at the age of seven, to become another page in Lord Ares' army. When I turned fourteen, I became an elite."

"And were then trained in the art of warfare," Leah supplied for him, for she knew the ways of the Spartan Army. Her eyes filled with compassion. "It is difficult for me to imagine what it must have been like for you, to find yourself torn from hearth and home at so young an age. And then, to spend year upon year in the midst of battle. My own childhood was both happy and unmarred by tragedy … until my parents were taken from me." There was a noticeable catch in her voice, and her eyes closed when Nicholas pressed a tender kiss to her temple.

"Were they both carried away by the war?"

"Yes. I miss them dreadfully still. My father was a good-humored rogue, handsome and proud and so full of charm that even his enemies could speak no true ill of him. My mother was much quieter, softer, a true beauty. It was she who taught me to sing."

"A gift for which I am indeed grateful."

"So it is my singing then that bewitched you?" she challenged in mock reproach, then gasped when his hand suddenly moved to clasp tightly at her bottom.

"I could well beat you, for both your disobedience and those absurd lies you offered the prince," he said threateningly. It was spoken, however, without any real mind to vengeance.

"They were not entirely falsehoods," she retorted. She pushed herself up on one elbow to cast him a defiant, wifely look. "I *did* seek to-to captivate you, even though it was not consciously done. What woman can in all honesty deny that she has done naught when it comes to such things?"

"And what man could have resisted the pleasure of conquering a Turkish wild nymph like you?" His eyes gleamed with wry amusement.

"If all Turks were 'conquered' with such sweet mastery, my lord, then I am convinced peace should be achieved by year's end." She was rewarded for the saucy compliment by the sound of his low, resonant chuckle. Her heart always fluttered wildly whenever he smiled or laughed. She would have to make certain he did so more often.

"I have little doubt that you shall lead me a merry chase." He smiled again before proclaiming seriously, "But It is one I welcome."

"We still have so much to learn about each other," she murmured, releasing a sigh as she settled against him.

"We have time enough."

They were silent for a few minutes then, each lost in their own thoughts while the night deepened and the blaze in the fireplace dwindled to a glowing mass of embers. Finally Leah stirred within Nicholas's arms again and asked softly, "Is it still your intention to send your sister back to Greece?"

"Yes." A faint smile of irony touched his lips, "yet there is something that might well prevent it."

"What do you mean?"

"Sir Josh Leonidas."

"Josh?" Her brow creased in puzzlement. "What can he—"

"He is in love with Thalia, Leah. I have suspected as much for some time now."

"But how can you be certain? And do you yet know if she returns his affection?"

"I have witnessed their regard with my own eyes. It was undeniably mutual."

"Then you must see that they are wed."

"No."

"Why not?" She drew away from him once more and sat upright in the bed. Tugging the covers up over her nakedness, she swept the wayward curls from her face and demanded, "Why should they not become husband and wife?"

"Josh has not yet sought my consent," he disclosed. He rolled unhurriedly to his side and braced himself upon one elbow as his eyes met hers in the candlelit darkness. "And Thalia is far too immature at present to—"

"Why, she is equally as mature as her brother!" protested Leah. "Are not many Greek women wed before they are allowed to mature? In Anatolia, it is expected that we marry young. Indeed, Langdon Fogus was most anxious. He feared that I would soon drift into spinsterhood."

"A most unlikely occurrence," said Nicholas, then acknowledged begrudgingly, "Greek custom is much the same. But Thalia is young in wisdom if not in maturity. She has led a sheltered life, one that has left her ill-equipped to assume the duties of a wife."

"I cannot believe her life has been so sheltered. I have heard of the many scandals and intrigues of the Greek court. Do you think her either so blind or naive that she will have remained unaware of them.

"She is immature, yes, but she is not a child."

His mouth twitched briefly, for he recalled having said much the same to Josh. Still, he was responsible for Thalia and would not be persuaded to relinquish his control over her welfare. "Even so, I cannot allow the marriage," he murmured, frowning again.

"Surely you will not seek to part them?" she queried in disbelief. Her eyes flashed down at him. "How can you consider such-such heartlessness? Josh is your top elite, but is he not also your friend? I cannot believe you would judge him unsuitable."

"I did not say that." He pulled himself into a sitting position now as well. "In truth, I felt nothing but pleasure when I saw them together.

Josh is more than even a friend to me. And Thalia I love. Yet what can the future hold for them?"

"The same as it holds for us."

"It is different for us."

"How so?" she shot back, her tone one of growing indignation.

"Thalia possesses neither your courage nor your strength," he replied quietly. "I have little doubt that you will weather the storms ahead. But I am not so certain of *her* fortitude."

"You underestimate her greatly," Leah insisted. "And if she loves Josh but a fraction as much as I love you, then I am certain she will summon the ability to endure whatever tribulations the fates may have in store for her."

"Though it pleases me to hear you say it, my mind is set upon withholding my consent."

"Then you must change it."

"No, Leah. Not even for you will I follow a course I believe at this moment to be wrong."

"Have you not already done so? Our marriage was forbidden, and yet you—"

"Forbidden, not wrong," he replied, with maddening calm.

"It is *wrong* to deny them the joy we have known," she maintained.

Her color was beguilingly heightened by now, and she had become too preoccupied to notice that the covers had fallen away from her body. Nicholas's eyes smoldered with renewed passion as they traveled appreciatively over the rose-tipped fullness of her naked breasts.

"Perhaps," he murmured. "We will speak of it no more for now." His hand moved along the curve of her hip, but she surprised them both by pushing him away.

"Do you think, Sir Nicholas Constinos, that you may end the quarrel so easily?" she insisted, not at all certain why she did so. Perhaps she wanted to taunt him a bit, to make him pay for his wholly masculine stubbornness. Whatever the case, she found herself slipping from beneath the covers. She scrambled from the four-poster, caught up the top quilt, and wrapped it about herself, then hastened to stand before the fireplace. Her eyes were wide—and glistening with a silent challenge—as she turned about to face Nicholas.

"Come back to bed, Leah," he commanded, his voice so seductive that she felt her resolve waver.

"No, my lord. Not until you have agreed to at least consider—"

"*Leah.*"

She felt a shiver dance down her spine. Her knees grew weak, but still she would prolong the game. For the first time in her marriage, she could be light-hearted. No longer did she suffer under the threat of seeing her husband forfeit his life for the crime of loving her. She could dare to dream now. She could dare to tease and play and test the newfound powers of her femininity.

"It is time, Sir Nicholas," she pronounced archly, "that you learned I am to be no meek and docile wife who would tremble at the darkening of your brow. I have opinions and am not averse to making them known. Nor shall I be content to sit at home with my sewing and leave you to your adventures."

"Shall you not?" His expression remained somber, yet his gaze held a disconcerting warmth as he climbed from the bed and leisurely advanced upon her.

Her own gaze traveled over his powerful, hard-muscled body. The sight of him never failed to send a liquid heat racing through her veins. "No, and I-I mean to ensure a better life for the people of Karabey." She moved behind a large, velvet-upholstered chair and lifted her head in a gesture of proud determination.

"A goal I share." A soft smile appeared upon his lips now, and he looked briefly to the fire before promising, "Tomorrow, we will plan for the good of the villagers. But I would prefer to think of other things this night."

"Indeed, my lord. You would prefer not to 'think' at all," she said accusingly, then felt her cheeks blush rosily at the look in his eyes.

"You have come to know me well."

"Not so well," she denied, heaving an eloquent sigh. "I fear you shall ever remain something of a mystery to me."

"Perhaps that is as it should be," he parried. "Now come, my love, for the hour grows late and I would make the most of the time left to us."

"Is your mind truly upon little else save *that* whenever we are together?"

"My mind is upon many things. Yet making love to you is by far the most satisfying."

The game was short-lived. Her pulse leapt as he gently took her hand and led her from behind the chair. He took a seat and pulled her down upon his lap. Her hands strayed up to his neck—and she offered but a feeble protest as he swept the quilt from her body.

"You are a wicked man, my lord," she murmured breathlessly, squinting with pleasure as his hand set up yet another bold exploration of her pliant, voluptuous curves. "I begin to see why you are called 'The Raptor'. And by all the gods, I cannot regret that I have become your prey."

His quiet laugh stirred her sweetly. She urged his head down toward hers, then delighted him with her bold, thoroughly inflaming kiss. Desire sparked and blazed with such swift intensity that, very soon thereafter, she found herself straddling his thighs. He took her there and then, while still seated upon the chair, but she had neither the will nor the inclination to offer any sort of complaint …

After receiving a promise from Prince Michael that he would honor them with a visit in but a few days' time, they left the palace the following morning and stopped briefly at Tykes' tavern. Leah retrieved her things—as well as Theresa's brooch—before offering first an introduction to Nicholas, then an explanation for her sudden disapperance the night before. "Truly, I am sorry if you were worried on my account, but my husband came for me," she told Dame Regina as the three of them stood together just within the doorway.

"I-I did not expect him so soon." The older woman subjected Nicholas to a swift, critical appraisal, then smiled. "It is easy to see why you were troubled at the parting. You have not long been wed, have you?"

"No," Leah confirmed, a faint color rising to her face. She managed a brief smile of her own before declaring, "I shall return the brooch to Theresa Unger. My gratitude once again for your kindness, Dame Regina."

"You will always receive a welcome here, child. Next time, Zeus willing, the night will prove less eventful," she murmured, her eyes traveling ruefully about the interior of the tavern. Cluttered with broken tables and benches, it gave indisputable evidence of the brawl. "Praise be to Zeus no one was killed. Though three Trojan men *did* have the misfortune to find themselves carted off to that damp, rat's haven of a jail. It makes little sense," she concluded, with a frown and a shake of her head. "More and more of late, the peace is shattered. But it was ever an uneasy peace at that."

"Perhaps the prince will be able to strengthen it," said Nicholas, his tone holding its usual authority.

Dame Regina could not help but warm to the sound of it, in spite of the fact that he was both Greek and a lord. "Since I assume you to be a loyal subject of Lord Ares, Sir Nicholas Constinos, I would expect naught else but such words from you. Still," she allowed begrudgingly, "I cannot deny that there are many who look to Prince Michael for a better peace." Turning to Leah, she promised, "I shall light a candle for you. You will, I think, have need of the guiding hand of the gods in the days ahead."

"Your words are kind," Leah thanked her.

They took their leave then, and were soon riding homeward. The morning was much the same as the previous one—gray and cold and devoid of any hopeful sign of a respite. Yet Leah's spirits had never been higher. She met Nicholas's gaze frequently as they rode; their eyes held the knowledge of what had passed between them in the night. They followed the road, and completed the journey in far less time than it had taken Leah the day before. Upon reaching the outskirts of Karabey, she reined to a halt and waited for her husband to do the same.

"I must return the horse to Theresa Unger, she announced, her brows knitting together in a frown at the thought. She was hesitant to face her friend—in truth, hesitant to subject herself to the rebuke she knew to be forthcoming. Was it possible that Theresa could understand why she had come back? "Her father will have need of it."

"I will arrange for it to be returned later," Nicholas assured her.

"Are you afraid that I may yet again be persuaded to take flight?" she teased, albeit half-heartedly.

"Not afraid. Merely cautious." He gave her a faint smile and led the way to the palace. She followed after him, her heart secretly thrilling to the familiar sight of the walled marble fortress that rose across the river. Thalia hurried forward to greet them when they dismounted before the keep. Her color was high and her eyes bright, and her relief was visible as she embraced Leah warmly.

"Oh, dear brother! Thank Zeus you have found her!" She cast a jubilant smile at her brother before launching into an interrogation of Leah. "Why did you run away like that? Where have you been? And where did you get such a truly *splendid* gown?" Her gaze widened in admiration while traveling over the cote-hardie fashioned of deep lavender silk.

"My own was sadly torn," answered Leah. "I received the loan of this one from-from a charitable gentleman."

"A charitable gentleman?" Thalia echoed in bafflement. "But who is this gentleman? And how did you—?"

"It is a long story." Nicholas cut her off, not unkindly. "One that can surely wait until after we have been granted a meal."

"Of course," said Thalia, appearing well-chastised for her impulsiveness She quickly recovered, however, and gave a soft laugh as she linked her arm companionably through Leah's and started up the steps. "Dame Frances shall most assuredly give thanks for your return. She complains hourly that she and the maidservants have far too much work to divide among themselves. I have done my best to assist them, of course, but I fear my housewifery skills are even more sadly lacking than your own. Now that you are back, we shall gladly give the kitchen duties to the women from the village."

Leah responded with a rather wry, noncommittal smile, for she was not at all certain that Theresa or any of the other Turkishwomen would ever willingly consent to return to the palace. Would they—upon learning that she meant to stay and assume her role as the lord's lady view her as a traitor, or as a valuable ally within the enemy's camp? It was impossible to predict with any real degree of accuracy what their reaction would be. They were fiercely independent, proud and stubborn, and far too uncompromising for their own good. And she loved them well for it.

Following a pleasant enough meal enlivened by the attentiveness of the elite, Thalia and Leah retired to a quiet corner of the great hall. It was time, the precocious brunette insisted, for Leah to reveal the particulars of her whirlwind courtship and marriage. Thus, while Nicholas related to his men what Prince Michael had said and told them of his plans for the immediate future—the two women settled themselves upon a high-backed wooden bench that had recently been drawn beneath the window. They were still close enough to the fire for comfort. And far enough away from the men for privacy.

"I took note of Sir Nicholas's interest in you," Thalia began, keeping her voice low. "Yet, at first, I believed it to be nothing more than the usual admiration of a man for a beautiful woman. Within scarcely a day's time, however, I suspected that it was much more than that. But how *did* it come about, and so quickly?" she asked. A mild frown of bemusement creased her brow. "I was surprised to hear of the new statutes. And, I must confess, my surprise increased tenfold when I learned that my brother was so willing to test the law. I have never known a man more committed to the good of his country. Indeed, I had begun to fear that he would remain wed to naught but his beloved honor and duty."

"He has not changed," Leah insisted, her mouth curving upward a bit. "What has happened … Our marriage … Oh, Thalia. It is difficult to explain." She released a sigh while her gaze strayed to where her husband still sat at the table with the elite. "There was a bond between us from the very beginning, a powerful attraction that lay far beyond what either of us might have expected. It was both unintentional and unavoidable. The fact that our love was forbidden was much considered, yet we could do naught to prevent it."

"And is it true then that you were not wed with the blessings of the gods?"

"Yes," Leah admitted reluctantly. "Under Byzantine law, a man and woman may become husband and wife by declaring themselves so.

They must both willingly consent, of course. And if they have done so, the marriage is both legal and binding—though, to be sure, the blessings of the gods are most welcome." Her eyes clouded at the thought, for she had always dreamed of a proper ceremony within the temple of Karabey's small, ancient square. But it mattered not, she told herself—for as Nicholas had said, Lord Zeus would bless their union.

"I think I should like it if this particular custom were adopted in Greece as well," Thalia remarked, her own gaze moving significantly toward the men. "Perchance I may yet convince a certain elite to embrace it." She looked back to Leah and blushed rosily. "In truth, Leah, I understand a good deal more than you might think. You see, I, too, have lost my heart."

"And does the object of your affection feel much the same?" Leah gave no indication that she already knew about the older woman's attachment to Josh.

"He does."

"Has he spoken of marriage then?"

"At present, he believes he is not worthy," Thalia replied, her tone disconsolate as she clasped her hands tightly together upon her lap. "But we have exchanged a promise. And if I could only persuade my brother ..." She paused and cast a meaningful glance up at Leah from beneath her eyelashes. "Will you not agree to intercede for us?"

"I-I." Leah responded with mingled surprise and reluctance. "Oh, Thalia I—"

"There is none better to do so," Thalia said, cutting her off and visibly warming to the idea now. "I should not think he cares for any opinion so much as your own. Surely *you* can prevail upon him to grant his consent."

"I fear he is much too headstrong to be swayed."

"Nonsense! Why, I know he will listen to you. And when he learns that it is none other than Sir Josh Leonidas who holds my regard, he cannot remain opposed—if he has a mind toward opposition. The two of them have endured much together these many years past. Josh is his trusted friend and advisor, is he not? He has no great wealth or influence, of course, but he is a good, kind gentleman who would suit me to perfection."

"Has Sir Josh broached the subject with my husband?" Leah felt a sharp twinge of guilt in that moment. Loath to reveal that Nicholas had already told her of the romance, and of his intent to withhold his blessing, she averted her gaze from the pleading brightness of Thalia's. "Has he yet sought Sir Nicholas's permission to court you?"

"No. Nor would he allow me to do so."

"Then you must be patient," advised Leah. On sudden impulse, she covered Thalia's hand with the warmth of her own. "Still, I give you my solemn oath that I shall do whatever I can to encourage his consent." The vow was uttered before she could reconsider it. Yet she knew that her words were sincere.

"Thank you, dearest sister!" Thalia replied, her brow clearing. She bestowed a quick, affectionate hug upon Leah before directing a nod toward the nearby table. "Perhaps we should turn our conversation elsewhere," she whispered. "I see that my brother watches us closely."

Leah turned her head—and caught her breath when her eyes met Nicholas's. Like her, he had exchanged his travel-worn attire for fresh clothing. He showed no ill effects from the journey. Quite the contrary. Her heart swelled with a hardy mixture of pride and love and admiration at the sight of him, and she longed for the coming of the night.

A short time later, after the others had taken their leave from the great hall, Leah stood alone with her husband near the fireplace and attempted to persuade him to postpone Thalia's departure from the palace. But he would not hear of it. At week's end, he decreed, his sister would be on her way back to the safer shores of Greece.

"You must not send her away," Leah persisted.

"How can I allow her to remain while danger gathers about us?" countered Nicholas, his tone quiet and his gaze darkening as he stared into the flames. "I should never have allowed her to come to Anatolia. Were it not for the prince's request, I would have prevented it."

"None in Karabey would harm her. We are not the savages you seem to think us, my lord." Frowning, she moved closer to him and lifted a hand to his arm. "Thalia has spoken to me of her love for Josh. Her heart is clearly set upon him."

"No, Leah," he said, covering her hand with the strong warmth of his.

"*Our* father would not have chosen to see her wed to a man whose connections are so far beneath her own."

"And do you think *my* father would have chosen to see me wed to a Greek man?" she challenged. She snatched her hand away, her eyes blazing resentfully up at him. "By all rights, you and I should not have wed. We have defied every rule and convention, both Greek and Turkish. We have defied the law itself. Would you now hold that the love Thalia and Josh bear for each other is any less significant than what *we* have found together?"

"How can it compare?" he replied, his arm slipping about her waist. He pulled her none too gently against him, and she melted inside at the fierce, loving gleam in his eye. "Still," he conceded, with a frown, "if they possess even a small measure of what we share, I suppose I must give consideration to it."

"Oh, Nicholas," she murmured happily.

"Mind you, I have not yet granted permission for Thalia to marry. *Nor* have I consented to the marriage."

"You shall!" She raised her hands to his chest and gave him a smile that was at once saucy and provocative. "You shall, my lord." Her mouth beckoned the caress of his, and she moaned in satisfaction as he most willingly obliged.

Thalia and Josh were similarly occupied at that moment, the two of them snatching a few secret moments together within the shadows of a corridor. But unlike Nicholas, Josh found his own passion tempered with guilt.

"No more, Thalia!" he grounded out, pushing her almost angrily away from him. She refused to be put off, however, and entwined her arms about his neck once more.

"Kiss me again, dearest Joshua!" she pleaded, her pretty face flushed and her eyes shining softly up at him.

"No!" Summoning all his strength of will, he shook his head and gritted his teeth while waiting for the fire within him to subside. He gently, yet firmly, forced her arms from about him. "I have work to do."

"We could be wed under Byzantine law!"

"By Hades, what are you talking about?"

"Sir Nicholas's marriage to Leah came about in such a manner," she told me. "We have only to agree that we are husband and wife!"

"Never would I agree to that," he declared, his tone low and simmering.

"And why not? If my brother—?"

"No, Thalia."

She watched in tearful frustration as he turned upon his heels and strode away. Catching her lower lip between her teeth, she crossed her arms beneath her breasts and walked slowly in the opposite direction. She drew to an abrupt halt in the next instant, however, while her eyes lit with a sudden, shocking idea. "Yes," she whispered, her heart racing with excitement as the plan took root within her mind. She looked back to where Josh had recently disappeared. "Soon enough, Sir Joshua Leonidas," she vowed.

"Soon enough, you will be persuaded."

Two days passed. Two days in which, still, none of the Turks crossed the drawbridge. Some of the elite clamored for a show of force, a punishment for the villagers' defiance, yet Nicholas ruled against any immediate retaliation. He was convinced that, in time, his marriage to Leah would find acceptance. Prince Michael had cautioned him to patience. Thus, for now they would play a waiting game. And in so doing, hope for a peaceful end to the stalemate.

Leah, meanwhile, could postpone her visit to the village no longer. She knew that Nicholas would not allow her to go alone, yet she was determined to do so. Her opportunity came one morning when he and Josh rode forth to pay a visit to several of the outlying farms.

Waiting until they had disappeared beyond the hills, she slipped out of the keep—careful to avoid Thalia—and hastened toward the village. No one tried to stop her. John, David, and Keith had gone hunting. Only Brian remained behind at the palace, and *he,* Leah had already noted, was preoccupied with listening to Dame Frances's instructions concerning the start of a much needed vegetable garden on the far side of the bailey. As before, her presence in the village drew a mixed reaction from the inhabitants. Polite greetings, curious glances, and venomous glares all came her way. Undaunted, she continued on to Theresa's cottage. Both of the elder Ungers were at home, in addition to three of the youngest family members, so Theresa hastily urged Leah to the far side of the street.

"I came to return this," Leah announced, proffering the silver brooch. "And to speak with you about—"

"Everyone knows you have returned to *him,*" said Theresa, her eyes bridling with reproach. "I thought you well away in Troy. Oh, Leah. Why did you come back?"

"Because I belong with my husband," she answered simply. "He came for me, Theresa. And, in truth, he convinced me that my absence would serve little purpose. I have returned to him for no other reason than the love we share."

"It is a cursed love."

"You are wrong."

"Am I? What shall you do then if Sir Nicholas Constinos loses his head because of the marriage?"

"That will not happen. Prince Michael himself has given his word."

"And you would believe the word of a Greek prince?" Theresa demanded scornfully. "You are a fool, Leah. May Athena's wisdom find you, you would risk all for the fleeting pleasures of a man's embrace."

"Do you not think—I."

"*Leah.*"

A sharp gasp broke from her lips. She whirled about, her eyes growing wide in mingled surprise and consternation as they fell upon Peatro Conrad

"I have waited many days to speak with you," he proclaimed in low, measured tones. His expression was forebodingly grave; his eyes held a cold glint as he approached her.

"We have naught to say to each other, Peatro," she insisted, endeavoring to keep her own voice steady.

"Langdon Fogus would have you come home."

"My home is at the palace now."

"Then you would still persist in your treachery?" he accused harshly.

"I have asked for your forgiveness, Peatro Conrad," she replied, with admirable composure, though inwardly her pulse quickened in growing alarm. "And for my foster father's as well. Truly, I am sorry to have caused you pain, yet my heart cannot change its course." She gasped anew when he suddenly seized her arms in a painful, punishing grip.

"Peatro!" cautioned Theresa.

"Do you think me witless, Leah Baal?" His expression had become menacing, and she blanched at the violence contained within his gaze. "I know that *Spartan* has seduced you into this traitorousness. I know that he has used evil trickery to keep you at his side!"

"You show yourself a fool," she charged furiously, struggling within his grasp. "Release me at once!"

"Peatro, please," Theresa appealed, clutching at his arm in a near frantic effort to make him see reason. "Would you bring Sir Nicholas' elite down upon us?"

"I would bring Lord Hades himself down upon us if it would purge her of this madness!" Still, he released Leah and stood eyeing her balefully while she, concealing her fear, rubbed at her bruised arms.

"Touch me ever again, Peatro Conrad, and I shall forget the friendship we have shared these many years past," she promised.

"Have you not forgotten it already?" he flung back, driven by pride and heartache and a thirst for revenge. "Stay with the master of Karabey awhile yet, Leah Baal. Linger within his bed. But know that your accursed marriage will soon come to an end."

"Do you dare to threaten me then?"

"I dare far more than you yet know." He compressed his lips into a tight, thin line of ill-disguised anger before vowing, "I will not be shamed by you. *Traitorous wench!*" With that, he turned upon his heels and stalked away.

"Peatro!" she called after him. But it was too late.

"I warned you that he had a mind toward vengeance," Theresa reminded her "He still speaks of a rebellion."

"He will suffer for such talk," murmured Leah, her eyes clouding at the memory of what had just occurred. "If my husband hears of it—"

"Will you be the one to betray Peatro?"

"No!" She shook her head in a vehement denial. "By all the gods on high, Theresa, how can you suggest it?"

"I have known you since we were children together, Leah. You were ever willful, ever high-spirited. But you have changed. I have seen the change in you. Since the day Sir Nicholas Constinos came to claim Karabey, you have seemed as though bewitched."

"I *have* changed, it is true. Yet the change required no magic—only a love so strong that I could not resist it. I am no traitor. I have forgotten neither my family nor my friends—nor all that has come before."

"You must seek to make amends."

"I shall do everything within my power to ensure a better life for the people of Karabey. If they see that Greek and Turks can live together in peace ..." Her voice trailed away, and she was silent for a moment before demanding softly, "Do you love Ronald Cayden?"

"What?" echoed Theresa, surprised at the question. "Why do you ask?"

"Because if you love him, you will understand." A faint smile touched her lips before she stepped forward to offer the other woman a quick, affectionate embrace. "You have always been a good friend to me, Theresa Unger I shall never set aside our friendship."

"Nor I," Theresa replied in all sincerity.

Leah headed back to the palace then, still greatly troubled by her encounter with Peatro. To make matters' worse, she crossed through the gates to find that Nicholas had returned unexpectedly. One look at his handsome, thunderous countenance made her whisper a prayer for guidance.

CHAPTER 13

▼

Before she could offer an explanation, he took her by the hand and led her up the steps of the keep. Once inside, he continued onward until they were within the privacy of their bedchamber. She watched in growing apprehension as he closed the door and turned slowly about to confront her.

"I did not think you would return so soon," she remarked, cursing the telltale quaver in her voice.

"My horse suffered an injury." He frowned darkly. His gaze seared down into hers. "Why did you go into the viliage alone, Leah?"

"I wanted to speak with Theresa."

"Have I not warned you—?"

"Yes, my lord. But would you keep me a prisoner within these walls?" she asked, her eyes kindling at the thought. "I am in no danger. Karabey is my home. If I were to shut myself away, to keep myself separate from them, then it would look as though I believed myself to be dishonored. I cannot allow it to seem as though I fear their judgement upon me. If we are ever to hope for an acceptance of our marriage, I must show that I am not ashamed."

"Perhaps you are right," he acknowledged, his brow creasing into a pensive frown now. "Still, you have disobeyed me again."

"And shall no doubt continue to do so," she parried, thoroughly unrepentant.

"Insolent siren," he murmured, with a low, resonant chuckle. His hands closed gently about her arms. She suffered a sharp intake of breath, dismayed to feel herself wincing in pain.

"What is wrong?" he demanded sharply.

"Nothing," she lied.

"You are hurt." He wasted little time in unfastening her gown and baring her arms. She looked down to see that her flesh bore the faint yet distinguishable marks of Peatro's hands. Her throat tightened; it was with dread that she looked up at Nicholas. "Who has done this?" His tone was one of deadly calm.

"No one."

"By Zeus and Hades, woman! *Who was it?*"

"It matters not," she exclaimed, hastily pulling her gown back up into place. She turned away, her heart drumming in her ears while she searched desperately for the correct words with which to diffuse his anger. "It was an accident, one best forgotten!"

"An accident?" he repeated, obviously disbelieving. He advanced on her again. "Tell me what happened, Leah."

"I went into the village to pay a visit to Theresa. While there, I-I did but collide with one of the older men. He reached out to steady me, and in so doing must have unintentionally offered me injury. I am in no pain, my lord, and implore you to forget the matter."

"You lie."

She whirled to face him again, her dread increasing at the piercing steadiness of his gaze. A sudden lump rose in her throat. She swallowed hard and shook her head. "It is the truth," she asserted, striving to do so with as much conviction as possible.

"Was it Peatro Conrad?" he suddenly demanded. He knew he had his answer when hot, guilty colors stained her cheeks.

"Peatro?" She quickly averted her gaze from his. "*No*. No, I have not seen Peatro since—"

"Whatever else has been between us, Leah, we have always been honest with each other." The look he gave her now was hard, compellingly intense. "Will you continue in the lie, or will you admit what we both know to be true?"

"Oh, Nicholas. You must not seek to retaliate against him." She raised her hands to his chest; her eyes were full of a heartfelt appeal. "He was angry. We quarreled. Yet I am certain he did not mean to harm me. Please, may we not forget it?"

"We may not," he decreed grimly. His eyes smoldered with murderous, white-hot rage, but he gave no outward indication of it as he started for the doorway.

"Where are you going?" she demanded, wide-eyed and breathless.

"At this moment, Leah," he paused to tell her, "I am not the master of Karabey. I am not the chief captain under Lord Ares. I am simply your husband, and as such I would punish any man who offers you insult."

"*No,*" she choked out. Terrified at the thought of what he might do, she entreated him to wait. "Nicholas, please!" But he was gone.

Her nerves were strung tight as a bowstring while she waited for him to return. Thalia offered her the distraction of a walk and pleasant conversation, but she could think of nothing save Nicholas. Her mind conjured up all sorts of horrible imaginings—she knew her husband to be capable of killing Peatro, and she knew that Peatro's thirst for revenge might well prompt him to further disaster. These thoughts, and others, haunted her throughout the next two hours. The minutes crawled by with agonizing unhaste. Finally she glanced up from her seat beneath the window in the great hall and caught sight of Nicholas as he strode inside. She leapt to her feet, racing across the room to fling herself upon his chest. "Sweet Hera, I feared you dead," she said.

"Have you so little confidence in my abilities, lady wife?" he teased, though without a great deal of humor.

"What happened? Did Peatro—?"

"Peatro Conrad was not to be found." He frowned, his eyes still gleaming hotly. "His mother claims to hold no knowledge of his whereabouts."

"He must have taken flight then," Leah murmured, flooded with relief. She was glad when Nicholas's strong arms came about her. "Perhaps he will not return."

"He will yet answer to me," vowed Nicholas. Releasing her, he moved away to take up a solemn, preoccupied stance before the fire.

"He-he spoke of a rebellion," she confided reluctantly.

"Yes."

"Do you not fear that he will gather others to rise against you?"

"I fear little, Leah." His mouth curved into a faint, ironic smile. "Save losing you."

"You shall never lose me," she promised. Swiftly closing the distance between them again, she lifted her hand to his arm and declared earnestly, "With all my heart, with all my body and soul, I love you."

"And I you." He drew her close again, the fury within him easing somewhat now. "I would have killed him, Leah. I would kill any man who dares to touch you." He released a heavy sigh and tightened his arms about her. "With you alone, I am at peace."

"It is the same with me." She smiled as she challenged in a playful tone, "And did you not find at least some measure of happiness among the beautiful, attentive ladies in Greece?"

"Never," he answered, pressing a tender kiss to the silken smoothness of her temple. He held her for several moments longer, until Thalia saw fit to intrude upon them.

"I would speak with you, my lord," she requested, not the least bit embarrassed to witness their embrace.

"Then do so." Reluctantly he allowed Leah to draw away. He wandered back to stand behind the table, his eyes traveling to his sister.

"Is it true that I am *not* to leave two days hence?" asked Thalia.

"I have decided that you may prolong your visit."

"Indeed? Perhaps, then, you might be prevailed upon to allow me to stay until the year's end."

"That is yet a month away," he pointed out.

"I would like to celebrate the eve of the new year here in Anatolia. I would like it very much."

"I have little doubt of that." His brown eyes glowed with a trace of wry amusement, but he schooled his features to impassivity. "I will consider it."

"Thank you, brother." She smiled at Leah. "I have every confidence that we shall manage to effect great and wondrous changes by then."

"The palace grows more comfortable with each passing day," Leah observed, determined that she herself would learn more about running such a large household. It was time she assumed the role of Lady Lord ... time she acquired more of the housewifery skills Dame Frances had hoped to find in her. "It may yet come about that Karabey Palace is known as a fine, welcoming place."

"Even if that were not so," said Nicholas, his gaze capturing hers once more, "I would consider Lord Ares' reward beyond compare."

Her heart fluttered at the sound of his words. And later, when the two of them lay together in the firelit warmth of their bedchamber, she pressed close to his lean, virile hardness and felt a contentment so deep, so pure and stirring, that she knew she would never regret the day the fates had thrown her across his path.

The following afternoon, she was pleasantly surprised when he suggested that the two of them ride alone. Excited at the prospect, she hastened to don her simple blue woolen gown and hooded cloak. Nicholas was waiting for her when she reemerged from the keep, and led her to where the saddled horses waited.

"Do you think it wise, my lord, for the two of you to be seen together?" Josh came forward to voice his concern. "It might well add fuel to the fire of discontent already burning within the village."

"It is time we demonstrated that we shall remain united," Nicholas replied. He exchanged a quick look of understanding with Leah. "As my wife has seen fit to advise me, the good people of Karabey will be far more likely to accept our marriage if we show ourselves among them."

"Still, it may yet be too soon," Josh sought to argue.

"I fear no attacks upon us." The ghost of a smile played about Nicholas's lips when he added, "I leave you to entertain my sister in my absence. She would, I think, enjoy a turn about the courtyard."

His eyes filled with an unholy light of amusement when he observed the dull flush that came over his friend's face.

Leah was quick to take pity on Josh. "In truth, Sir Josh," she offered amiably, "Lady Thalia *did* make mention of a desire to assist Dame Frances in the planning of the garden. Perhaps the two of you may discuss it with her."

"Perhaps," he murmured, responding to her suggestion with a rather wry smile of his own.

With Nicholas's assistance, she mounted up and reined about. He rode at her side as she set off across the drawbridge. The sky had threatened rain for most of the day, but there was as yet no scent of it in the air. The cold November wind swept across the countryside, bringing with it the promise of a frost in the coming night. Leah reveled in the freedom she felt as the horse carried her swiftly away from the palace and beyond the surrounding hills. She bent low in the saddle, doing her best to outpace her husband, but he had soon overtaken her. After calling out a protest for his ungallant behavior, she laughed and watched as he slowed his mount to a canter.

The two of them visited three of the outlying farms during their ride. At each one, Leah was treated with a wary distrust. But she remained cordial, inquiring after the health of each family and the success of the harvest, and in so doing sensed that she had made at least some small measure of progress in showing herself to be no different from the Leah Baal they had known for so long. She was both pleased and proud at the manner in which Nicholas treated the farmers and their wives. He spoke to them more as equals than servants, never once displaying anything other than a genuine regard for their welfare. If they would but give him the chance, she reflected with an inward sigh, he would prove himself a kind, just master.

"There is need of a school in Karabey," she told him as they left the third farm behind. Her words were prompted by the fact that she had just witnessed half a dozen children, all of them poorly protected against the winter, toiling outside the thatch-roofed cottage. She made a mental note to see that they were provided with warm clothing … though she would have to tread carefully in order to make certain the father's pride did not prevent an acceptance of the gift.

"Is there not a school at the temple square?" asked Nicholas.

"Yes, but very few can afford to seek attendance there. The children of the farmers have little hope of learning to read and write. Too often, they are left to grow up ignorant, with naught in their future save more of the same."

"I fear many would be reluctant to send their children to a village school." His brows knitted together into a thoughtful frown.

"Especially one of my making."

"And they may well resist traveling so far for something they consider insignificant. But still, we must try. None would have to know of your involvement." Her eyes sparkled as the sudden idea took hold. "I could speak to Oracle Victoria. She would—"

"Next, perhaps, you will insist upon a school within the palace walls." His tone was affectionate, teasing, and she could not help smiling in response.

"Do you dislike children, my lord?"

"No. And you, Leah?" His eyes met hers, and she was startled to hear him ask, "What if my child already grows within you?"

"A-a child?" she stammered. Her heart pounded fiercely; she felt a warm joyfulness spreading over her at the thought. *A child.*

"The idea does not displease you then?" Nicholas queried, watching her face closely.

"Not at all." She smiled again. "It is too soon to know yet," she cautioned.

"Then we shall continue to do all we can to ensure success." He gave a quiet chuckle at the sight of her rosy blush.

Twilight was fast approaching as they headed back toward the palace. Leah was surprised when, instead of approaching the gate, Nicholas set a course for the woods on the other side of the village. He led the way to the edge of the thick cluster of trees, then swung down from the saddle and waited for her to do the same.

"Why have we stopped here?" she asked, drawing her mount to a halt before him. "Darkness will soon fall. Should we not return to the palace?" With a mild frown of bemusement, she felt his hands close about her waist. He lifted her down and gathered up the reins of both horses.

"It was here that your singing beckoned," he reminded her. Looping the reins about the branch, he took her hand and urged her along with him into the cool, fragrant shadows of the forest. "Or have you forgotten?"

"You know I have not." She did not protest as he led her through the thick tangle of underbrush to the stream. The memory of what had happened between them there set her pulse to leaping wildly.

"Never did I think I would find my privacy intruded upon that day," she recalled, her crystal blue eyes aglow. She sank down upon the grass and trailed a hand lightly within the water as she faced her reflection.

"And I did not expect to be forever captivated by a golden-haired Turkishwoman who sung like a muse," said Nicholas. He bent to one knee beside her, his gaze following the direction of hers. "I had never heard or seen anything so beautiful."

"Perhaps that was how my mother bewitched my father as well."

"I do not doubt it." His arm caught her about the waist; he smiled tenderly down at her. "I suppose, like me, he had little chance of escape."

"Were you seeking escape, sir?" she demanded in mock indignation.

"In the beginning," he admitted. "But only because you were forbidden to me."

"It is a cruel statute that would make love a crime," she opinioned, her gaze momentarily clouding.

"Yes. For what it is worth, I intend to use any influence still within my possession to see that the new laws are struck down. No doubt there are others who find themselves caught in the midst of a similar quandary." His other arm came about her now as well, and he gave her a slow, thoroughly disarming smile as he drew her against him.

"But let us not talk of that. Not now."

"Very well. What *would* you prefer to talk about?" Already breathless, she allowed her arms to steal upward about his neck.

"Talk is not required at all." He lifted a gentle hand to caress her cheek. "Perhaps I should discover if your lips still taste as sweet as they did before."

"Have you not discovered the answer to that often enough these past several days?" she pointed out, her voice lowering to a seductive level.

"I have, but I would know if these woods possess any particular magic that aided in my 'entrapment,'" he replied huskily.

"Pray then, Spartan—do what you must to set your mind at ease."

She had no sooner offered the challenge than Nicholas accepted it. His mouth captured hers, his powerfully muscled hardness molding with perfection against her supple curves. In no time at all, the two of them lay together upon the thick cushion of grass. Briefly Leah thought to protest that they might be seen, but she was soon past caring as Nicholas's fierce, skillful lovemaking took her to dizzying new heights of passion. She gasped at the rush of cold air upon her bare skin as he raked up her skirts, and she squirmed in restless pleasure, her cheeks flaming, when his mouth roamed hotly—wickedly—across the saucy curve of her bottom. An unspoken question rose within her mind when his fingers urged her hips upward, but her bewilderment was not of a lengthy duration. A soft cry escaped her lips when he thrust into her from behind, his manhood slipping easily into the moist, silken warmth of her feminine passage. His hand delved between her thighs as she strained back against him, and her eyes closed once more while she surrendered herself completely to the heart-stopping ecstasy that carried her skyward.

A short time later, after they had returned to the horses and mounted up, Leah could have sworn she heard the sound of something—or someone—moving about within the forest. She tensed.

Her eyes filled with apprehension before making a hasty, vigilant sweep of the nearby shadows.

"What troubles you?" Nicholas demanded, his own gaze narrowing imperceptibly as it searched her face.

"I thought …" She shook her head and gave him a smile, gathering up the reins more tightly. "It is nothing. My ears have deceived me."

"I should not have forced you to tarry so long in the cold," he remarked, with a frown.

"I do not recall the use of 'force' at any moment. And in truth, I found myself warmed." She was delighted to hear his soft, resonant laugh.

"Still, I have become careless since my arrival upon these shores."

"There *is* magic here," she warned him, her beautiful eyes dancing "Many have found themselves powerless against it."

"Yes. I begin to understand why the statutes are so anxious that we should keep ourselves separate."

They began riding toward the palace, yet Leah's gaze was drawn back to the woods one last time. She felt an involuntary shiver run the length of her spine—and turned away before she had caught sight of the man who stood watching her from just within the cover of the trees …

She was easily persuaded to sing after the meal in the great hall that evening. Her spirits soared when the elite, even Keith Robards, pronounced themselves willing to learn the lyrics to some of the ancient Byzantine ballads. The remainder of the evening passed in a pleasant whirl of songs, games, and conversation. For the first time since her marriage to Nicholas, Leah could tell that the resentment of some of the Greek men had begun to fade. Zeus willing, she thought hopefully, they would never have cause to bear her any more ill will.

She and Nicholas retired to their bedchamber, and soon slept peacefully in the warmth of the bed. It was nearing midnight when she was awakened by the sound of footsteps in the corridor. Her eyelids fluttered open; she cast a swift look down at her husband in the darkness. He slept on. She heard the sound again. Her curiosity well-aroused by now, she slipped carefully from beneath the covers, and tip-toed across to the door. She held her breath and pressed her ear against it, all the while wondering who would be roaming about at so late an hour.

On the other side of the door, Thalia crept past and continued on her way down the corridor. Her heart pounded erratically within her breast, and she knew a moment's true fear at the thought of what lay ahead. Her brother would be furious. The elite would be scandalized at her bold, shameless behavior. Even Leah was bound to disapprove. And Josh ...

Josh. She swallowed hard, paling as his face swam before her eyes. She knew that his anger could be fierce indeed. He might well lose his temper completely. Yet still, he could not deny the love they shared. He would have to agree to her plan. He would have to!

Quickly regaining both her courage and her determination, she drew her cloak more closely about her. She wore nothing save a delicate, white linen shift beneath it, and she had neglected to don a pair of slippers to shield her feet from the cold marble floor. Thus, she shivered a bit as she reached the winding turret stairs and descended to the rooms below.

Finally, she reached the small, private bedchambers that lay just off the great hall. After much work, they had been made habitable for the elite And Josh, she knew, slept alone within the one closest to the staircase She paused before it, the torchlight flickering softly downward from above. Her fingers were shaking as they closed about the outer handle. The door was unbolted. Her eyes lit with triumph at the discovery. She eased the door open and slipped into the cool darkness of the room. With great care, she closed the door behind her and leaned back against it for a few seconds, while her knees trembled and her throat tightened. "It is now or never," she whispered to herself bracingly. She drew off her cloak and lowered it to the floor. Her long chestnut tresses were unbound; they shimmered about her as she crossed slowly to the bed. It was not nearly so large as Nicholas's; in fact, it was scarcely spacious enough for Josh's tall, muscular frame. Thalia gazed down at the prone form of her beloved As was his usual custom, he wore nothing while he slept. One sinewy arm rested atop the covers. His sword lay close by in readiness on the far side of the mattress. His breathing was strong and steady, his features relaxed and looking much younger. Her heart swelled with the force of her regard for him. She was no longer afraid. Offering up one last prayer for success, she pulled up the covers and lay down beside Josh. He stirred, only a little at first, and then rolled to his side, his arm falling across her slender waist. Smiling, Thalia moved even closer. She caught her breath when her thinly clad curves pressed against his hard, naked warmth. Her pulse leapt in excitement—and in truth, no small amount of maidenly apprehension and she lifted a tentative hand to his shoulder. In the very next instant, he tensed. His eyes opened wide, and he came bolt upright in the bed. "What in Hades—?" he grounded out. Before Thalia could say anything at all, he caught up his sword and scrambled from the bed. She sat up and stared breathlessly across at him in the darkness. "Joshua?" she whispered, her voice tremulous and her eyes round as saucers.

"Thalia?" His own tone was one of stunned disbelief. He quickly lowered his sword to the bed and lit a candle. His gaze met Thalia's and he blinked hard, as though she had somehow stepped out of his dreams instead of through his doorway. "What are you—"

"I would marry you this night, Joshua," she proclaimed. She tilted her chin up to a defiant angle.

"By all the gods on high, have you gone mad?" he asked, his own eyes filling with incredulity.

"Indeed, I have not! I knew that you would not yet speak to my brother. I knew that he would be reluctant to agree to our marriage. So I have come in order that the two of us may wed under Byzantine law." A fiery blush stained her cheeks as her eyes strayed with a will of their own over his exposed, undeniable masculinity.

Josh muttered a blistering oath and snatched up the quilt. Abruptly wrapping it about his lower body, he stood scowling down at her with such obvious fury and reproachfulness that, had her determination not been so strong, she might well have taken flight.

"I told you I would have no part of this, Thalia," he reminded her.

"You must leave."

"Not until we are husband and wife," she insisted stubbornly. She took a deep, steadying breath and flung back the covers. Rising from the bed, she stood before him and asked, "Do you not wish to take me this night, dearest Joshua? Am I so undesirable to you then?"

Josh gave a low groan. His eyes smoldered as they raked over her, his blood running hotly. The linen shift concealed little from him. The candlelight played softly across her beautiful face, her full breasts, her sweet hips, and slender thighs. He wanted her more than he had ever wanted any woman. Zeus help him, he loved her. His heart told him that she was his for the taking. But his head-his head urged him to embrace honor and reason.

"Go back to your own room, my lady," he commanded grimly, giving little evidence of the battle raging within him. He moved to retrieve her cloak. He held it out to her and gave her a faint, sad smile. "This is not the way."

"You do not love me," she charged, hurt and angry that he should reject her. "You have captured my affection falsely. You have—"

"Accuse me of whatever you wish." He was so infuriated with her that he could have easily turned her across his knee as he had been threatening to do. But he knew that if he dared to set the flat of his hand upon her pretty backside, he would not settle for that alone. The image conjured up by such thoughts served to further inflame his desire. "I will not be a part to your dishonor!"

"How can I be dishonored when you refuse to touch me?" she retorted, unaware of how close danger lay.

"The fact that you are standing alone with me in the privacy of my bedchamber, in the middle of the night and clad as you are, would be more than enough to bring Sir Nicholas' wrath upon me."

"So you reject me because you fear my brother?"

"I reject you because when we *do* wed, Lady Thalia Constinos, it shall be with the blessings of both your brother and the gods."

"Oh, Joshua! I knew you loved me!" she cried, impulsively throwing herself at him.

He stiffened, gave another low groan, and tried to prevent his arms from gathering her close. But they would not be stilled, and he knew a moments exquisite torment as he pulled her against him. The quilt tumbled to the floor.

"You must go now," he said, his voice edged with barely controlled passion. "Before you are discovered here."

"There is no one about," she assured him. She entwined her arms about his neck and cast him a look that was innocently seductive.

"Please, my love. May I not stay with you awhile yet? We are betrothed now, albeit secretly. There can be no true sin if you would but hold me."

"Thalia ..." With remarkable self-control, he pushed her firmly away from him and drew the quilt about him once more. "You have much to learn about men."

"Have I not already declared myself a willing pupil?" A loud gasp broke from her lips then, for the door suddenly swung open behind her. She whirled, her countenance reflecting both startlement and dismay when she saw that it was her brother who stood ready to confront them—with sword in hand.

"Sir Nicholas!" she exclaimed.

"It is not what you think, my lord," Josh hastened to declare. Showing no fear, he pulled the quilt more securely about him and stepped forward. "We did but talk—"

"I would have a word alone with Sir Josh," Nicholas announced grimly as Leah now swept into the room.

"Please, my lord," she entreated, her arms slipping about Thalia's shoulders when the younger woman hastened to her side. "May we not speak of this in the morning?"

"We may not." The tone of his voice filled her with dread. She cursed her own unintentional part in the discovery. If she had not slipped from the bed in an effort to satisfy her curiosity, he would not have awakened and insisted upon investigating the footsteps in the corridor. He would not have eventually descended the stairs, drawn onward by the sound of voices.

"Joshua has done nothing wrong," Thalia proclaimed feelingly. "It is *I* who am to blame. Indeed, I came uninvited to his bed in the hope that we could be wed as you and Leah were."

"See that my sister returns to her bedchamber," Nicholas directed Leah.

"I will not leave you alone with him," Thalia protested. She narrowed her eyes at him and vowed hotly, "If you dare to harm him, my lord, I shall never forgive you!"

"If my mind were set upon revenge, your threats would sway me little." He allowed the merest ghost of a smile to touch his lips.

"Come, Thalia." Leah urged her gently. Though reluctant to do so, she led her from the room. The door closed behind them.

"Oh, Leah. What do you think he intends to do?" Thalia asked, her bright, anxious gaze straying back to the door.

"I do not yet know my husband as well as I should like," confessed Leah, "but I do not believe him capable of any true violence toward a man who is the same as a brother to him." She released a sigh and shook her head. "Whatever possessed you to do such a thing, Thalia?"

"I could endure no more of waiting." She was grateful when Leah helped her don her cloak. The two of them started back up the stairs.

"I feared that it might well be years before we could gain Sir Nicholas's consent for the marriage. And Josh would be patient."

Leah led the way into her own bedchamber. She and Thalia crossed to sit before the fire. Save for the crackle of the blaze and the faint whisper of the night wind, they heard nothing.

"I suppose I am to be sent back to Greece," Thalia said despondently.

"Perhaps not," Leah replied, trying to sound encouraging. She pulled her own shawl about her shoulders and stared into the flames.

"I have not forgotten my promise to plead your case whenever possible."

"I fear it will do little good now."

Mercifully they did not have to wait much longer. And when Nicholas strode into the room, Leah was relieved to note a glimmer of wry amusement within his dark brown gaze.

"Well, my lord?" demanded Thalia, rising to her feet to face him. Looking anything but contrite, she folded her arms across her chest and lifted her chin proudly. "What is to be my punishment then? Am I to be banished from Anatolia on the morrow? Or perhaps sent into a temple in order to reflect upon my transgressions?"

"You are ill-suited to the life of an oracle," Nicholas observed. He came forward to join them in front of the fire. "Your betrothal to Sir Josh Leonidas will become known without delay."

"My betrothal to—" Thalia started to echo, only to break off and fling her arms about his neck in supreme happiness. "Oh, dearest brother! I knew you could not be so cruel!"

"But," he stipulated, gently prying her arms away so that she would meet his gaze, "the marriage will not take place for a years time yet."

"What?" she cried indignantly. She whirled away from him and shook her head in disbelief. "Why? Why may we not be wed before then?"

"Because Sir Josh and I have agreed that you are not ready yet."

"Joshua would not agree upon that," she argued, yet knew in her heart that he had done so.

"One year, Thalia."

"I am certain it will pass quickly," Leah reassured her.

"Well …" Thalia murmured, her anger diminishing a bit as she cast another—more fair-minded—glance toward Nicholas. "At least you have spared him."

"Or perhaps merely sentenced him to a lifetime of torment," he parried dryly.

And so it was settled. Thalia returned to her bedchamber, happy in the knowledge that she would, indeed, become the wife of Josh, yet dreading the prospect of twelve long months in which she could only dream about what it would be like to share his bed. Once she had gone, Nicholas drew Leah down upon the fire-warmed rushes with him and wrapped his strong, loving arms about her.

"What prompted you to give your consent to the betrothal?" she asked, both puzzled and delighted at his change of mind.

"In the end, my love, I had little choice." He smiled and explained, "As you have told me, they care deeply for each other. And if my sister is set upon him for a husband, then Zeus help anyone who would seek to keep them apart. How can I hope to argue against such determination?"

"So his 'unsuitability' no longer matters then?"

"I did not say that. But perhaps, if they remain devoted enough to each other, any other impediments to the match will be overcome."

He reached for her. "Josh would have them live here in Karabey. If, that is, you do not object?"

"Object?" She stirred within his embrace and cast him a look of playful, wifely disdain. "I should like nothing better."

"Still, I must send her back to Greece for a time," he said, a mild frown creasing his brow. "And we must pray that Lord Ares will permit the union. It might well be that he is reluctant to do so once he learns of my own marriage."

"He would punish Thalia because of you?" Leah asked, her eyes bridling at the mere thought or such injustice.

"That, I cannot say." He climbed to his feet and pulled her up as well. "It grows cold. We must return to bed."

"But I am no longer sleepy."

"Then we will not sleep." He bent and scooped her up in his arms.

"I think, Sir Nicholas, that you are well-accustomed to having your own way," she said accusingly, though without any true grievance.

"I am," he readily admitted. His eyes burned down into the soft, luminous depths of hers. "But in this, my love, I would give pleasure as well as take it." And as he proved once more, he was ever a man of his word.

CHAPTER 14

▼

True to her determination, Leah set about assuming a greater role in her position as the new mistress of the household the very next day. Dame Frances, upon being asked, was only too happy to provide guidance in such matters. And Thalia, remarking that she, too, had a good deal to learn about housewifery before she married Josh, added her own enthusiasm to the tutelage.

A few of the men from the village finally drifted back to work at the palace, but none of the women saw fit to present themselves there. Leah knew it would be hardest of all to win *their* favor again. She was troubled by that thought, yet remained convinced that they would eventually unbend. Sooner or later, of course, Nicholas would have to put an end to their disobedience—by force, if necessary, in order to show that he would be master. And that was something she desperately wished to avoid.

When he suggested another afternoon ride, within the presence of Josh and Thalia as the four of them sought a well-earned respite within the courtyard, she colored faintly and whispered in his ear that he was wicked beyond belief. But he smiled and declared himself innocent of the charge. In truth, he told her, he wanted to visit Ponceel House.

"You wish to speak to my foster father?" she asked in surprise.

"Yes. And to see where you grew to womanhood."

"He will not welcome us there." She drew in a ragged breath, her eyes shadowing at the painful memory of Langdon Fogus's *fury* and recriminations. "I am certain he would be angered by the visit."

"At first, perhaps," conceded Nicholas. He drew her arm possessively through his again. His own gaze filled with a darkness as he noted her disquiet. "But I would still seek to make peace between us. I know your heart to be heavy at the separation."

"Yes," she replied, then lapsed into thoughtful silence for a moment before adding, "I suppose it would do little enough harm to go." In truth, she had already begun warming to the idea. A reconciliation with Langdon and Louise would do much to lift her spirits. She wanted nothing more than *for* them to realize what a good, noble man she had wed. And if Langdon could somehow be won over, then there was every reason to hope that others would follow his lead. Though not quite so beloved as Viggo Baal had been, he was nonetheless well-respected by his friends and neighbors.

They took their leave of Josh and Thalia shortly thereafter, and were soon riding past the village. Leah was nervous at the prospect of facing her foster parents again. Her apprehension increased as she and Nicholas drew closer to Ponceel House. The sight of it, nestled like an old faded jewel within the green-mantled swell of the hills, brought a lump to her throat. She fought back sudden tears and reined her mount to a halt but a short distance away.

"It is not nearly so grand as it once was," she told Nicholas. "Yet I love it well."

"Then so shall I." Their eyes met, and she drew strength from the tender look he gave her.

Continuing down the hill, they rode to the front of the house and dismounted. Leah's heart was drumming in her ears as she stepped up to the weathered, iron-banded door and raised her hand to knock. After what seemed like an eternity, the door was opened by her foster mother. "Leah!" Louise exclaimed, both joy and astonishment written on her face. She did not hesitate before catching her up in an affectionate embrace.

"I have missed you, Louise," Leah murmured, relief washing over her at the lack of either anger or reproach in the older woman's greeting.

"And I you," said Louise. She held her at arm's length now and appeared pleased at what her eyes beheld. Her gaze traveled past Leah. "This is your husband, then?"

"It is," Leah confirmed, casting a glance back over her shoulder at Nicholas.

He stepped forward and offered Louise a polite smile and nod. "I have long desired your acquaintance, Dame Louise," he told her quietly.

"I-I thank you, my lord," she stammered. She subjected him to a swift critical appraisal before commenting on his superior height.

"You are quite large!"

"He is, indeed," Leah replied, with a soft laugh. Her smile faded, however, when she queried, "Is Langdon not at home?"

"He is home," Louise answered, then frowned worriedly. "I fear he will not be pleased that you have brought Sir Nicholas with you. Though he would have you home again, he has not yet forgiven you for your disobedience."

"And you, Louise?" she asked in earnest. "Have you forgiven me?"

"I have done so. Sweet Hera, child! Was I ever capable of bearing you a grudge? Yet I cannot deny that I am troubled by your marriage. You have broken the promise given by your mother. And Peatro ..." She heaved a sigh and lifted a hand toward the room that lay just off the entrance foyer. "Langdon is within the library at present."

"Then we shall seek a meeting with him."

She was grateful for the warmth of Nicholas's hand upon her as they stepped inside. Louise, anxious to avoid any role in the confrontation, escaped to the sanctuary of the kitchen, leaving Leah to open the door to the library. Her gaze sought and immediately fell upon her foster father, who stood from his desk and reddened with anger.

"What are you doing here?" he demanded, his narrow, wrathful gaze slicing to Nicholas before fastening on Leah once more. "Have you so little regard for my feelings that you would bring this Spartan into my house?"

"He is my husband, Langdon," she reminded him, lifting her head proudly. "I would have you—"

"Do not take that tone with me!" he growled, turning abruptly toward the window.

"If you will not speak, then you must listen." She moved away from Nicholas and crossed to the older man's side. Her hand touched his arm, her eyes full of a heartfelt entreaty. "May we not have peace between us, Langdon? I love you well, and I would see you happy. But I could not have wed Peatro Conrad. If I have shamed myself, then so be it." When he maintained his obstinate silence, she demanded more sharply, "Will you not at least pay respect to my husband?"

"By the blood of the gods, girl, you go too far!" Langdon thundered, rounding on her in a burst of fury.

"Leah, please leave us," Nicholas commanded in a voice of calm authority

"Leave you?" She stared up at him in bemusement. "But I would stay."

"Leave us," he reiterated, not unkindly.

She obeyed, though with a visible reluctance. When the door closed behind her, she did not move away, but rather leaned against it in an effort to hear what was being said in the library. It was unworthy of her, and she knew she would suffer a pain of guilt for it later, yet she would know if there was any hope of a truce—however precarious—between the two men she loved best.

"I will speak plainly, Langdon Fogus," Nicholas began, his eyes holding a steel glint. "Leah is my wife. She will remain so. Your lingering anger wounds her greatly, and *that,* I will not tolerate."

"You will not tol—?" Langdon started to echo in disbelief, then reddened anew. "Your threats do not frighten me, Sir Nicholas Constinos."

"I have not come to threaten. But I will not see her hurt. So we must understand each other—I will honor you as her foster father, and you in turn will honor me as her husband. There is no need to pretend any friendship between us. Only a mutual, albeit grudging, respect."

"And if I do not agree?"

"Then she will be forever lost to you."

"You would deny Leah her own family?" demanded Langdon.

"No. *You* would do so." He slowly closed the distance between them, a faint smile touching his lips. "Karabey is mine now. I will not leave I would have us live in harmony, yet I know there are those who would destroy any hope of peace."

"We are not all so inclined," the older man insisted.

"Perhaps not. I know you to be a good man, else Leah would not love you as she does."

"You stole her from Peatro Conrad," Langdon suddenly accused, unable to forget how his plans had been thwarted.

"Yes, and would do so again."

"Then you are no better than the others who have come before."

"I have never claimed to be so," replied Nicholas, shaking his head. "Still, I would try. With Leah at my side, I am convinced that much can be achieved."

"She was ever headstrong," Langdon recalled, half to himself, as the rage finally began to subside.

"She has not changed." Nicholas's gaze lit with a touch of humor at the thought. He quickly sobered again, however, and asked in a quiet, level tone, "Shall we not have an agreement between us then, Langdon Fogus?"

The Turkishman appeared to be pondering all that he had heard. His brows knit together into a deep, pensive frown, and he breathed an oath as he folded his arms tightly against his chest. "It is not so easy," he muttered at last, his gaze falling beneath the steadiness of Nicholas's.

"Nothing of any true worth is easily obtained."

"She is happy?" They both knew he spoke of Leah.

"She is."

"And you will not set her aside?"

"Never," vowed Nicholas.

"Peatro Conrad will not rest until he has gained his revenge," Langdon warned him. "I … You should take care, for there are rumors that some would take up arms against you."

"I have heard the rumors. But it changes naught."

"And what of the danger to Leah?"

"I will protect her," he promised, his features looking quite solemn.

"None shall harm her."

Langdon appeared at least somewhat satisfied with that answer. His brow cleared a trifle more; he uncrossed his arms. Following another long moment of silence, he turned back to Nicholas and released a long pent-up sigh, more of weary resignation than contentment.

"I know you have both the power and the right to do as you please," he said stiffly, "but I would ask you to treat her as befits the mistress of Karabey."

"I give you my word that she will never know anything save honor and devotion at my hands," Nicholas assured him.

"And what of the law you have broken?"

"I have spoken with Prince Michael of Thrace. It may yet be that I am to forfeit my holdings as a result of the marriage. But even then, Leah and I will not be parted." He decreed it with so much resolve, so much assurance, that Langdon could not help believing him.

On the other side of the door, Leah's eyes glowed with mingled elation and relief. She whirled about, anxious to share the good news with Louise.

By the time she and her foster mother returned to the entrance foyer a short time later, their husbands were emerging from the library.

"It would please me to see the remainder of the house now,"

Nicholas requested of Leah, his manner casual but his eyes telling her of his satisfaction.

"And you must have some bread and wine before you are on your way again," offered Louise, then ventured a quick glance at Langdon to see if he would dare to say otherwise.

"I fear our wine may not be fine enough to suit the lord," he put forth gruffly. "Still, they are welcome to it."

Leah impulsively pressed a kiss to the roughness of his cheek. He allowed his arm to stray about her waist before declaring himself too busy with his books to spend any more time upon leisure.

Apollo had already begun to draw the sun low upon the horizon by the time Nicholas and Leah left Ponceel House behind. He announced that they would detour through the village on their way homeward; Leah's stomach knotted anew at the prospect, but she voiced no argument against it.

They reined to a halt and dismounted upon reaching the edge of the village. Leading their horses behind them, they set off toward the market square. At that late hour of the afternoon, many of the Turks had already sought the warmth of their homes in preparation for the coming night, but there were still a number of people wandering about the streets and alleyways.

Leah's gaze remained wary and vigilant as she walked alongside Nicholas. Though she did not believe anyone would be so foolish as to offer them insult, she knew that there were some who would look upon them with unmistakable hostility or resentment. They passed several whose astonishment at seeing them there was apparent, and when they stepped into the square, it was to find a small crowd of men and women who abruptly ceased their conversation when their eyes fell upon the newcomers. A few of them appeared ready to offer Leah a greeting, but thought better of it when they realized that they could not do so without speaking to the Spartan as well. Silence, they concluded, was perhaps the best weapon of all.

"You have made yourself scarce enough here, my lord," Leah murmured to Nicholas as she took note of the familiar faces about them. "Were it not for my presence at your side, you might well pass unrecognized as the lord"

"I begin to think my patience has lingered too long," he remarked, his voice holding an edge.

"Leah Baal!" someone called out unexpectedly above the silence.

Leah's gaze quickly discovered Oracle Victoria in the midst of the crowd. She hastened toward her. "Though, I suppose it is 'my lady' now," she amended, smiling as she warmly clasped her hand. She turned to Nicholas and declared, "I have not yet made your acquaintance, my lord. I am Oracle Victoria."

"Oracle Victoria," said Nicholas, giving her a curt nod. "I would have a word with you soon."

"Indeed? Then I shall call upon you tomorrow." She shivered and clutched the edges of her cloak together when a sudden gust of wind swept through the square. "Winter fast closes in."

"I pray that it will not be so harsh as the one we endured last year," Leah remarked, still acutely conscious of the many eyes upon them.

"Well, I shall leave you to be on your way," the elder oracle announced. She directed a polite nod of her own toward Nicholas, then took Leah's hand again. Her eyes were kind, her manner genuinely compassionate when she told her, "You are always welcome at the temple. And in time, with Lord Zeus's help, you shall once again find yourself welcomed in Karabey."

"Thank you, Oracle Victoria." She smiled in gratitude and watched as she hurried away.

"It is a beginning," Nicholas observed, with a faint smile.

"Yes," she responded, her beautiful eyes softly aglow. "It is a beginning."

Another two days flew past. Leah's time was much occupied with household matters, while Nicholas's duties as the new lord kept him equally busy. Most of the Turks continued to defy the law and did not present themselves to him for the required settlement of rents and taxes, yet the few who did come were greatly relieved to find him every bit as fair-minded as Leah had known he would be. Oracle Victoria, of course, knew no such qualms about venturing inside the great hall where Nicholas and Josh awaited; she looked upon her own visit to the palace as an opportunity to set a much needed example for her stubborn, recalcitrant flock. If she could show herself willing to cooperate with the Greek, then perhaps the barriers would finally begin to tumble.

Though Leah was not present at the meeting between them, she demanded a full accounting of it from Nicholas afterward. He told her that they had spoken of a school, of repairs to the temple square, and of other matters as well. When pressed to clarify what these 'other matters' might be, he would only say that she would not be displeased when the time came to reveal them. She chided him for his reticence—and would not permit him to take her in his arms as he would have done. But later, when he caught her up against him in the shadows just beyond the great hall, she gave a soft laugh and did not protest at the boldness with which his mouth roamed across the creamy flesh swelling above the neckline of her bodice.

Life settled into a routine of sorts, though one overshadowed by a pervasive, inescapable feeling of uneasiness. There had been no word concerning the rumored insurrection, no reports of rebel armies gathering or suspicious amassment of weapons. For now, there was nothing to do but wait.

In spite of the worry, Leah was happier than she had ever been.

She would not have thought it possible, but her love for Nicholas grew stronger with each passing day. They delighted in making new discoveries about each other—and were ever anxious for the moment each evening when, once the palace was quiet and the other members of the household had retired for the night, they could seek the sort of intimacy that only the truest of lovers can know.

The elite offered more than one favorable, lighthearted comment regarding the changes wrought in their lord—no longer, they said, did he scowl and curse as often as he had once done. Leah had coaxed forth the warmth and humor within him. And in so doing, had found her own peace. There were other changes to be celebrated as well. Three days after she and Nicholas were seen together in the village, Leah was treated to the sight of Mabel, Mildred, Angela, and Theresa crossing the drawbridge together. None of them had stepped foot within the temple square since before the feast of *Artemis.* Their return to the palace was particularly significant, for they were the first women from the village to break the stalemate.

Her eyes sparkling with both pleasure and surprise, Leah hurried forward to greet them as they approached the kitchen building. The late afternoon sky was choked with heavy, ominous gray clouds; the coming night threatened to bring with it a torrent of wind and rain. But she took little notice of the storm that was brewing, for her spirits were much lightened.

"I am so very happy to see you," she exclaimed sincerely, smiling at the four women. They each wore heavy woolen shawls to protect them from the November chill.

"We have not come to please you, Leah Baal," Mabel declared sourly, her gaze narrow and belligerent.

"Still your tongue, Mabel Dorrance," Mildred said quickly. She returned Leah's smile, though tentatively, and said, "Some of us were of a mind to return before now. But ..."

"You are truly wed to him, Leah?" Angela asked, her normally serene expression replaced by one of incredulity.

"Truly," Leah confirmed, then admitted, "I feared I would never see any of you here again." Nicholas had said that time and patience would do much to heal the rift, she recalled. Zeus be praised ... If he had consented to the elite's demand for a show of force, there was every possibility that calm would have proven forever impossible. Her heart swelled with immeasurable pride and love and admiration for his wisdom.

"It was Langdon Fogus's doing," Theresa now revealed, her eyes full of warmth. "Once it was known that he had made a truce with Sir Nicholas, others were persuaded to follow his lead. And Oracle Victoria has told everyone of the school. I cannot say that they are prepared as yet to offer your husband the loyalty and obedience he seeks, but I think many are no longer ready to risk everything for a moments useless defiance. May Lord Zeus bless us all. Come the eve of the new year, we will have at least the start of peace in Karabey."

"I would be glad of it," Leah replied. She embraced her affectionately, whispering close to her ear, "Perhaps now, Theresa Unger, you begin to see why I could not leave him."

"Still, we must pray none will rise against the Greek," Mildred cautioned. She frowned and shook her head. "Peatro Conrad holds influence. If he is not willing to abandon his quest for revenge, there may yet be some who would join with him in rebellion."

"I doubt those in Karabey would do so," Theresa insisted. "In spite of what has happened, I do not think any man here either brave or foolish enough to—"

"There are others in Anatolia who have waited for such a time," said Mildred. "They would use Leah's marriage to Sir Nicholas as an excuse to revolt."

"And would meet with naught save tragedy," murmured Leah, her gaze clouding at the thought.

"Have we not work to do before night falls?" Mabel reminded everyone with her usual sharpness.

"Who has done the cooking of late?" Angela asked, looking to Leah again.

"A Greek woman called Dame Frances has taken charge of the kitchen, aided by two maidservants. Sir Nicholas's sister, Lady Thalia Constinos, and I have mastered a few skills. But in truth," she concluded while the sparkle returned to her eyes, "I am convinced that the elite shall offer a prayer to Demeter for your return."

"They deserve naught better," Mabel muttered under her breath.

"No, Mabel," Leah scolded her, quietly yet firmly. "I shall hear no more against them."

"You would place them above your own people then, Leah Baal?" the older woman accused in anger.

"It is Leah Constinos now." Her eyes kindled with a fiery determination, while her tone was quite low and level. "And, but for Sir Nicholas Constinos, I would place no man higher than another."

Mabel appeared ready to say more, but Mildred would not allow it. She took her by the arm and propelled her into the kitchen. Angela gave Leah a rather weak, timid smile before following after them. Theresa tarried with Leah for several moments longer, anxious that they should have no lingering ill will between them.

"It was wrong of me, urging you to leave Sir Nicholas as I did," Theresa confessed, then heaved a long sigh. "I have thought much about what you said. About Ronald Cayden and myself. About love."

She paused, visibly searching for words while her gaze fell. "You spoke the truth, Leah. If we have not love, then what else can matter? The heart chooses the man, neither his duty nor his position."

With another sigh, she raised her eyes to Leah's once more.

"Perhaps I begin to understand."

"Oh, Theresa," said Leah, touched by her friend's words. She clasped her arm warmly and offered her a smile that told Theresa all she needed to know.

The meal that night was not so very much superior to the ones Dame Frances and the maidservants had prepared, yet Thalia made the mistake of declaring it the most superb she had enjoyed since leaving Greece. There were hurt feelings to be soothed afterward, and it was necessary to assure Dame Frances that her position within the household had suffered little as a result of the Turkish-women's triumph in the kitchen, but order had been restored by the time everyone within the palace sought their beds.

Nicholas had been nearly as pleased as Leah when she had told him of the women's return. Like her, he recognized it as an important step toward harmony.

"Much has changed since you came to Karabey," she remarked, sitting with him before the warmth of the fire in their bedchamber. She cherished these times when the two of them were alone, when they could share their thoughts and plans and dreams.

"For me as well." Seated upon a great carved chair, he held her upon his lap and gazed deeply into the flames. The storm had broken but an hour ago. The air was filled with the scent of rain. The sound of it drumming upon the roof above was at once steady and soothing.

"Have you yet received no word from Prince Michael?"

"No. He has much to occupy him in Troy at present."

"Nicholas?" She stirred within his arms now, her gaze soft and inquisitive as she turned her head to face him.

"Yes, my love?"

"If we were forced to leave Karabey, would we truly remain in Anatolia?"

"I do not know," he answered honestly. Frowning, he gave a slight shake of his head. "There is little to call me back to Greece. My sister may not welcome a return home—of that I am certain. But I would not wish to find out."

"The Baals still hold land in the north country," she told him.

"Perhaps we could—"

"Would you have me seek the charity of your kinsmen?" he demanded, feigning considerable annoyance.

"It would not be charity," she said, quick to deny. "We would but receive my father's portion, to do with what we will."

"So you intend for us to farm."

"And why not?" She slid from his lap and wrapped her shawl more closely about her linen-clad body. "I am not afraid of hard work, my lord. We could have a good life there." Drawing nearer to the flames, she did not realize how appealing a picture she made.

The soft, flickering glow revealed the delectable curves beneath her thin shift and lit gold within the thickness of her hair. "I desire comfort as much as anyone else, but I would make whatever sacrifices were necessary in order to find happiness."

"Do you think you have wed a penniless man, Leah?" Nicholas asked, his tone vibrant and laced with an undercurrent of amusement now.

"You are but the younger child of a nobleman, are you not? And I know that Spartans often take a vow of poverty when they enter the service of Ares." She watched as he, too, stood and idly raised a hand to the mantelpiece. He wore nothing save his braies; his upper torso gleamed all hard and muscular and bronzed in the firelight.

"Karabey was given to me as reward for that service," he pointed out, his eyes glowing down into hers.

"Yes, and you now stand in peril of losing it."

"Even if that were to happen, I would still be no pauper."

"What do you mean?" she asked, gazing up at him in puzzlement.

"I mean, lady wife, that I possess enough money to purchase ample lodgings of my own—whether it be in Anatolia *or* Greece."

"But how can that be?" She shook her head—and was thrown into further confusion by the tender, indulgent smile he gave her. "If you have such wealth, then why did you choose to accept Karabey?"

"Because it was what Lord Ares wished. And because I was searching for something I had not yet found." He smiled again, his hands closing about her shoulders. "My elder sister inherited my father's estates, but my mother's fortune was left to me. I have had little need of it these many years past. Perhaps it can now be put to good use here."

"Why have you never told me this?"

"Would it have made any difference?"

"You know it would not have done so," she asserted, her crystal blue gaze kindling at the suggestion. She released a sigh and cast him a reproachful look. "It is only that I never would have thought myself married to a man with a fortune."

"Does it trouble you to learn that you will not have to toil in the fields?" he said, teasing.

"I would have done so, and gladly."

"I know." He reached for her, drawing her close while his expression grew more serious. "By Zeus, you are a woman like no other. Even if you had not captured my heart, you would have earned my admiration long ago."

She rested pliantly against him for several long moments. Then, her thoughts were drawn back to the surprising news she had just been given.

"If you do indeed possess such a fortune, my lord," she pondered aloud, "we shall be able to make a great many improvements to the palace, to the farms and the village, and even—"

"You *will* make a pauper of me yet," he chided.

The sound of his low, resonant chuckle made her knees grow weak. She tilted her head back to look up at him, a tremor of emotion—all of it pleasurable—coursing through her body when her eyes met the deep, provocative steadiness of his. "I would love you no less," she avowed softly.

"Then I have wealth above all others." He sat down in the chair again and cradled her upon his lap once more. She released a long, contented sigh "Nicholas?"

"My lady?"

"Now that Josh is to wed Thalia, do you not think it imperative that your other elite find wives as well?"

"I have given it little thought," he replied, his mouth twitching.

"I suppose it is unlikely any among them would be allowed to choose a Turkish bride," she murmured.

"The law still stands." He gave a slight frown as he stared into the flames. "Though I have been dealt with mercy, it would be unwise for them to follow my example. Zeus willing, the statutes will be struck down soon enough. But it would be folly to tempt the fates until that time."

"Then we must set about finding them Greek brides."

"There are none to be found in Karabey," he reminded her unnecessarily, his voice laced with wry amusement.

"No, but there are a goodly number of Greek women in Troy," she pointed out. "And in the northern territory as well."

"Perhaps so. But do you believe them incapable of conducting the search without your assistance?"

"I believe them reluctant to do so. without *your* blessing!"

"Tomorrow then, I will send them forth on the quest."

"Tease me if you must, but now that it appears there will be no rebellion to threaten us—"

"We have a beginning to peace, Leah," he cautioned her. "Nothing more. It is too soon as yet to know if any will rise against us."

"So you think the danger still present?"

"I am not yet prepared to believe it past."

"But you are optimistic, are you not?" she persisted, raising her head to search his face again.

"Yes," he conceded, with a faint smile. "Cautiously so." She knew she would have to settle for that.

Sighing again, she leaned her head upon his shoulder and closed her eyes. His strong arms tightened about her. The fire crackled and hissed softly, filling the room with light and warmth, chasing away the cold and the darkness and adding to the sweet contentment of the moment.

CHAPTER 15

▼

The remainder of the week passed in a continuing whirl of activity. And on Saturday morning, not long after the drawbridge had been lowered, more than a dozen Turkishmen crossed into the square to add their efforts to the work. Leah's eyes lit with pleasure and satisfaction at the sight of them. Her own optimism increased daily; she dared to hope that the coming of a new year would bring with it the peace and prosperity for which the villagers had so long waited. Oracle Victoria had returned to the palace twice more, and even Langdon and Louise had promised to visit soon. Theresa and the other women came daily. Indeed, it was beginning to appear as though they took considerable pride in their kitchen tasks. Mabel, in particular, seemed no longer of a mind to poison the Greek men. Her culinary skills were much praised by the elite. There were still a few dissenters in Karabey, of course, those who would not be silenced in their murmurings against the Greek, but the atmosphere had become far less volatile. And would, prayed Leah, continue to improve. She had been told that her marriage to Sir Nicholas Constinos, while initially viewed as traitorous, had done much to encourage the truce. But she knew that Peatro Conrad would never accept it. He had not been seen since the day he had threatened her in the village. She hoped that he would start a new life elsewhere, that he would find someone to ease his pain. A pain of guilt still gripped her heart whenever she thought of him. She told herself that she had never meant to cause him any suffering. Still, she felt the loss of his friendship acutely.

Winter was closing in rapidly now, the days growing shorter and the air snapping with the cold. Life within the palace, however, was warm and comfortable. Leah enjoyed the evenings spent in the great hall with Nicholas and Thalia and the elite. She took pleasure in her deepening acquaintance with the men, and could not help but smile at Thalia's attempts to provoke Josh. It was clear that their marriage would be something of a battle of wills. It was equally clear that Josh, though both adoring and indulgent, would always possess the upper hand.

By late in the afternoon upon that Saturday, the work within the courtyard had ceased. The villagers had returned to their homes. The drawbridge was raised and the portcullis lowered as darkness fell. Night deepened, the clear and endless sky lit by a host of twinkling stars. After the evening meal, Leah joined Nicholas where he stood before the fire in the great hall. He had received a message from Prince Michael but a short time earlier, informing him of a royal visit three days hence.

"Does the prince say nothing then of a decision regarding Karabey?" she asked, her gaze wide and anxious.

"No. Nor would he do so in a letter."

"It is cruel to keep us ignorant."

"Ignorant?" His mouth curved into a soft smile of irony, his eyes glowing hotly as they moved over her upturned countenance.

"Perhaps it would have served me better to wed a woman who lacked the ability to think so much."

"One does not exisist," she retorted saucily.

"I will exact revenge for that impertinence once we are abed, my lady," he promised, his vibrant tone lowering for her ears alone.

"Will the prince bring with him much of an entourage, do you think?" Keith wondered aloud. He sat opposite Brian at the table, a chessboard set up between them.

"You mean, will he bring *women* with him?" John corrected, a sly smile playing about his lips as he sprawled negligently back in his chair nearby.

"Do not ask us to believe that the same has not been upon your mind," Keith replied, with a challenging frown.

"More than upon yours, good Sir Keith."

"Women?" David echoed in his usual energetic voice. "Zeus bless them!" He raised the tankard of ambrosia to his lips and drank deeply.

"Faith, we cannot all possess the good fortune of Josh," said Brian, casting an envious glance toward the spot where Josh and Thalia sat together upon the bench beneath the window.

"Nor the courage and daring of our liege," John added, then proceeded to down the last of his own ambrosia.

Overhearing the conversation, Leah smiled knowingly up at Nicholas. "Did I not tell you of the need for matchmaking?" she whispered, folding her arms beneath her breasts.

"Zeus help me if we are to have four other ladies beneath this roof," he remarked dryly. Unmindful of the witnesses, he slipped his arm about her waist and drew her against him. She protested, albeit halfheartedly, and would have pulled away, but he would not allow it.

"I would see the palace filled with the laughter of children," she told him in earnest.

"And are we to begin yet?" His eyes searched her face closely.

"It is still too soon to know," she answered, then felt a rosy blush staining her cheeks. She had begun to suspect … No, in truth she knew already. A *child*. She was carrying Nicholas's child. All day long she had held the truth close to her heart. But she would not tell him now. Not until they were alone. The knowledge filled her with such happiness that she could scarcely conceal it. Her child, a child conceived in love, would have the best of both worlds. Turks and Greek. A *new beginning*.

"Leah?"

She was drawn *out* of her reverie by the sound of her name upon Thalia's lips. Turning her head, she saw that the older woman stood looking quite annoyed beside a solemn-faced Josh.

"Yes?" Reluctantly Nicholas let her go. She moved across to speak with Thalia.

"If you please," said Thalia, casting a reproachful look at her betrothed, "I would have you settle a quarrel."

"A quarrel?" Leah repeated. Hesitant to become involved, she shook her head. "Oh, Thalia. I fear—"

"Joshua would have me believe that I can better learn to become a dutiful wife if I am first shut away within a temple," the petite brunette declared indignantly.

"I said only that I would prefer for you to spend time there instead of returning to Greece," Josh reiterated, a discernible edge to his voice. His gaze was full of remorse when he told Leah, "It was not our intent to involve you, my lady."

"I need you to offer no apologies on my behalf, Sir Joshua Leonidas," said Thalia, her eyes kindling with anger.

"What you *need*, Lady Thalia, is something I have as yet no right to offer," he countered.

"Perhaps," Leah hastened to intervene, "it troubles Josh to think of you in the company of the handsome young gallants in Greece. Would you not allow that a man in love can be jealous?"

"Is that so, Joshua?" Thalia demanded, rounding on him again. She saw that he looked uncomfortable, but also that his eyes held the truth. Instantly contrite, she heaved a sigh and murmured, "I am sorry, sir, for having doubted you."

"By all the …" he muttered. He met Leah's gaze and his features suddenly relaxed into a crooked smile. "I am not at all certain, my lady, that a man likes his emotions laid bare with such ease."

"No doubt my husband will offer that same complaint," she replied, her blue eyes sparkling brightly.

"I think not," Josh insisted. A look of complete understanding passed between them in that moment. Thalia frowned in bemusement and impulsively grasped Josh's hand with her own.

"I know not what you mean," she confessed, "but mayhap I shall reach a greater comprehension of such things once we are wed."

"First you must school that accursed temper of yours," Josh put forth sternly.

"Does it not require *two* to make a quarrel?" she shot back, though with a playfulness that made his heart stir.

Leah left the two of them alone again. Returning to Nicholas's side, she caught a glimpse of the humor in his own gaze.

"I suppose this is but a taste of things to come," he grumbled. "I see before me a life made all the more unsettled by the presence of the brides you are determined to welcome here."

"Ah, but that life shall never be dull," she predicted in response.

"And in truth, I know you to be glad of it." She watched as a slow, thoroughly disarming smile spread across the rugged perfection of his face.

"You know too much." He drew her close once more, and this time she did not care who saw them.

Much later, long after everyone had settled into their beds for the night, Leah was once again awakened by the sound of the wind. It howled through the cracks in the great marble walls and whipped down the chimney to stir life within the dying embers. The air was heavy with the chill of it, the night sky clear and marked only by the curlings of smoke that rose from the village. Leah rolled to her side and snuggled closer to Nicholas's naked, hard-muscled warmth in an effort to sleep again. But her mind was racing too much to allow a return to slumber. The memory of Nicholas's joyful response to the news of her pregnancy was still fresh; she knew she would never forget the light in his eyes, or the deep-timbered resonance of his voice when he had declared himself the most content of men. Her hand moved instinctively to her abdomen and she smiled in the darkness. "Our child," she whispered, her heart swelling anew. Tears started to her eyes when her mother's face suddenly swam before them. She felt her sweet, loving presence and knew that she shared in the happiness. Casting a swift glance down at Nicholas, Leah climbed gently from the bed and tossed her cloak about her shoulders. She paused to don a pair of slippers, then eased open the door. Impulse called her forth, and she found herself descending the turret stairs to the great hall. A fire still burned within the massive stone fireplace. She immediately drew close to its warmth and stared into the flames while her thoughts drifted idly back over the events of the day. Her ears detected a sudden noise behind her. She turned her head, but had no time to react before a hand clamped with brutal force upon her mouth.

"Make a sound, Leah Baal, and you shall have cause to regret it!" a familiar voice hissed against her ear.

Her eyes opened wide, her pulse leaping in alarm.

Peatro Conrad!

His other arm snaked about her waist from behind, tightening until it threatened to cut off her breath. She felt her head spin and began to struggle. But he dragged her across to the far side of the hall and pulled her into the shadows. The thundering of the wind taunted her, drowning out the sound of Peatro's voice to all save herself. He held her there in the cold darkness, well away from the bedchambers where the elite lay sleeping.

"Did you think I had forgotten my vow of revenge?" he said with a sneer, startling her when he removed his hand from about her mouth. She sucked in a deep, ragged breath and sought desperately to remain calm. "You must leave, Peatro!" she told him in a quavering undertone. "Before it is too late. Before—"

"It is already too late," he said, cutting her off. He abruptly forced her about to face him, his hands seizing her arms in a hard, bruising grip "You are mine, Leah. You have always been mine. And before this night is through, you will know it!"

"No!" She shook her head in a vehement denial, then raised her own hands to his chest and appealed, "I know not how you came to be here, but you must leave before you are discovered. I shall tell no one." She spoke the truth, well aware that Nicholas would not hesitate to kill him this time.

"It was easy enough to gain entrance. To these Greek bastards, I appeared to be but yet another Turkishman, come to do their bidding along with the others. I had only to conceal myself and bide my time." His mouth curled into a bitter, humorless smile. "And soon enough, there will be no one to tell."

"What do you mean?" she gasped.

"I have come for you, Leah. I have come to claim my bride, the bride stolen from me by Sir Nicholas Constinos. But first, you will be made a widow."

"Dear Zeus, no!" Her eyes filled with horror; her heart twisted painfully within her chest. *Nicholas.* Her eyes flew upward and she opened her mouth to scream. But Peatro, anticipating her response, silenced her with the cruel pressure of his hand. He yanked her against him once more, his features ugly with hatred.

"There are four others with me this night," he revealed triumphantly.

"Four others who would see all Greek driven from these lands. The elite will be slaughtered in their beds, their throats cut as befitting such unholy swine. But I have saved for myself the privilege of killing the master of Karabey. By all that is holy, I will make him pay for what he has done!"

Stricken with terror at his words, Leah renewed her struggles. She twisted violently within his grasp—and managed to free an arm with the intent of striking him as hard as she could. But he suddenly pressed the tip of a knife to her throat. The feel of the cold, sharp steel against her flesh made her stiffen in fear. She thought of the child she carried.

"I watched you with him, Leah. I watched the two of you together in the woods. Can you not think of the torment I suffered when I saw his hands upon you? Once he is dead, the spell will be broken. The bewitchment will end. You will be free. I will send him to Hades and you will be free." Still holding the knife to her throat, he now forced her back across the hall. She felt sick with dread and glanced toward the elite bedchambers. She saw no one. The thought that her husband's men might already lay dead caused a sob to well up in her chest. She closed her eyes and offered up a desperate, heartfelt prayer for guidance. *Dear Zeus, what should I do?*

"Do not think to resist me, Leah," Peatro cautioned as he compelled her toward the stairs. "If I am not to have you for my own, then I would see you as dead as the man who took you from me."

Feeling as though lost in a nightmare, she was pulled along with him up the torch lit steps. Her throat constricted painfully when they approached the door of the bedchamber she shared with Nicholas.

Nicholas! Her heart called silently out to him. She knew that she could not let Peatro harm him. But how was she to prevent it without endangering the life of her child? Zeus help her, how was she to warn Nicholas?

Peatro removed his hand from her mouth, but kept the knife poised menacingly against her while he opened the door. She held her breath and felt a violent tremor shake her. Her wide, fearful gaze shot to the bed where she had left Nicholas sleeping peacefully.

He was gone.

She had no time to think about the significance of it, no time to call out or react with anything more than a sharp intake of breath. Peatro thrust her roughly aside. She landed hard upon the floor. And when she pushed herself up into a sitting position, her eyes searched for—and found—her husband in the candlelit room.

"Nicholas!" she cried brokenly.

Clad only in his braies, he stood with a sword clasped in his right hand. His features were a grim mask of fury, his eyes filled with a hot, murderous gleam. Peatro had drawn his own sword by now. He faced Nicholas with a virulent intensity of his own.

"It is time, *Spartan,* you were made to pay for your crimes," he spat out.

"I will kill you for daring to touch her," vowed Nicholas, his tone one of deadly calm. His fingers clenched about the hilt of his sword.

Shaken, Leah climbed to her feet. She swallowed hard and told Nicholas tremulously, "I am unharmed. But he has brought others with him."

"Enough to ensure that your elite will never awaken," boasted Peatro. Filled as he was with hatred and the desire for revenge, he gave no thought to the fact that Nicholas was the far superior warrior.

He raised his sword and lunged forward.

"No!" Leah gasped out. Staggering backward, she clutched at the bedpost, her fear for Nicholas's safety alone. Her breath caught in her throat as she watched him easily deflect his opponent's first attack.

"For my wife's sake, I would yet be merciful," Nicholas offered, though with considerable reluctance. He desired nothing more at that moment than to run the man through. But the sight of Leah's pale, horror-stricken countenance prompted him to make one last attempt at reason. "Surrender, and you—"

"I ask for no mercy," Peatro flung back defiantly. "Nor do I offer any of my own!'"

With that, he sealed his fate.

Leah recognized the inevitable, yet she still hoped that Peatro would somehow turn from his determination. She stifled her cry as she watched him strike at Nicholas again—and her eyes closed tightly against the awful scene when Nicholas's sword found its target. She remembered the boy she had grown up with, remembered the happy times they had once shared. A sharp pain sliced through her heart as surely as the blade had sliced through Peatro's chest.

Nicholas spared only a brief glance at the man who lay sprawled, still alive yet unconscious and bleeding heavily from the wound, upon the floor. He closed the distance between himself and Leah, catching her up against him.

"You are truly unharmed?" he demanded. His gaze raked anxiously over her upturned face.

"Yes." She nodded, her eyes filling with dismay again. "Oh, Nicholas! The elite—"

"Stay here."

She sank wearily down upon the bed as he left her. Then she moved to kneel beside Peatro. Removing her cloak, she pressed it to his wound in a futile effort to staunch the flow of blood. The tears finally came; she felt their liquid heat upon her skin as they coursed down the smoothness of her cheeks.

After what seemed like an eternity, Nicholas returned. Leah went into his arms gratefully. She was lightheaded with relief when he told her that Peatro's scheme had been met with defeat.

"His fellow rebels were careless, ill-prepared to carry out the task he had set for them. John was ever a light sleeper. He awakened and sounded the alarm for the others."

"And what of the Turkishmen?"

"One was injured, the others are dead. They will be taken to Troy."

"Peatro ..." she murmured, her voice trailing away as she looked to where he lay.

"The decision was his alone," Nicholas asserted quietly. "I have instructed David to summon Oracle Victoria. If Peatro lives, he will face the charge of treason as well."

She nodded silently and drew away, watching as he knelt to examine Peatro's injuries.

In the next instant, Thalia and Josh hurried into the room.

"Oh, Leah! Are you all right?" Thalia asked. She immediately flew to Leah's side and embraced her warmly. "I could scarce believe it when Joshua told me what had occurred!"

"It is over with," murmured Leah. "Thank Zeus, it is over with."

Josh and Nicholas carried Peatro from the room and downstairs to the great hall. Oracle Victoria was not long in coming. She had brought two of the village men with her, and together they conveyed Peatro back to the square, promising to tend to him and make certain none spirited him away.

Once she and Nicholas were finally alone once more, Leah lay within the strong, loving circle of his arms and felt the horror of the night finally subsiding. "Never before have I been so frightened," she confided, shuddering at the memory of Peatro's treachery. "I would have gladly sacrificed my life for yours. Yet I feared for our child, and—"

"I know, my love," he told her, his tone low and vibrant with emotion.

"How is it you were prepared when we came into the room?" she asked, her brow creasing in puzzlement.

"I heard someone upon the stairs. When I awoke to find you gone, I was intending to go in search of you. But then, the sound I heard filled me with unease."

"And you are long accustomed to obeying your instincts," she observed. She released a sigh and settled her body even closer against his. "I pray that no others will seek to destroy the peace."

"They will have the example of this night to dissuade them." He frowned, his gaze darkening when he confided, "Your fear was no greater than my own, Leah. When I saw that Peatro Conrad held a knife to your throat—" He broke off abruptly as the vengeful, white-hot rage swept through him once more.

"I do not truly believe he would have harmed me. Yet he was no longer the Peatro I knew." Her voice held a telltale note of sadness.

"We must put all thought of it behind us now," Nicholas exhorted tenderly, his arms tightening about her. "And think only of what lies ahead."

"I shall be glad when the prince comes. If we are forced to leave Karabey—"

"Then we will make a new life elsewhere." Cupping her chin gently, he tilted her head back so that their eyes could meet. "We have each other, Leah. What else can matter?" He gave her a smile that set her heart wildly aflutter. "As I have said before—for the remainder of my days upon this earth, I will give thanks to the fates that brought you to the palace. And for the song that drew me to you in the woods."

"My mother would be pleased to know that her gift was so treasured," Leah replied softly. "But then, I think she knows it well."

She settled her head upon his chest and closed her eyes. With the sweet, lilting resonance of music echoing deep within her mind, she drifted off to sleep. Her heart beat in unison with Nicholas's, her dreams the same as his own.

CHAPTER 16

▼

Twelve months later.

The wedding was not so very different from the one that had preceded it some twelve months earlier. Just as Leah and Nicholas had been joined in marriage (a "proper marriage") by Oracle Victoria within the beautiful, ancient temple at the square, Thalia and Josh were now charged to love and honor each other as well. Thalia looked beautiful in a gown of cream silk, while Josh would surely have broken the hearts of any former ladyloves who set eyes upon him that day.

Once the newlyweds had been toasted with a celebratory meal at the palace, they retired to the same room where Thalia had once boldly sought to convince Josh to introduce her to the mysteries of the marriage bed. She would not be disappointed this night—nor would her new husband have any cause for complaint.

Leah excused herself from the company of the revelers within the great hall. Climbing the stairs to the room she shared with Nicholas, she thought briefly of Theresa, whose own wedding to Ronald Cayden would soon take place. It had required another *few months* to convince the two lovers that the bonds of holy matrimony were not so fearsome after all. Her eyes sparkling with wry amusement, Leah reached the bedchamber and eased the door open. She slipped quietly inside to check upon her sleeping son.

"You may retire now, Dame Frances," she whispered, smiling in gratitude at the older woman who had proven to be a devoted attendant to the child.

"He was but fretful for a time an hour ago," Dame Frances advised her in a hushed tone. "No doubt, the wee master thinks himself unfairly excluded from the festivities below." Her skirts rustled softly as she crossed to the door.

"Good night," said Leah.

Once Dame Frances had gone, she sank down into a chair before the fire and gazed lovingly at the baby who had brought her more joy than she would have ever thought possible. Karlos Viggo Constinos looked a great deal like his father. He was a healthy, happy child. And had, so it was said, added considerable impetus to the elites' courtship of several young Greek ladies recently brought to grace the prince's court at Troy.

"You are tired?" Nicholas asked softly, his tall frame filling the doorway behind her.

"Only a little," she replied. She watched as he closed the door and moved forward to stand before the fire. "The wedding was beautiful, was it not?"

"Second only to our own." He smiled and folded his arms across his chest "Prince Michael will be sorry to have missed it. Yet his presence was required in Greece."

"Will he be away long?"

"A month or two at most."

"I shall be forever grateful to him for his intercession on your behalf. It still seems a miracle to me that you were allowed to keep Karabey.

But then, any other decision by Lord Ares would have aroused ill feelings that he would have found difficult to soothe. You have far too many supporters, both here and in Greece, to—"

"And what makes you so certain of that?" he asked, his gaze lighting with fond amusement.

"Josh told me," she revealed, with a mock defensiveness. She cast another affectionate look down at their son before admitting, "Nicholas, I-I have been thinking of Peatro Conrad of late."

"He is safely within the prison at Troy."

"I know. But I would wish that he were free."

"Free?" Frowning, he uncrossed his arms and raised a hand to the mantelpiece. "He must serve his sentence, else others will think justice easily thwarted."

"That may well be true, but I have received a letter from him. And before you become angry," she hastened to plead, "you must hear what I have to say."

"By Zeus, Leah. You cannot—"

"He expresses remorse for his deeds. He asks only that I forgive him."

"Forgive him if you will. But he will not be free."

"Do you not think it possible that these twelve months past might have changed him?"

"I do not." A faint smile touched his lips now. "You possess a soft heart, my love, and I am glad for it. But we have more to consider than our own feelings in the matter. Karabey has finally come to know peace, and I will not jeopardize it."

"I suppose you are right," she conceded, with a sigh. She rose from the chair and placed her hand upon his arm. "Perhaps, in time, even the most obstinate of the villagers will acknowledge your wisdom."

"It would please me more if my wife would do so," he said teasingly, then covering her hand with the warmth of his own. "I have yet to tame you."

"I told you once before that I would not be a meek and entirely dutiful wife."

"True." He slipped an arm about her waist. "Still, I would have you no other way."

"Indeed, Sir Nicholas, you have 'had' me little enough these past several days," she retorted archly, referring to the fact that she had been far too occupied with the preparations for the wedding.

"I am prepared to remedy that at your command," he offered, his magnificent brown eyes holding the promise of passion.

"Then I do now command it."

With a quiet laugh, he scooped her up in his arms and carried her toward the bed. Their gazes flickered in unison to where their son lay close by, beneath the window. Once more, their hearts were warmed by the memory of the first song that had brought them together.

"Our sweet son is calmed by your singing," noted Nicholas, then gave her a smile that quite nearly took her breath away. "Yet I find that I am still much stirred by the sound of it."

"It is a blessing then, and not a curse," she whispered, her arms reaching for him as he lowered her gently to the bed.

"Did you ever doubt it?" He lay down beside her and gathered her close.

"A little, perhaps," she confessed. "But I shall not do so again." She lifted a hand to the clean-shaven ruggedness of his cheek. His own hand, warm and strong and possessive, closed about her fingers.

"I love you, Leah," he declared solemnly, his deep voice much the same as music to her ears. "Lord Zeus has indeed blessed our union. And it will always be so."

"Yes, my lord." A sigh of pure contentment escaped her lips— and her eyes told him all he needed to know. "It will always be so."

Ten years later. Nicholas Constinos' adventure continues in

Kingdoms.

A coward turns away, but a brave man's choice is danger.

Kingdoms!

One dying wish from a desperate soldier allowed him to survive, but brought him a lifetime of despair.

"By the gods, what have I become?"

Now, the only way to right the wrongs of his past is to conquer the challenges set forth by the Gods of Olympus.

In an epic adventure of conquest, destiny, and revenge—war-ravaged Karabey, legions of Turkish soldiers, and a desperate god, are no match for the fury of one … vengeful … warrior …

Kingdoms!

Kingdoms

by Tino Georgiou

Available soon in your local bookstore.

978-0-595-46433-3
0-595-46433-5

Printed in the United Kingdom
by Lightning Source UK Ltd.
126139UK00001B/46-63/A